Remedy is None

FATHER DYING. COME HOME AT ONCE.

Charlie Grant had only gone to University because his father had scrimped and saved to send him there. Now he was left with the old man's blessing – 'You'll be a' right Charlie. Wi' a University education. You'll no' be like me. The guid jobs. The big money.'

Was this all, then, that remained to his father? A few shibboleths and magical words which he had had to learn to bolster his failure. When Charlie thought of the man his father had been the injustice of it 'cleft his mind like lightning'. He could think of nothing except setting the injustice right.

WILLIAM McILVANNEY

REMEDY IS NONE

Since for the Death remeid is none,
Best is that we for Death dispone,
After our death that live may we:
Timor Mortis conturbat me

WILLIAM DUNBAR
(1465-?1520)

RICHARD DREW PUBLISHING
GLASGOW

REMEDY IS NONE

First published 1966 by Eyre & Spottiswoode

This edition first published 1989 by
Richard Drew Publishing Ltd
6 Clairmont Gardens
Glasgow G3 7LW
Scotland

The publisher acknowledges the financial
assistance of the Scottish Arts Council in the
publication of this book.

British Library Cataloguing in Publication Data

McIlvanney, William, 1936-
  Remedy is none
  I. Title
  823′.914 [F]

  ISBN 0-86267-246-5

Printed and bound in Great Britain by
Cox & Wyman, Reading

To my Mother

Part One

Chapter 1

'OF COURSE, GENTLEMEN, AT THE BEGINNING OF THE play you will remember (those of us who have read the text) that Romeo is in love not with Juliet, but with someone called Rosaline. In fact, it might be truer to say that at this point his love is not so much directed at any specific person as at woman in general. The American writer William Saroyan has a short story entitled *Seventeen* which effectively conveys the state of mind we may assume him to be in. I think we all know it. Do not all young men fall in love first with a chimera . . .?'

'I am a chimera,' Andy said, raising his hands like claws, putting on his monster's face. 'I was a teenage chimera.'

'I'm in love with a darling young chimera,' Jim sang quietly.

'It is only later that this idealized woman transmigrates to the body of a living person – and the trouble starts. At this point in the male's life there enters the unknown Max Factor.'

Dutiful laughter was struck up in the lecture-room, disconcerted by a jeering bassoon from the back, closely followed by an operatic facsimile of agonized death.

'Hey, Charlie,' Andy said, nudging him. 'Waken up. Ye're missing all the riotous fun. We've just had a joke.'

'Ah wondered what the smell wis,' Charlie said. 'Hell, Ah wish he would give ye some sign, like dropping a hanky or something. Ah always miss his wee jokes.'

'Ah know why *you* missed it, too,' Jim said. 'You were off to Mary-land there again.'

Jim's guess was right. Charlie had been thinking about Mary. Since her last letter his mind had developed a kind of stutter and he couldn't get past thinking of what she had written. He closed his mind on the lecture-room again, locking out Professor Aird's insistent voice. He thought again of

3

the sentence that his mind had been pushing out like a mad teleprinter for three days until he had barely room for another thought. 'It's five days since "you-know-what" was due and didn't come and what do I do?' Well, what did she do? Take up knitting? He liked the euphemism – 'you-know-what'. He knew what, all right. She had always been very regular, she said. Maybe a day either way. This was five. And now three more. That made it eight – the simple arithmetic of paternity. Five plus three equals daddy. Every day was another step up the aisle. He didn't object to marrying Mary. He wanted to marry her – eventually. He had calculated on that pleasure coming along in time. But he didn't want his future express delivery. He couldn't use it just now. He had two more years of university after this one, if he took honours. It was a good thing it wasn't a course in premarital relations. He wouldn't win any medals for that. Even if he told his father – who had enough to worry him without the patter of tiny bastards – and even if he squared it up with Mary's folks, where was the money to come from? What did you do? Sue the contraceptive makers for the price of the reception? It was hopeless. Why did even the most natural things you did have to pivot on economy? They had you every way. All the good things were either padlocked with morality or tagged with money. Money. Mon-ey! God of our fathers, we worship thee in all thy glorious manifestations, from the mighty fiver to the sterling pound, yea even to the little pennies of the pocket. Without thee, what is man? He is even as a pauper and the glories of the world shall not profit him, neither shall they yield him aught of joy. Without thee, what may a man do? Pray. That was all you could do. Pray to Nature to take her erratic course. And Nature said, let there be blood. And there was blood. That was all he could hope for. That was all he could do. Pray. 'More things are wrought by prayer than this world dreams of.' Well, he would put it to the test.

'Of course, it is hoped that Juliet will marry Count Paris. But in reciprocating Romeo's love she helps to create the microcosm of sanity and love within the macrocosmic hate and senseless conflict of Verona.'

The voice droned on, buzzing against Charlie's brain like a fly against a window-pane. He was worried about telling his father, not because of what he would say, but because he set so much store by Charlie's going to university, and it was enough of a struggle without adding mendicant grand-children. That was the worst part of all, the way you inevit-ably impinged on other people in these things. If it had just been a matter of themselves it wouldn't be so bad. But you were all connected by invisible wires so that anything you did provoked a response in others. He could imagine Mary's father doing his fireside Stoic about the whole thing, bleeding quietly all over the place, stabbed to the heart by Charlie's treachery. And her mother. That was going to be worse. Mrs Littlejohn. She was bad enough at any time. She was a conning-tower for misfortune. She saw it coming when no-body else could, dim in the distance, and she put out the welcome mat for it. Charlie could almost sense the forth-coming cataclysm, like earth termors. Her shock would be seismic. It always was, even in trivial matters. She enclosed herself in a crinoline of rigid convictions and seemed con-stantly offended that the rest of the world was out of step. Every time she moved, she rustled with bigotry. In her presence Charlie always felt like being in a room cluttered with ornate bric-à-brac of cut glass where you couldn't make a wrong move or say a wrong thing without another trans-parent prejudice being smashed. When she heard of this, the noise was going to be deafening. Charlie didn't relish playing the bull to her china shop.

'But can he, in fact, openly profess his love for Juliet? Today, no doubt, things would be different. But we must try to think ourselves into the social climate of his time and society. We must try to appreciate that the very air he breathes has a texture different from that which we inhale at this moment in this room. In our society, for better or for worse, the reins are being given more and more into the hands of youth. Or perhaps it would be more accurate to say that crupper, bit, and bridle are being dispensed with altogether and the individual clings only to the mane of natural instinct to guide the course of his life. This is doubtless a sad reflection on the social horsemanship of your elders. Be that as it may. It is not so in Verona. For Romeo, personal choice is gravely restricted because of the social pressures under which he lives. Authority is to a degree sacrosanct. Romeo owes allegiance to his father, who in turn owes it to the duke. He is subject to a strict authoritarian hierarchy. So too, of course, is Juliet. Witness old Capulet's outbursts at her unwillingness to accept Paris as a husband. How then, in this atmosphere of claustrophobic conformity, can Romeo fulfil his personal feelings without coming into direct and open conflict with this hierarchy and authority? Here lies Romeo's problem.'

Stuff Romeo, Charlie thought. He thought he had problems. He didn't know the half of it. 'Oh, speak again, bright angel,' and tell me that 'I-know-what' has come at last.

'Montague and Capulet are the pincer-jaws between which Romeo and Juliet are caught, crushing them in the end, but also in so doing squeezing out of their tragic love an intensity and a poignancy which would not otherwise have been."

Montague and Capulet? They weren't in the same league as Mrs Littlejohn. She was Verona all on her own. Maybe she was just sharpening her pincer-jaws at that very moment, and looking out her thumbscrews.

'Accident plays its part, it is true, and the play is the weaker for it. Nevertheless, the tortuous sequence of events that culminates in a double suicide as well as the deaths of Paris and of Tybalt to balance that of Mercutio stems directly from the need for constant subterfuge that is imposed on the two lovers. Therefore, where does the blame finally lie?'

With the rubber tree? Perhaps that was it. His tragedy might have its origin in the dim recesses of some Malayan forest where one tree among thousands had been smitten with the dreaded rubber-worm. And now he was reaping the fruits. 'Fruits' was right.

'Accident, yes. But accident nurtured by hate. Accident which has as its foster-parent human error. Notice that accident enters into it only *after* the initial damage has been done by human agency. Notice human error. Notice human guilt. Notice . . .'

'Notice the time, Jimsy,' Andy muttered. 'For God's sake, man, even intellectuals have to eat. Ah'll be reduced tae gettin' beetled into this desk in a minute.'

Charlie smiled to himself. Andy's voice summoned him back to commonsense. He looked at Jim and Andy, waiting like horses at the gate to go and get fed. There were only a couple of minutes to go. Just being with them helped. With them, through banter and familiar jokes and clowning, he could build up a synthetic atmosphere, like an oxygen tent, in which he could breathe easy again and the pulse of panic could settle back to a contrived normalcy. All he wanted was for things to go on the way they were going without disturbance. He would be happy to go on like this for another two years, attending lectures, carrying on interminable conversations of abysmal profundity in the Students' Union, working in the reading-room, having a drink with Andy and Jim in the beer bar, going home for a week-end every month or so. It was a good set-up. He had no complaints, if only this thing would blow over. And there was still some hope. Perhaps the crisis was over already and he didn't know it. Perhaps a letter was on the way, telling him it was all right. He hoped he knew for certain before next week, anyway. He had examinations then. And he couldn't settle to work with this hanging over him. Perhaps he would know before then. He might go home at the week-end, although he hadn't intended to be home for a fortnight yet. If he hadn't heard by the week-end, he would go home and see Mary. Having made a definite decision, however small, he felt a little better. That meant he had three more days before he could do anything positive, and the best thing he could do meanwhile was to try and carry on just as usual. There was no point in doing trouble's work for it. If the situation was going to give way under him, it would. And when it did it would be bad enough without his making it worse by anticipation. There was nothing he could do just now. Any minute they would be going down to the Union for lunch and maybe have a game of snooker before going up to the reading-room to work.

'But Verona can only be purged of its evil hatred through the deaths of these two people, people themselves innocent of that hatred.'

'Come on, come on,' Andy said. 'Ring the bell, verger, ring the bell, ring.'

'Hell, we're gonny have tae shoot this man,' Jim said.

'Through these scapegoats a corrupt community is shriven.'

Professor Aird shuffled his notes and took off his glasses, looking round the students. Charlie liked these moments. The professor could express more with his face than with words. Charlie remembered the time he had demolished the Chicago school of critics with one eloquent eyebrow. Now his face seemed to express regret at the atavism which put food before Shakespeare.

'Dinner is served,' he said.

There was a respectful pause as he left the rostrum and headed for the door of his side-room. But before he could escape he was ambushed by three girls with ears asinine for learning. Those less dedicated made for the door.

Andy was one of the first to get out. He raced across the quadrangle and through the cloisters, dodging students and moaning, 'Food, food!' Jim and Charlie came up with him at the top of the hill and fell into step. University Avenue was busy and they walked quickly, knowing there would be a queue at the Union.

Jim held out an invisible microphone to Andy and said, 'And would you like to tell the viewers something about the life of a chimera in our day and age? Would you recommend it to others?'

8

Andy assumed what were apparently the rough tones of the professional chimera.

'It's like any other work, really. Ah mean we do a lot that isny appreciatit by the public, ye know? We have our own kinna more or less union, certainly. N.I.C. National Incorporatit Chimeras. But, eh, Ah personally would like tae see chimeras gettin' the vote. Ah mean tae say . . .'

But Jim suddenly lost interest in chimeras and gave his attention to a tight-skirted girl just ahead. As they came abreast of her, he fell into step with her, smiling inanely into her face.

"Excuse me, modom,' he said, twirling an imaginary moustache. 'Could I carry your briefs-case for you?'

She gave him a chilly look and his smile went stalagmite. Then he ran after Charlie and Andy with a gust of demonic laughter.

'You better watch it, freen,' Charlie said to him as he caught up. 'You'll get what yon other wit got that spoke tae the lassie with the sweater.'

'What was that?' Jim asked.

'The royal order of the boot.'

'Ye mean sent down?'

'That's right.'

'Just for talkin'? He musta been some talker right enough. What did he say, like?'

'Well, she had oan this sweater. Ye know? Which I am led to believe she was causing to protrude in two places. And directly over the left hoodjykaplonk –' Charlie made a vague mamillary gesture – 'she had neatly inscribed the initial "T" – no doubt referring to her monnicker. Well, this very witty fella comes up to her and says "What do ye get out the other one – coffee?" There you are. Bob's yer uncle, and farewell to the student life.'

Jim rasped his tongue derisively.

'And the band played believe-it-if-you-like,' he said.

They had reached the Union. It was crowded already. Many groups were standing about in the hall, chatting. Andy gripped Charlie's arm.

9

'Come on downstairs with me,' he said, 'till Ah get ma sandwiches out the locker.'

They all went down to where the lockers were, beside the toilets. While Andy was opening the locker, somebody tapped Charlie's shoulder on the way past. It was Alec Redmond.

'Yes, Charles,' he said. 'Working hard?'

'Hullo, Alec. Oh it's the old Trojan stuff, definitely.'

'Oh here, Charlie.'

Alec was half-turned in the doorway of the toilets. He snapped his fingers.

'Mickey – the porter – told me there was a telegram just come for ye,' he threw back as he went on.

Charlie's first thought was, God, that's what you call premature. He was convinced it must be from Mary. He turned round abruptly to go up and get it when he bumped into Mickey, who was holding the telegram.

'Ah seen yese comin' in therr,' he said, 'an' Ah thought Ah better get this to ye as fast as possible. It's like fightin' yer wey through Hampden Park up therr.'

'Thanks, Mickey,' Charlie said, taking it.

The name looked strangely formal – Mr Charles Grant. He couldn't find a way into it at first.

'Ach aye,' somebody said philosophically on his way past to the toilets, 'in one end and out the other'.

Charlie managed to get it open and unfolded it. He was so sure of what it was going to say that at first all he could understand was that this was not the message he had anticipated. Spelled out on the strips of pasted paper, as if from some malevolence that wished to remain anonymous, were the words: FATHER DYING. COME HOME AT ONCE. JOHN. Slowly, Charlie brought his mind into focus. The first thing he thought was that he couldn't take his lunch here, but would have to leave right away. Then he thought he might have to leave university. Then he thought that he would see Mary sooner than the week-end. On the heels of these came shame that he should have thought of them at all. But it was almost impossible to grasp what these words meant. He stared at the

10

message again. The words seemed to buckle, distend elastic-ally, defy meaning. How could this piece of paper he held in his hand above the tessellated floor, with people shouldering past him, come to mean so much? FATHER DYING. Father dying? With people talking and laughing and Andy closing up his locker and giving it a parting slap as if it were something animate and Jim putting his hand on his arm? Father dying?

'What is it, Charlie?' Jim said. 'What's the matter?'

Charlie enunciated the words gradually, as if telling him-self as well as Jim and Andy.

'My father's dying,' he said.

In one of the toilets someone was singing, 'Hear my song, Violetta.'

Chapter 2

'ARE YOU SURE YOU HAVE EVERYTHING, NOW? AND whatever you do be sure and write as soon as you get there and tell us if everything's all right. Your father and me'll be worried until we know for sure.'

'Yes, Mother, yes,' the young woman said through the small opening in the window. She had slid back the pane, and her mother stood on the platform outside, hopping with maternal solicitude in case the guard should flag short her advice. 'Now don't worry about me. You would think I was going to the North Pole. I'll be perfectly all right. Oh, excuse me, I'll shift that,' she said, lifting her hat from the seat opposite hers and putting it on the rack above her head beside the new tan suitcase.

Charlie sat down on the cleared seat like a somnambulist. He hadn't noticed the hat. He hadn't noticed much between the university and the railway-station, only spasmodic and incomprehensible fragments of what was going on around him, an Underground map, a mother nursing her child on her knee, a ticket-collector's hands clustered with warts. These things occurred as shapes and shadows against his frosted perception, threatened dimly without admittance. His awareness had frozen on the fact of his father dying, and impressions only skimmed the surface of his consciousness like skaters seen from underneath the ice. He still couldn't realize it. FATHER DYING. Two words that detonated in his mind, exploding his concentration to smithereens, and left him searching the debris for fragments of understanding. How could he be dying? He had seemed all right the last time Charlie was home. But that was more than a month ago. Did people pass from apparent health to imminent death in a month? It seemed somehow unjust, somehow too casual.

Death was something august and terrible, a climactic presence heralded by long illness. How could it come suddenly, unannounced like this, ensconce itself in your house behind your back? It was a possibility Charlie had never really contemplated. It wasn't easy to start contemplating it now. But he tried to adjust to the fact towards which he was moving relentlessly.

The train exhaled steam and lunged forward, leaving the young woman's mother to run a few paces along the platform, throwing snippets of advice that the wind scattered like confetti. The young woman closed the pane with a sigh of relief and sank into her seat. She looked at Charlie, shaking her head, trying to form an alliance of understanding with him on the difficulties of having mothers. Charlie stared past her through the window. The old woman in the corner opposite them looked across deliberately, appointing herself chaperone while the young woman unbuttoned her costume jacket to reveal a lace blouse. The compartment door slid open and three businessmen came in, laughing. The youngest of them chose the seat beside Charlie so that he was facing towards the young woman. They had an air of mildly alcoholic carnival about them, as if they were wearing paper hats. One of the older men was smoking a cigar and its lengthening ash stayed miraculously intact in defiance of his gestures. He was telling a joke, the climax of which was imparted in a whisper that punched their heads back, leaving them groggy with laughter. The youngest one directed his laughter at the young woman, taking a side glance at Charlie to check the competition.

Charlie's impassivity made it obvious that he wasn't entering. As the train gathered momentum, he strove to analyse what the news meant to him. With the numbness of the initial blow wearing off, his mind prodded tenderly at the pain, trying to determine the extent of the damage. There were certain obvious consequences. He might have to leave university. They had been very tight for money as it was. There was the house to keep. With only himself and Elizabeth living in it, that wouldn't be easy. At eighteen, Elizabeth wasn't making much of a wage. The mess he had made with Mary was going to be impossibly complicated. It was some time to get pregnant.

But these were merely abrasions. The sheer fact of his father's dying must cut a lot deeper than that. He was almost afraid to examine it to the marrow. He thought tentatively what it would mean to lose his father. He tried to consider it not in the practical terms, but simply in human ones. At first, in the absence of any definite reaction to something so unassimilable, his mind struck a vague, eclectic attitude towards it, one derived from dim, subliminal sources. Death was a terrible and awesome thing. Without any experience of it, he knew that. It was the ultimate mystery, recurrent theme of poets and preachers. His thinking had been subtly conditioned to endorse a vague, idealized image of it by what he had read in books and seen in films and overheard in occasional muted references. As a boy, he had been aware of it as a furtive presence in adult conversations, accompanied by lowered voices or significant looks or suggestions that he go out and play, as if this was too fiercesome an ogre to be admitted to the understanding of a child. He had witnessed the heroism of countless cinematic deaths from decorously positioned arrows or invisible bullets, which caused the life-blood to bloom as formally as a flower on the victim's breast, while angelic voices choired man's majesty and the glycerine grief of women registered irreparable loss. And he had seen most of them at an age when the moment of lonely communion in the dark was still too powerful to be dispelled by the need to evade 'God save the Queen' or by the glib cynicism of the foyer. He had learned of death's stature at second-hand from the broodings of the Metaphysicals and the declamations of Shakespeare. Now he was to meet his magnificence in person.

But, sitting in this compartment – death's mobile anteroom – with the insistence of the wheels imposing their practical rhythm on his thoughts, what gradually impressed itself on his mind was simply the depressing ordinariness of it all. There was no sense of grandeur about it. Nothing was any different. The random chords of the day did not combine into any impressive overture to death, but remained casually dissonant. In a station they passed through, a porter lounged in the doorway of a waiting-room, picking his teeth. Two horses stood immobile in a field, distinguishable from statues only by tail and mane. Everything that could be seen, through the patch Charlie's hand had automatically cleared in the misted glass, was the same as ever. Was this how death happened, in the middle of a bright day that was too busy to notice? It was somehow shocking. What made it worse was that Charlie's shock included himself. He was like a child who has closed his eyes against the imminent pain of a doctor's touch, and opens them again in disbelief, surprised to find that it can hurt so little.

He was ashamed of himself, ashamed not because he had dreaded pain, but because his feelings didn't justify that dread. How could he be so callous? How could he have been so callous in the past? For this callousness must have developed gradually in his relationship with his father, and was like a hard skin formed on his affection. How had it happened? He seemed hardly to have thought about his father as himself for as long as he could remember. The selfishness of it was shattering. He had known the last time he was home that his father had been X-rayed, but he had somehow assumed that it had been all right. His father had been very off-hand about what he called 'just a check-up', probably because he didn't want to disturb Charlie's studies. To Charlie's father, 'the studying' was sacrosanct, a mysterious activity involving some miraculous act of concentration. And Charlie had let himself be convinced that there was nothing to worry about. The truth was that in the last few days his own problems had left no room for his father's in his mind. But that was no excuse. For a long time now, he had been concerned almost exclusively with himself, living his separate life in Glasgow. It was so easy to become isolated. He had an

...ablished routine and it was a pleasant one. His only real worries had been examinations. And they were the kind you could defer until they gathered in one week and were over the next. The rest of the time he enjoyed just being a student. Certainly, he could have gone home more often. He thought again of how long it was since he had been home. Over a month, and it was only a short train journey away. But he had discussed it with his father and Elizabeth, and they had all decided that with important class examinations coming up it would be a good idea for him to stay in Glasgow and work at the week-ends. Mary had agreed reluctantly. She had come up to Glasgow for the day once or twice since then. It might have been better if she hadn't, he reflected ruefully.

He should have gone down more often, he told himself. He should have gone down much more often. How was it possible to have been so thoughtless and indifferent about his own father? Their relationship had been so tacit and casual, confined to meetings at the tea-table or the occasional brief exchange when Charlie came in late at night. The whole relationship had become a cliché for Charlie, as incidental as the talk between these people with whom he happened to be sharing a compartment.

'They're making some drastic changes here,' the one with the cigar said to the man beside him, indicating a street in the town they were going through.

'Yes. It's high time, too.'

'Those buildings must have stood for seventy years, anyway.'

'More like eighty.'

'Yes. They're very old.'

They nodded knowledgeably, the motion of the train prolonging the action until it looked like the perpetual acquiescence of dotage. Their jollity had lapsed before the seductive torpor of a long journey, and they sat recharging their batteries. The one with the cigar held it burnt out between his fingers, his trousers stained haphazardly with ash. The youngest one was making a show of looking out the window,

16

conducting an optical conversation with the young woman. The old woman sat blinking in her corner like a cat, having a dignified disagreement with her eyelids, which kept insisting on sleep, although she jerked herself awake repeatedly.

Charlie sat staring out the window at himself. He wasn't exactly enamoured of what he saw. A selfish taker, whose habitual gesture towards his father was an extended hand, palm up. It wasn't as if things had been so easy for his father. Apart altogether from the money, it must have been hard going. Especially over the past six years. Was it six? Perhaps it was more. Charlie had trained himself not to think about it. That part of his memory was fenced off from everyday contact. It had left its effect on all of them when it happened, and each had had to make his own peace with it. They seldom talked about it. But he found himself wondering how big a toll it had taken of his father, while Charlie had been too busy to pay it any attention.

The telegraph poles outside went past more slowly now, measuring the progress of his private journey as well as that of the train. The coaches ricocheted to a standstill, waiting for the signal that would bring Charlie home not only to his father, but to himself. In the stillness, a wagon clanked somewhere in a siding and a man shouted some words that the wind pared to a shapeless sound. Then they could hear the signal swing down on its metal joint, and the train pulled in to the platform.

As they drew in, Charlie stood up, thinking for a second of his brief-case before he remembered that Andy had put it in his locker. He slid open the compartment door and went into the corridor. He left at a run, his tie flapping like an oriflamme, as if he could outpace the last six years or so.

'Where's the fire?' said one of the businessmen, shutting the door.

The old woman, briefly disturbed, settled back into herself.

The youngest businessman looked at the young woman and winked at the other two. He slid casually into the seat

17

opposite her that had been vacated by Charlie, wiping the pane unnecessarily with a prefatory hand.

'That's better,' he said, smiling at the young woman.

She smiled back, not taking her eyes from his. She shifted slightly under his gaze. Her skirt moved a tantalizing inch and she let it lie. The other two nudged each other and got up.

'We're going out for a breath of air in the corridor, Ted,' one of them said.

'Right, John. Don't walk off the end of the train.'

They left. The old woman had succumbed at last to sleep. As the train drew out, Ted leaned forward to look out of the window, accidentally brushing the young woman's knee. She didn't move.

'Hm. Kilmarnock. How far do *you* go?' he said. While Charlie ran.

Chapter 3

'HE'S AWAKE UPSTAIRS,' JOHN SAID. 'THE DOCTOR WIS in this mornin' tae give 'im morphine, but he wouldny have it till he'd seen you. He hasny long, Charlie. Maybe a matter of hours.'

John was wearing his good clothes. He couldn't have been to work at all that day. He had an air of harassed competence in his official capacity as elder son. Elizabeth was sitting in statuesque misery by the fire. Her cheeks looked as if there had been acid on them. She had started to cry all over again when Charlie came in, as if his presence brought the fact of her father's death nearer.

'Why the hell wis Ah not told aboot this, John?' Charlie said, filibustering with the facts. Now that he was here, Charlie felt himself inadequate to the moment of facing his father, and instinctively postponed it a little longer. 'Ah knew nothin' aboot it. Then Ah get this telegram. Ye coulda told me sooner than this, John. Ma feyther musta been ill for a long time. How long has he been lyin'? Whit is it, anyway?'

'Look, Charlie. You musta had some idea. Ye kent ma feyther had T.N.T. poisoning durin' the war. An' every night fur mair than fifteen year he coughed for hours in that bed up there. Ye don't go on like that an' nothin' happens. Somethin's got tae happen.'

'So what? Am Ah a clairvoyant? How does it happen *now*? Whit is it, anyway?'

'It's cancer, Charlie,' John said. 'That's whit it is.'

Charlie's ears suddenly had hands of silence to them and sound was a closed circuit inside his head. He was aware of the pneumatic thrust of blood against his brain and the metallic click of his tongue sticking and unsticking on the roof of his mouth and his throat constricting on a lump of panic it could not swallow. The word 'cancer' kept blaring in his head like a klaxon, startling into his mind confused images of emaciation and the memory of a poster showing a man caught in the coils of a green snake.

'Cancer?'

John said nothing. Charlie stood enclosed in that moment of bright silence like a thrown net. That word conveyed his father's death to him, was as final as if it had been carved in stone. Cancer? he asked the wooden figure of a woman with a child on the mantelpiece, who had always been like a cipher of security for him. Now she stood there like a sinister totem, carved out of indifference. The enormity of the situation grew around him like a glacier.

'Ah shoulda been told,' Charlie said suddenly, chipping at it with the first thought that came to hand. The sheer fact of his father dying was too much to be withstood, swept all re-actions and attitudes before it, and he had to canalize it into something more manageable, anger that he had not been told sooner. 'This musta been goin' on for some time. Ah shoulda been told sooner.'

'That's the way ma feyther wanted it, Charlie. He knew ye had examinations comin' off an' he didny want tae worry ye.'

'Didny want tae worry me? For God's sake, John. Didny want tae worry me.'

'Ye know whit he's like about university an' that. Ah mean a' he wants is for you tae make the grade. That's what's been really preyin' on 'him. He wisny wantin' tae let anythin' put ye off. Ah think he felt he could hold out all right tae after yer exams were finished. Ah don't think he realized how near it was. Ah don't think anybody did. Ah mean, maybe *Ah* shoulda told ye sooner, Charlie. But this was the way ma feyther wanted it. An' it meant an awfu' lot tae him. So Ah went along with it. Whit else could Ah dae?'

Nothing else. Charlie's brief recriminations turned shame-faced from John's question. Behind it, making it unanswer-able, lay the attitude of his father, and Elizabeth and, to a lesser extent, John himself to all that the university meant. To them it was something of immense importance and impregnability, a fortress of fabled knowledge that they could never gain access to, and they never quite became blasé about the fact that one of their family had managed to penetrate it. They maintained a certain deference, not to him (for he was still to an extent the familiar fixture he had always been about the house, reading and self-absorbed, to be met with suddenly, vegetating quietly in a chair, and everywhere he went books and magazines and ties and pullovers grew like a fungus, so that Elizabeth had to keep following him up and pruning his untidiness before the furniture got submerged), but a deference to that part of his life that took place in Glasgow, that consisted of lectures and notes and books with portentous titles. Because of this, he was accorded certain concessions. Into their thinking had been introduced a special clause of consideration that affected their reactions to many of the things he did. If he were short-tempered or inconsiderate or uncommunicative, allowance had to be made. He was 'studying', he was 'at university'. And had Charlie done anything to discredit this attitude? Had he not enjoyed to a degree this special consideration for what he was doing? Had he not on occasion fostered it by deliberate reference to some abstruse work or to 'Anglo-Saxon', which he knew would create a measure of awe among them? He couldn't now blame John for something which emerged from a situation he had himself helped to create. John's question was unanswerable. It stood like a wall before his recriminations, the stronger because he had helped to mortar it himself, and his anger struck ineffectually against it and washed back on himself. For his anger was really directed against himself, he realized. It was not so much that he blamed John as that he had sought to divert any blame from himself, and now he admitted to himself that he was in part to blame. He was the one who had been content to stay in Glasgow and concern himself almost exclusively with his own problems and his own life. John and Elizabeth had been here, knowing and worrying about his father, and trying to look after him. What right had he to blame anyone?

'An' anyway,' John went on superfluously, 'it's all happened so quick. Ah mean, ma feyther got the X-ray, and then they had him in for observation fur a wee while, and then they just sent him hame tae dee. There wis nuthin' else fur it. They said it wis too late. Ah think ma feyther musta been nursin' this fur a long time, Charlie, without tellin' anybody.'

'Ah know, John,' Charlie said. 'It's just somethin' ye canny get tae believe all at once.'

Elizabeth was still sitting staring into the fire, clutching her handkerchief in a wet ball. Charlie stood looking at her, and in the firelight tiny filaments of vein scarred the whites of her eyes.

'Ye better go up noo, Charlie,' John said. 'The doctor said he would be back in this efternin tae give 'im the morphine. He might no' come out it again. This might be the last time he talks. He might be in any time now.'

Charlie nodded. He felt like some sort of prodigal son. Well, he was here now, anyway. A trifle late, it was true. But he was here. He went up the stairs slowly, over the worn flowers of the carpet, and he was thinking that his father would never step on them again. Each step seemed to settle in a slough of reluctance to face what was ahead.

'Charlie?'

Charlie stopped as if trying to locate where the voice had come from. It seemed to dirl from a distance further than the room above him. The door was open, but he knew he wouldn't see his father until he was in the room, because of the position of the bed behind the door. He went on up and stood still a moment at the door. In the wardrobe mirror he could see the outline of his father's legs beneath the covers and one hand laid waxen on the counterpane. It looked as fine as filigree. Illness must have sculpted long and patiently at the flesh to make anything as pale and fragile for aesthetic death. It lay motionless, as if life had already left it.

'Is that you, Charlie?'

The voice drifted thin as smoke from the room.

'Aye, Feyther. It's me,' he said, and went in.

Nothing could have prepared Charlie for this. In his youth his father had made a fetish of fitness because, being little more than literate, he carried most of his assets in his body, a body made hard by the pits and pick-and-shovel labouring through many years before he was smitten by the dream to be his own boss, to 'branch out' on his own. It had taken little more than a month of sickness to make a mockery of sinew and muscle and reassert the bone so that the hard muscular form Charlie had said cheerio to now lay skeletal, barely giving shape to the sweat-stained pyjamas, protruding sticks of wrist that even those frail hands seemed too heavy for. The face was a sharp miniature of what it had been, dominated by the eyes, hollowly dark, like twin tunnels to nothing.

'Hullo, son,' and a smile came like a scar across his face.

'Hullo, Feyther,' and Charlie carved a careful answering smile of his own.

His father was laboriously pretending to feel no pain, pursing his lips. There was a chair beside the bed with a newspaper lying on it. 'Tragedy in a Tenement', Charlie noticed before he sat down.

'Is everythin' a' right at the university, Charlie?'

'Aye, Feyther, it's fine,' Charlie said, wondering what difference that made to anything.

It occurred to Charlie that it might be difficult to find things to talk about. What did you say to someone who was dying? Everything he could think of was double-edged, and did not mean for his father what it meant for him. But his father solved the problem by easing himself up in bed, ready to talk. He obviously had something he was very anxious to say. Charlie saw that he was excused clichés. This was to be a monologue.

'Ah didny send for ye. Sooner, Charlie,' his father said, pain punctuating his breath at random. 'Ah knew ye wis busy at the studyin'. An' Ah didny want. Tae gie' ye any more worry than Ah had tae.'

23

'Aw, Feyther,' Charlie said. What did he think, anyway, that he rated lower than class examinations? That he had to die out of term time, organize his death to suit the syllabus?

'Naw, Charlie, Ah didny want tae do that. But Ah don't ken how much time Ah have now. An' Ah wanted to see ye.'

'Ah, mebbe ye've some time yet, Feyther,' Charlie said, the sight of his father denying the words as he said them.

'Naw, son, naw. Ah ken. An' Ah've had a long time to think. Lyin' here. A long time.' Pain suddenly prompted him to hurry. 'You keep an eye to Elizabeth, son, will ye? She's a good lassie an' Harry's a nice boy. She'll be all right. She's mature now. A sensible lassie for her age. She's had to be, God bless her. Takin' a mither's place before she was a woman. Doin' two jobs. She's made a good job of herself. She'll be all right. As long as you're there just to look after her a wee bit. John's got his ain family now, ye see.' Pride flickered for a moment in his eyes, the ghost of an emotion. 'He's got his wife an' son to look after now. God bless them.'

He paused, fighting the pain. It was harrowing to watch him, a man numbering his children in his will. All he had to give them were blessings.

'An' yersel', Charlie. Now. Ah want ye to keep in. At the university. It'll no' be easy. Ah know. It's no thanks to me if ye do make it. Fur it's little. Ah can leave ye. But listen, Charlie. In the jacket of ma blue suit. In the wardrobe. Fifty pounds. Inside the lining o' the sleeve. It'll be a help. An', Charlie. The funeral's all covered. By the insurance. There'll be no expense whatsoever from that. There'll maybe be somethin' left over.'

It was all arranged. His death was to cause them as little inconvenience as possible.

'Feyther,' Charlie said. 'We'll be all right. Don't worry about that.'

'An', Charlie. In the inside pocket of the jacket. A key. To ma lock-up down at Fore Street. There's a lotta metal there. Mick an' me stripped it off old gas-masks. Ye'll get a few pounds for that. But Mick. He's got to get his share of it. He helped me. The key's in the inside pocket.'

Charlie looked down at his hands. Why was he so concerned with money at this time? The key to the lock-up. It was like a macabre mockery of a fairy-tale – the legendary treasure told of by a dying man. A few bits of metal. He was apportioning his worldly goods. Everyone was to get his share, even Mick, the model-lodging ne'er-do-weel who had played Sancho Panza to his father's Quixotic dreams of financial success.

'It's no' much, Charlie. But it'll help to tide ye over just now. Ye must stick it. At the university. Ye've got to, Charlie. Ye're no' goin' to be like me. A nobody. You'll make a success of your life. You'll be different from me, son. You'll be different.'

'Ah don't want to be different from you, Feyther,' Charlie said. He couldn't believe that his father was saying that. Why was he speaking like this? 'What is there to be different about?'

'Naw, son. You'll be different. You'll no' make. The mistakes Ah made. Ah can see ma mistakes now. Ah see them. When it's too late.'

'Ye never made mistakes, Feyther. Don't say that.'

'Aw naw, son. Ah was wrong. All ma days. All the time Ah was wrong. Full o' mistakes. Ah see them now. Ah see them.'

Charlie said nothing, struck to stone by the terrible sincerity of his father's voice. He saw with sudden horror how real these 'mistakes' were to his father's mind, like spectres gathered about his bedside. He sensed how they must have haunted him these past weeks, the agony they were giving him at this moment. This was really what he wanted to tell Charlie. And Charlie listened in disbelief while his father talked on through his pain as if he had something terrible to confess before he died.

'Don't be like me, son. Ah never did anything wi' ma life. Ah had nae education an' Ah never made anything wi'

25

whatever Ah did have. Whit's ma life, Charlie? Where is it? Ah wis a terrible failure, son. Nae money fur ye, nae security. Whit wis Ah ever use for?'

Use for? He was use for being a man, that was what he was use for. He was good at just being a man. All the times Charlie remembered him by were all just human moments. He remembered him laughing, moving, talking. He knew him by his courage and his physical strength. He remembered long before, when Charlie was small, how he would come in, muscled like a pony from the pits, and dispense good humour through the house. He remembered his kindness, his presence like a lightning conductor for trouble, making them safe. And wasn't that enough? Who said it wasn't? Who made it that a man had to measure himself against money in the bank or what he owned or how far he 'succeeded' or 'security'? Who decided that a man had to be judged in terms that had no connection with manhood, that coinage was a yardstick for a man? When had it happened that this man had accepted that everything he had was nothing when set against what he didn't have, an eight-room house with his name on the door, a car, a bank account? Who passed that judgment on him? How did it happen?

'Ah know now where Ah made ma mistakes, Charlie. Ye see –' Charlie saw by his father's face that what he was going to say was made difficult by more than the pain – 'ye see, whit yer mother did that time. Goin' away.' Pain gave way to hate on his face. 'Wi' that bugger Whitmore!' The words shot out like bile, and he subsided. 'That was me, Charlie. It was me. She wanted things. An' Ah jist couldn't get them. She was used. To them, ye ken. Everybody wants them. Don't blame 'er, Charlie. Everybody wants them. An' she wanted them. An if Ah couldn't give her them. There was somebody who could. It was ma fault, Charlie.'

That was it, a poison six years in taking effect. A kind of hemlock. Slow death. But leaving no trace. She left him and gradually he came to believe that she was right to leave him. And why shouldn't he believe it? What did he have to dispute it for him? All around him, that was the only measurement he could see. And he didn't fit it. He was a failure. Charlie remembered how he himself used to be exasperated at how often his father changed work. That would be mainly at the time before his mother left. He had always had a slight suspicion that it had been part of the reason for his mother's leaving. Now he saw that it was the other way round. It had been his father's pathetic and desperate attempt to be what he thought he ought to be, what he had been convinced he should be. He started several 'businesses', trying to sell cars, or ice-cream, or fruit and vegetables. They all folded. Charlie had found it laughable at the time. When he was given a form to fill in at school he was uncertain what to put for 'father's occupation'. He knew now. His father had never been anything more than a full-time human being. And it had never been enough. Now he realized the lonely desperation that must have been behind what had seemed to him laughable whimsy. He saw the reason for it. His mother went away and his father was left with something that had lived inside the banter and the clichés all this time, quietly doing its work. And nobody had paid much attention. Not even Charlie, himself. It was all done so neatly and skilfully, you could hardly tell. Now, six years later, with his mother married to someone else and living in another town, his father was dying quietly in this room and it wouldn't be noticed. That other married couple somewhere else could not be connected with this husk of a man dying here. No one would notice or see any connection, except Charlie. He noticed. He sat staring at his father, seeing a connection between him and those other two, somewhere in a brighter room.

'You'll no' be like me, though. You'll stick in, son. You'll get the education an' the good job. You'll make somethin' oot yer life. Ah ken ye can dae it, son. You'll have the university an' the education . . .'

So that was what he had been left with, a mouthful of shibboleths, a few magical words that he kept muttering like an 'open sesame', that he was passing on to Charlie as if they

27

were the keys to all the doors he had always found closed, had bled his fists against. That was how he had been left to finish, mouthing a few empty incantations, broken and bemused, surrounded by the painful mystery of his 'failure'. He wasn't just allowed to die. A man had to die. That was nothing. But nobody had the right to destroy a man before he died. And he had been destroyed. This wasn't the way he should have died. It had been made this way. This wasn't something just happening now. It must have happened a long time ago, and no one had noticed. A man had had everything taken from him, had been destroyed, and nothing had been done.

'You'll be a' right. Charlie. Wi' a university education. You'll no' be like me. The guid jobs. The big money.'

The last will and testament, a few words they had taught him painfully, punishing him when he neglected their importance. That was all he had left. When Charlie thought of the man his father had been and realized what he had been made now, and then thought that it had all happened in the utter isolation of his lonely self, he seemed to understand something for the first time. He knew what it must have been to be his father. And the insight was blinding, seared his mind, cauterizing it clean of every other thought. The injustice of it cleft his mind like lightning, and something vague and terrible followed in its wake, like distant thunder. But he could give it no shape, could form no definite thought from it as yet. Only one bitter word kept hammering on his mind as on an anvil. Bastards. Bastards. But what it was forging there he did not know. He just sat looking at his father, branding that image of him on his thoughts, and the small wooden carving on the bedhead above him, a cross inset in a diamond, stamped itself on his mind like a hieroglyph of hate.

His father's voice was petering out, but he was still trying to talk on, as if it mattered. He had lost the grip he had been keeping on his pain and his body was visibly racked. Charlie thought of the agony he had suffered to wait and talk to him. And what could Charlie say that could be commensurate with what his father had suffered? Nothing. He felt more bitter than he had ever felt before. He choked with inarticulate rancour. This was so wrong. His father was completely mistaken. But he had neither the time nor the words to tell him so. Nothing Charlie could say to him would make any difference. Speech dwindled to meaninglessness dropped into this chasm. Words withered in his breath. This was beyond talk. Something else was necessary. Something else.

Charlie just wanted his father to sleep now. That was all that could help him. As if from a great distance, he heard a car draw up outside the house. The front door was opened. Footsteps came slowly up the stairs, and Charlie felt that he was in a room where they could never join him. As the doctor came in, Charlie's father reached out to hold on to Charlie, as if not wanting to be gagged with morphine.

'Ah'm talkin' tae Charlie,' he said.

He was groggy with pain. Charlie barely noticed the doctor. He had hold of his father's hand in an incongruously formal gesture of handshake.

'It's a' right, Feyther,' he said. 'Ah hear ye. Ah'm listenin',' pushing back the pyjama sleeve. 'Ah know whit ye mean. Ah know it, Feyther. Ah know.'

The doctor came forward. Come on, Charlie thought, give it to him. Let him sleep. It's over for him. But not for us. Not for us.

'God bless ye, Charlie,' his father said. 'God bless ye.'

John stood in the doorway awkwardly. The needle searched a second in the puckered skin and submerged. Charlie felt the hand go rigid and relax, as if passing its pain into his. The lips kneaded themselves in silence as if trying to say more. Then the mouth went slack. He was asleep.

Chapter 4

HE NEVER RECOVERED CONSCIOUSNESS. AS THE DAY
progressed and as the family, making from time to time pathetic pilgrimages upstairs to his room, sensed him going in-
exorably from them down a lengthening corridor of cold and
clinical fact, the practical requirements of the situation impressed themselves on John. Most of the immediate family
knew that their father was within a day or two of dying and
had been calling in at the house each day or so to find out
how he was. In the late afternoon John left to go round them
all and inform them that his father was not expected to last
out the night. It was a laborious business and he had to be
careful to omit no one who would expect to be told. To many,
such an oversight would be an offence that no bereavement
could extenuate. Even grief had to be practical.

He was gone a long time and he was hardly back before the
first of the mourners followed on his heels. For an hour after
that they made a solemn, uneven procession into the house.
There was an indefinable sameness about the way they filed
upstairs, as if all their thoughts were dressed in uniform black.
Every negotiable chair had been taken from other parts of the
house and placed in a wide semicircle round the bed and
when there were no more chairs left they sat on cushions on
the floor or squatted on their haunches against wall or wardrobe. New arrivals were greeted with a muted murmur, a
slow sough of sound in which no words were decipherable, a
communal sigh which drew the newcomer into it as if their
grief were swollen by his. The room filled slowly till it brimmed with people. At other times they met each other only
fitfully, in street or shop or at the football or on a quick visit
to borrow a tool or bring a little news. Each had his own
concerns. For each, habit had laid private roads that none of

the others frequented. Old familiarities that they had had with each other in their youth were neglected, became overgrown in disuse. Each grew apart into his separate life. Often when they met in the street they would greet each other almost grudgingly, like toll-tax paid for roads they didn't use. Some did not even like each other. Some remembered the bitter word or imagined slight and filed it away for ever in their minds under the appropriate name. Some were merely indifferent. But all came together unquestioning for this, like amoebae in reverse. And their presence seemed to assume a single pulse that moved in time with that of the man who was dying.

No one spoke. Someone might offer round his cigarettes to those who were nearest him. Then they were lit and smoked, with the lengthening ash tipped into cupped hands. Small gnats of sound and movement flicked at the grave stillness from time to time. Someone coughed, and the sound was gagged with silence almost at once. Someone eased the position of a leg that hurt irreverently. Someone was picking fragments of clotted dust from the turn-ups of his trousers. For the body had to be occupied, was a troublesome encumbrance here, too skittish to submit for long to this solemnity. Hands moved of their own accord, roamed into pockets, furtively searching for occupation. Feet tapped on empty air, forgetting where they were. Eyes studied palms, escaping through an old scar to the past. It did not matter that the body misbehaved. No movement lived long in the face of that awful quiet. Only the small metal clock was insistent, relentlessly whittling the seconds from a life.

They sat on through the evening while outside the changing sounds recorded the time in the street. Children clattered past on imaginary hooves, shooting from inexhaustible guns, their voices changing from whoops to raucous argument because someone refused to be dead. A lawn-mower whirred spasmodically. The whistling of an ice-cream vender shifted deceptively, farther and nearer, elusive as a grasshopper. Sounds became less frequent. The voice of a strident mother

31

called her laggard child back home to his bed in the gathering dark. Someone whistled jauntily up the dark street, his heels clanging metallically on the pavement. A drunken man sang a broken verse of nostalgic song. Milk bottles put a full stop to the night in someone's house. Still they sat on, watching the man in the bed, who lay in troubled sleep, drawing up strained buckets of breath from an emptying well. Occasionally, he gasped and shuddered like a landed fish, hooked mercilessly to his own dying. They sat like children in church, concentrating on a solemnity that was awesome, incomprehensible, and not to be evaded. All evening no one had moved except one woman who rose every so often, wet her forefinger in whisky, and rubbed it round the dying man's mouth. This was Aunt Ella, a condor in bombazine, circling round their lives, alighting where trouble was, feeding on the carrion of other people's lives. She was Uncle John's widow, one of the family's professional mourners. Broken marriages, accidents, illnesses, deaths, they were all meat to Aunt Ella. She came in corbie-black and took her perch in sick-rooms and broken homes, zestful in grief, avid in consolation. She knew what had to be done in times of trouble the way other women knew how to turn the heel of a sock or the best way to remove a stain from clothes. Now she was officiating here with her bustling, busy sadness. When she got up to perform her ritual again, a harsh voice stopped her half-way to the bed.

'For God's sake, lea'e him alane!' Charlie said.

She sat back down and closed her hurt upon him like a door. But her pursed-lipped umbrage was lost on Charlie, whose attention barely flickered from his father. All evening he had sat concentrating on his father dying, not missing an agonized breath. He was hardly aware of other people in the room. Only his father lying on the bed was fully present to him. All other thoughts and awarenesses were incidental, mere doodles on the margin of his mind. Everything that happened in his father's body was transcribed to Charlie's mind, the soft hiss of air oozing from the raddled lungs, the features knotting on a sudden pain and unravelling slowly, the frequent

32

spasms that took possession of the body, causing it to convulse as if labouring to give birth to death, each macabre detail meticulously recorded. It was as if he was keeping an account. Why he should do this never occurred to him. But his mind of its own volition entered everything that took place as if against some future reckoning.

After Aunt Ella cloistered herself in her hurt pride, Charlie's father lay easy. Every time the whisky had been put to his mouth, he had girned under its touch, like someone not wanting to be wakened. Left alone, he seemed less troubled, except when the pain reached its spasmodic climax. The pain seemed to attack him like that, to hit him suddenly, rack his body for a time and then leave him. His body wrestled on the edge of the grave and it was impossible to tell whether it was struggling to hold on to life or gain possession of death. Often it seemed as if he couldn't die, as if all the pain was because he couldn't make his body yield to death. It went on into the early morning, fierce bouts of pain, until the watchers sensed the last struggle coming. They rose and gathered round the bed as if to lend him their strength. Hands reached out to touch him. Pain arched him upwards from the bed and they took him in their arms. Some of the women were moaning and keening, urging him to die. For a long moment, wet with their tears, he hung on to life by a thin chain of breath that rattled in his throat until the last link snapped and he was gone. Death shook the body as a dog shakes a rabbit and then dropped it, broken and empty, back into their arms.

In that moment all the grief that had stayed dammed in them during his dying seemed to break. It was as if his death, which had been happening through many hours, had all the time been unexpected. Women wept terribly. Their faces, abandoned to the distortions of grief, ran with tears and their mouths gave out an inhuman wailing. It reminded Charlie strangely of a word he had always remembered from a Latin textbook at school – *úlulare* – to wail. The sound they made was what it meant. The men stood silent, though some of them too were crying quietly, trying to comfort their women.

Gradually they filed past the bed, laying their last respects like wreaths beside him. Some touched him gently.

Downstairs, the women went into the living-room and sat nursing their sorrow and commiserating with Elizabeth, who was inconsolable. The men went through to the kitchen. It was done by ritual, as though the two groups had separate functions to perform. A bottle of whisky was produced from somewhere and drinks were distributed. They made a strange tableau, standing sombre in the little kitchen, as if drinking a dark toast to the dead man, while on the table the uncleared remains of a meal testified to the normalcy that would soon resume.

'He wis jist wan o' the hardest wee men in Kilmarnock in his day,' Charlie's Uncle Hughie said, his eyes moist with memory.

The others nodded and some said 'Aye', and they listened, looking at Hughie looming above them, while he talked of his prowess as a fighting man, which in his young days had been considerable. Hughie was brother-in-law to Charlie's father, married to his older sister, and he had probably been closest to him. They had been born within a year of each other and no more than two pubs and a pawnshop apart. They had experienced the same social crises from the same position. They had both been too young to be fully aware of the reverberations of the Sarajevo bullet. They had gone on strike from the pits and queued at soup-kitchens. They had gone in groups up Sunday morning roads and watched greyhounds chasing hares. They had stood at bookies' corners, following the progress of the favourites through the card more concernedly than the fate of nations. Something of the waiting at corners and the months without work and the long grass-chewing talks in the park had always remained with them. It was as if all their lives they had waited for things which had never happened, for the Utopia prophesied in bothy and bar-room, for the chimerical equality of men, for the manifestation of God's grace through the treble chance, or for the smaller miracle of the three-cross roll-ups that would give

34

them independence. And as Hughie spoke, telling of small incidents from Charlie's father's life, those who remembered added other parts from that past. They took their farewell of him, remembering what was best in him. It was their own funeral service.

When they were finished, they went through to the living-room. John had phoned for the undertaker and went upstairs with him when he came, to lay out his father and dress him for burial. Charlie stayed in the living-room with the others. From time to time he could hear John and the undertaker move quietly upstairs, arranging his father's body, plugging in the smell of decay. In the living-room grief was slowly exhausting its first throes, but there was still the unbearable weeping of women, wrapped in their elemental misery like a shawl, rocking back and forth, cradled in sorrow. Only Charlie was apart from it in a way he couldn't understand. He had not wept at any time, had not come near to doing so. He could not come to the easy and honest emotion of his Uncle Hughie. That seemed somehow a self-indulgence, a luxury he couldn't afford at the moment. His feelings were somehow too serious for tears. What he felt was like grief, yet more still than the others', quieter, unable to make itself seen or heard, like tears dripping inwards.

Chapter 5

'LET NOT YOUR HEART BE TROUBLED: YE BELIEVE IN God, believe also in me. In my Father's house are many mansions: if it were not so, I would have told you. I go to prepare a place for you.'

The voice rose and fell with mechanical regularity, dispersing its words like seeds from the hands of a sower. Rigid as rock, Charlie stood by the window, trying to take the meaning of the words to himself. The others in the room seemed to form a unity with the words of the minister, and one of which Charlie did not feel himself a part. They sat in hypnotic sorrow while the minister gave articulation to their grief, and the old words gave meaning to their misery. Some of the women were crying, but in a restrained, an almost formal way, so that no one's personal grief obtruded, but their weeping had a choric dignity. The men were very still and stiff in dark clothes, impassive as befitted death's retainers for a day.

The whole thing seemed curiously irrelevant to Charlie. The etiquette of death was new to him, and he had waited throughout these strange proceedings for something that would enable him to endorse their validity, to accept them as an expression of what he felt. He was like an unbeliever in a church, witnessing the elaborate ritual of a service, waiting for the experience that would change him from onlooker to participant. He wanted a sign, anything that would strike a responsive chord in himself and bring him into harmony with the others here, enable him to share their acceptance, make what had happened bearable.

But nothing that had taken place in this room seemed to have any connection with the man who had lain upstairs with his private agony. All of this decorous ceremony was like a deliberate mockery of what his father had been. It suggested a fulfilment and a culmination that belied the desperate and unfulfilled longing that had been his father. It was a pretence so contrary to the truth that Charlie couldn't begin to accept it.

Nothing here had any relevance to his father. The minister who presided over their sorrow had remained for Charlie no more than a kind and considerate man, administering mouthfuls of solace from his markered bible. He quoted beautiful archaic words at them. He gave up prayers of thanksgiving, raising his hands in benediction, quoting verses in his pulpit voice. But he didn't know for what he was giving thanks. He didn't know the years of suffering, the unnecessary despair. He thanked God. But God was not the only one to whom the thanks were due. You couldn't just make out all grief to the Almighty and expect Him to honour it. That was too easy. Your involvement went a lot deeper than that. Grief was your responsibility as well as His, and it wasn't enough to put it all to His charge.

But that was what they seemed to be doing. There was a vagueness about the whole thing, as if it didn't relate to anyone personally, but was merely a dismissal of anonymous remains. The minister's inaccurate and generalized eulogy typified it. This was a service dedicated to some uncertain and idealized image of a man that bore no resemblance to Charlie's father. Charlie tried to go along with it, but he couldn't recognize his father in any of it. He found himself wondering if this was all there was to be. He wanted desperately to accept this, to believe in its significance as the others seemed to. But by the time the minister brought his service to a close, Charlie was still unconvinced.

The men filed out into the waiting taxis and they moved slowly through the top part of the town with the traffic giving them precedence, and an old man at the kerb taking off his cap. The cars stopped just inside the gate because where the grave was could only be reached on foot by a narrow path. The cemetery was wet and very green after the recent rain as

37

they came out and took the coffin. They carried it upwards to the new grave which was half-way up the hill, and laid it on the ground while the minister spoke. Charlie remembered what the card given him by the undertaker had said: 'Please take cord 2.' They lowered the box, and the minister dropped dirt on to the wood. While the minister spoke for a few moments they stood around awkwardly, each with his own thoughts.

Charlie heard the minister's voice taking place far away, listened to rooks in the near-by trees, saw the clouds move together dark, conspiring rain, heard the horns of the traffic which passed, one graveyard away, and it wasn't enough.

Nothing here was enough. Something more than sanctimonious mutterings was needed over this grave. It was like a confidence trick to keep his spirit quiet. It would have been more honest to try to summon his ghost from its grave to haunt the actions that lived after it until it was blessed with meaning and had been given justice. Anything would have been better than this hypocrisy.

Charlie looked round the others at the grave. Their faces were as impassive as masks. What was taking place behind the masks? Did they know what had happened to the corpse that was lying in that coffin? Did they know what he had been and what he had been made into before he filled a box? Were they prepared simply to accept it as the way things were? Their faces showed nothing. They stood in their dark clothes like sentries barring the way to honesty, guardians of indifference and pretence.

Charlie felt antagonistic to their very presence. They were part of the lie that had destroyed his father. Their impassivity was a denial of what had happened. They thought it was enough to stand for a little while round this grave down which they flushed the refuse of their lives. But there was more to it. Death wasn't an end in itself. Lives were more than boxes of worm-food or elaborate manure. People mattered, and accounts had to be kept.

The minister was finished, and two men in overalls started

to fill in the grave. The others began to leave slowly like oxen yoked to an invisible burden. Charlie still stood beside the grave.

'Come on, kid,' John said to him quietly. 'It's finished.'

'It's no' finished,' Charlie said, shaking his head.

John did not know what he meant. He could see the others moving towards the gate, outside which the cars were drawn up, waiting.

'It's no' enough,' Charlie said simply.

On a plot of waste ground opposite the cemetery, two boys were calling to their careering dog.

'Sheena, Shee-na, Shee-na!' They yodelled through cupped hands.

It ran in crazy circles, cornering into the sound each time they called, tethered to their voices.

One of the men filling the grave glanced up at Charlie, and John touched his arm.

'Come on, Charlie. Come on.'

'Ah'm tellin' ye, John,' Charlie said. 'It's no' enough.'

Chapter 6

'AYE, MAGGIE GOT A QUICK CALL, TOO,' HIS FATHER said. 'Big Tam fairly went doon the brae after that. He used tae be a great case before it. Mind it was him that showed us yon trick wi' the egg, Charlie?'

Remembering the scene, Charlie was able to recall it complete, existing as it did bright and separate in his memory, like a room where the same people sat for ever saying and doing the same things. All he had to do was re-enter it and set them into motion. His memory, like a skilful stage director, established time and place, arranged them in their positions, gave them their cue. Saturday night. He had come in after seeing Mary home. In the living-room, his father, Uncle Hughie, and Elizabeth. Elizabeth, reading a magazine with that air of detached concentration as if something else was happening at the same time, like having her hair done. His father and Uncle Hughie sitting at the fire with the coffee table laid between them. They collided intermittently on Saturday nights, about half-a-dozen times a year, as if under some planetary influence, and inevitably finished up here, counteracting alcohol with tea. The crumbs on the table-cloth and the ash in the saucers indicated how far they had travelled towards cold sobriety. Charlie sat between them, listening to them pontificate on the General Strike, and local worthies, thoughtfully repeating names from the past, paging images through rooms of memory. Then, in the middle of the perfunctory conversation, his father's remark about the egg suddenly opened up a whole new moment. It was one of those 'open sesame' remarks through which the trivia of a night suddenly fall apart to reveal something memorable. One moment they were seated by the fire talking with perfect sanity, and the next were witnessing

40

something utterly unforeseeable and magnificently ludicrous.

'What wis this about an egg?' his uncle Hughie asked. He had an insatiable passion for all tricks, riddles, and feats of general curiosity.

'Ye must've seen it done,' Charlie's father said. 'It's just a matter o' tryin' tae break an egg longways.'

'An egg?' Uncle Hughie said incredulously.

'A comming or garding egg,' Charlie's father said, warming to the fact that it was new to Uncle Hughie. 'Ye just haud it at the two tips between yer hands. And ye canny break it. That's a fact.'

Charlie's father demonstrated the prescribed method of holding the egg.

'Ach, get away wi' ye!' Uncle Hughie's lip curled sceptically.

'That's as sure as Ah'm sitting here, Hughie. Ah've tried it maself.'

Uncle Hughie appealed to an invisible synod. As he looked back at Charlie's father his scorn was tempered with sympathy.

'Ye mean tae tell me, John, that you're goin' tae sit there, a grown man, an' tell me that ye couldny break an egg?'

'Ah'm tellin' ye mair than that. *You* couldny break an egg, if ye haud it the way Ah'm talkin' aboot.'

The slur on his manhood was too much for Uncle Hughie, six feet in his woollen socks, half as many broad, with arms like pit-props, reputed to be one of the strongest men in the shire in his prime, who had made a habit of lifting derailed hutches loaded with coal back on to the lines single-handed, who had once carried a huge concrete ball thirty yards from one gatepost to another, whose party piece was so to fill his jacket-sleeve with a flexed forearm that you couldn't move the cloth a millimetre (though some of the family were cynical about the last achievement, believing it to depend on the connivance of Uncle Hughie's tailor). Uncle Hughie's past prowess rose crowing in him like a cock.

'Ah'll lay a' the tea in China that Ah can break every egg

41

frae here tae John o' Groats. An' the hens that laid them.' The last thrown in as a magnanimous afterthought.

'Ye can have London tae an orange,' Charlie's father said adamantly, not to be outdone in generosity.

The rather intractable geographical dimensions of the wager were scaled down to the more finite terms of an even dollar, and four bright half-crowns were tiered ceremoniously on the mantelpiece.

'Elizabeth,' Charlie's father said. 'Would ye go through an' bring us an egg, please, hen?'

'Oh that's no' fair, Father,' Elizabeth's lips pursed righteously. 'You ken fine it canny be done.'

'Are you anither yin, Lizzie?' Uncle Hughie looked like Samson among the Philistines. 'You go through an' fetch me an egg, an' we'll see if it canny be done. This man's got you as bad as himself.'

'Anyway,' Elizabeth said, 'we don't hae eggs to throw away like that.'

'Ah'll buy ye a dozen eggs wi' ma winnings, hen,' Uncle Hughie promised.

'Yer egg'll go back the way it came, Elizabeth,' Charlie's father said. 'Don't fash yourself aboot that. I'll have it for ma breakfast first thing the morra mornin'.'

'I'll get ye an egg,' Charlie said.

'All right. All right.' Elizabeth could hold out no longer against a united front. 'I'll fetch it for them.'

Uncle Hughie took advantage of her absence to pivot on his chair and fart thunderously, as if it was some kind of inbuilt fanfare-system.

'Well, if ye haven't burst yer farting-clappers already, Hughie,' Charlie's father said jocularly, 'ye'll do it when ye try to break this egg.'

'Better wi' a toom hoose than a bad tenant.' Uncle Hughie said cryptically, taking off his jacket prefatory to combat.

'Homespun proletarian wisdom,' Charlie said.

But his Uncle Hughie was absorbed in his preparations. He was rolling his already rolled-up sleeves even higher.

'Ye'd better strip to the waist, Hughie,' Charlie's father said seriously. 'It'll make an awfu' mess when that egg bursts.'

Uncle Hughie took him at his word. He peeled off shirt and vest as one, and stood naked to the waist, revealing a huge craggy torso with fine dark coal-scars running over the left shoulder, and tattooed forearms. On his left forearm what looked like some sort of dancing girl stood with her arms tirelessly upraised, a faded relic of the romantic past who had aged with Uncle Hughie. On his right forearm two pale pink hearts had grown anaemic with the years.

Elizabeth entered like a handmaiden, carrying the egg. A space was cleared in the middle of the floor, and Elizabeth sat down beside Charlie on the settee like a ringside seat. Everything was done with formal propriety, as if it was all according to the eggbreakers' handbook. Uncle Hughie was set in the middle of the cleared space and Charlie's father stood with his hand on his shoulder, giving him a brief run-through of the rules. Uncle Hughie was nodding quietly, not missing a trick. Charlie almost expected to see him shake hands with the egg, and started to give a tense sibilant commentary in Elizabeth's ear.

'I want a good clean fight,' he was saying. 'And break when I say "break". You both know the rules. I won't hesitate to disqualify either you or the egg. So come out fighting and may the best egg win.'

Uncle Hughie was ready. He laced the fingers of both hands carefully together and held them cupped upwards while Charlie's father painstakingly placed the egg between his palms. Uncle Hughie's hands closed impatiently on the egg, but Charlie's father halted him and ran his fingers lightly round the edges of the egg to make sure that it was being held only by the tips.

'Right, Hughie,' he said. 'Away ye go.'

Uncle Hughie started to press.

'Feeling is running high at the Garden tonight,' Charlie resumed in Elizabeth's ear. 'This is something of a needle

43

match, Hughie versus The Egg. Human dignity hangs in the balance.'

Uncle Hughie was now visibly putting on the pressure. The dancing girl writhed sensuously. His right forearm had angina pectoris in duplicate. Huge veins rose and fell on his neck like organ-stops. His forehead, ploughed with effort, slowly took on a faint dew of sweat. His body, like an overheated boiler, became suffused with an unnatural red glow, as if combustion was imminent. And at the middle of this gigantic exertion, in the still centre of the hurricane, lay the egg, a tribute to the grit of Danish hens.

Uncle Hughie relaxed and took a breather. His palms glittered decoratively, sequined with sweat, and he wiped them on the seat of his trousers.

'Ah wouldny have believed that,' he said.

'There y'are,' Charlie's father said, vindicated. 'Ye'll maybe no' be so cocky the next time.'

He resumed his grip on the egg, with Charlie's father sitting confidently watching. Charlie became aware that Elizabeth was struggling to hold in her laughter. She snittered once briefly, like a horse neighing, and cut it short. Glancing at her, Charlie saw her lips twisting nervously in an attempt to suppress the laughter which showed beneath her composure like a kitten under a coverlet. Then he felt laughter lit like a slow fuse in himself, rising steadily, coming nearer to ignition, until it flashed and exploded from his mouth, simultaneous with Elizabeth's. Just at that moment the egg slipped in Uncle Hughie's perspiring hands and burst. Egg-yolk exploded dramatically like shrapnel, and catherine-wheeled in all directions. It spattered sideboard and mirror. It clung like a canker to an artificial flower. A fragment of it fried merrily in the fire. It spotted Uncle Hughie like an exotic acne. The laughter of the other three overtook the last particle of it before it found a resting-place. They hosed Uncle Hughie mercilessly with laughter, while he stood in the centre of the floor, dripping egg. They laughed and coughed and gasped for breath and laughed again. Charlie fell off the settee on to the floor and lay there helplessly, epileptic with laughter.

'For my next trick . . .' Uncle Hughie said.

And they became a quartet of laughers in unison, modulating, improvising, giving new interpretations to the situation through their laughter, until Uncle Hughie went through to get washed and returned spruce and eggless. While he was putting his shirt on again, Charlie's father tried to give him back his money but he insisted it had been fairly lost. In the end it was decided that the money should be given to charity, namely Charlie and Elizabeth. The incident had generated laughter that lasted throughout that night and beyond.

As he remembered it, Charlie's smile was an ironic echo of that laughter. Lying alone in his room, he thought himself through that occasion and others like it as if it were a form of penance. Since his father's death he found himself brooding over past incidents like that, fingering them over and over in his memory, like rosary beads, as if mysteriously they could somehow help him to understand what had happened to him, help to resolve the enigma his feelings had become even to himself. Something about all of these moments drew him, seemed to promise to help him come to terms with the amorphous feeling of utter deception that he felt. Somewhere in them was the reason for his inability to participate as he had done before in his own life. And the incident of the ludicrous egg-breaking contest was typical of them all.

He remembered how they had all felt after it. They were all conscious of having made something among them. A night had been baptized. That was The Night That Uncle Hughie Fought The Egg. It was salvaged from the anonymity of other nights. It would be remembered, along with The Night The Dog Took A Fit, when John, playing vets, muzzled Queenie with an elastic band, and its head inflated ominously and it frothed like a drawing pint, charging chairs, butting sideboards, running a canine reign of terror until his father came in and unloosened the elastic; The Massacre Of The

45

Chickens, when his father put a hundred day-old chickens in a ramshackle hut with a floor like a sieve and during the night the cats pulled them down through the floor like manna and his father came out next morning to a cenotaph of feathers; The Siege Of The Lavatory, when Elizabeth locked herself in the toilet and couldn't get back out and the rest of the family spent most of an hour huddled round the door broadcasting instructions to her and sending messages of hope, and in the end his father had to climb the rone and break a window to get her out, tear-stained and penitent; The Quest For The Canary, when the pet canary, which had the run of the house, flew out of a window inadvertently left open and the scheme turned out to watch his father, holding aloft a cage and rattling a packet of birdseed, wander the streets calling 'Joey, Joey, Joey', to the roof-tops until Joey alighted on his head and he nudged him back into his cage and returned home in an aureole of Franciscan awe.

To their canon of occasions another night had been added. That was how they had felt. That was how they all remembered each other, haloed in a certain incident, incarcerated in an anecdote. They met each other fitfully, in the cleft of a phrase, in casual moments. When Charlie thought his way through the past six years, trying to place the terrible image of the father he had found in that death-room, trying to match it with another, he could not. All he could remember were those brighter rooms, moments of laughter, incidents that refused to be taken seriously. He could remember many things about his father, but almost all of them seemed redolent with humour. He could remember the time his father had risen at three in the morning to listen to the world championship fight from America. He made tea and sandwiches, arranged his armchair by the wireless. He filled a pipe meticulously. He sat with his tea before him, the quilt from the bed draped round his shoulders, the wireless tuned in, and, with the match raised to light his pipe, the fight was finished in the first round. Charlie remembered his father sitting there, resplendent in bedclothes, the match burning his fingers, his

46

face sagging with disbelief, crowned with rumpled hair, King of Incredulity. He remembered the time his Uncle Hughie had interrupted their record session with some folk-singing of his own. They had all been listening to the records which seemed to have been in the house before they were, when his Uncle Hughie had dropped in, almost literally, and insisted that they should listen instead to his own repertoire of favourites for inebriates. He asked them, with unconscious irony, what was their pleasure, and proceeded to sing his own. 'The Lea Rig.' He rearranged himself in his chair, coughed the loose phlegm from the back of his throat, and swallowed it, kneaded his lips, fluttered his eyelids, and started to sing (with Charlie's father descanting at the ends of lines and interpolating ironic commentary, 'On ye go then . . . Can ye beat 'im . . .? Awfu' guid . . . Clear as a bell . . .?'):

> 'Whe-hen owes the hull yon eastren staaar
> Tells bughtin' ti-hime is near my Jo-ho . . .'

His Uncle Hughie never actually sang a song. He simply shouted the words as loudly as he could and left the notes to fend for themselves. His eyebrows assumed an acrobatic existence of their own, lifting and lowering with random suddenness. His Adam's apple bobbed alarmingly like a float under pressure from a porpoise. His eyes scuttled in their sockets like mad mice. Convulsive breathing made a bellows of his body, and huge arms were liable to be flung straight out at any moment in massively dramatic gestures. To anyone new to the experience it must have been a fearsome prospect, like the death throes of a mammoth. But through it all there was a ponderous sincerity to his performance. He was able to let a song possess him utterly, like an insane demon, so that once started nothing would stop him till the last line had been exorcized. He sang on relentlessly and where he didn't know the words he simply improvised with a weird keening mouth-music of his own, or else stretched one word out like elastic until it filled a line:

> Down by the burn where yon birk trees
> Wi' dew are ha – a-a-a-aangin' . . .'

That ludicrous sound had never faded from his memory. It was strange how he could remember so much that was casual and trite. He seemed to move among memories of his father that mocked the enormity of his dying. He found only trivia to recall. Broken fragments of small enjoyment littered his memory like a child's discarded toys, aimless and inconsequential, seeming to have no connection with what had happened in that final room, with what must have been happening for years inside his father, while no one had been taking any notice. To have had laughter was good, but when the banter and the jokes were set against his father rotting twice in that little room – when they were all there was to set against it – they seemed a bitter insult to his dying. It was like a conspiracy of smiles against the truth. Something terrible had happened to his father, perhaps because six years ago his wife had left him, perhaps because of other things, perhaps because of many things. But it had happened. He had been destroyed as a man and the fact had registered nowhere except in himself. His own family had not even acknowledged it. Their lives had gone on superficially while he had lived at that awful depth, completely alone.

He thought of his father nursing the broken pieces of himself and being jocular. Even when he talked of himself as he did sometimes, perhaps sitting by the fire with Charlie, he would talk mainly of times far in the past, as if at some point something had happened that negated himself and he had only those things to remember from a better time. When he talked like that it was like a ritual. The same stories recurred and Charlie came to learn them, his father's private mythology, the accidental debris of a man that he took out from time to time to look at and be nostalgic over. They were pathetic in their motley variety of the funny and the ridiculous and the gently sad. He might recite the one about Lubey's fabled methods of obtaining drink. How he once told a barman that for a half of whisky he could rid him of the flies which came in plagues from a rubbish-dump behind the pub. The barman, like most figures of authority in legend, must have been somewhat gullible, for he duly set up a half. Lubey downed it, jumped back, put up his dukes, and said, 'Send the buggers out one by one'. There was the series about Alec Nine-toes, whose boyhood must have been like a sort of re-enactment of the plagues of Egypt. He was a walking monument to human vulnerability. He broke limbs as casually as matches. He once broke both legs simultaneously, jumping a wall to evade the police. He got his nickname from the time when he was looking down a pen for frogs and the grid fell and consigned a fair proportion of his big toe to the sewers. He went on from boyhood to manhood, living always between the plaster and the poultice, weaving uncertainly along his private zodiac, until one night, when he was drunk on the money from a modest pools win, he and a double-decker bus converged on King Street and it was as if all his past life had only been a rehearsal for that moment. He was the incarnation of the god of chance in the private pantheon of Charlie's father, and the evocation of his image was always accompanied by reverential shakings of the head, as if to appease his spirit.

But the part of the past Charlie's father returned to most frequently was properly not one story at all. It was rather a small plexus of memory, and to touch any part of it would stir a series of connected responses. It concerned Sanny, the younger brother of Charlie's father, and it was sensitive to a variety of pressures. You might touch upon it by an incidental reference to the past or by reiterating a saying which for Charlie's father belonged essentially to his brother's canon or by mentioning the war. The war was the commonest point of contact. Sanny had been killed at Monte Cassino and Charlie's father still kept the last letter he had written – a letter Charlie had seen many times himself – on thin, unlined paper fraying along the folds so that you had to open it very carefully, in pencilled words that the years since the war had all but erased, in illegible handwriting, with wrong spellings, and with almost no punctuation, but suffused with a courageous unconcern that made it for Charlie's father like an illuminated manuscript. Usually when he spoke of it he would rise at some point to fetch it from the drawer that held the photographs, bringing as illustrations to its text a dun photograph, scarred with handling, that showed Sanny in battledress, flanked by two anonymous comrades, all three grinning determinedly out from a frame of flags. He would hand you the letter as if it were an undiscovered manuscript of the Apocrypha. When you had read it for yourself, he would read it to you. And when he came towards the end where it said not to worry because Sanny didn't think the German was born that could kill him, Charlie's father always commented that that was right enough because he had been killed when the British mortar he was loading backfired and exploded in his face. There was no sense of bathos or ludicrous irony in it for him. It was simply a vaunt fulfilled.

Charlie had often enjoyed listening to his father talking about these things. Taken together, these anecdotes of his father and those Charlie had garnered for himself had formed a sort of composite picture of his father for him, had provided a fixed point from which to see him and understand him. But listening to his father as he died had pulled the pin away on that image, had somehow shattered it. Now when he drew these thoughts from his memory it was like picking bits of shrapnel from himself. Their familiar composition had been destroyed in the explosive experience of sitting in that death-room with his father. They had shifted into unfamiliar positions, no longer rested comfortably in his mind but rubbed and irritated there, barking against each thought, suppurating in his subconscious. Their former levity and ease of acceptance were the very things that made them seem alien now that their coherence had given way to a tunnel of doubt, to the dark hole blown in them by his father's death. It was this dark void that Charlie was aware of facing him when he

50

thought of his father's life. It was this void he was concerned to penetrate, to follow wherever it led.

Did his father's suffering have no meaning? It could have no meaning if everything else was to continue exactly as it had done. Was it simply to be accepted with the reflection that this was the way things were? Did a man's life mean so little that it was not even to be acknowledged? A man had been destroyed through no fault of his own. He had been made to believe devoutly in his own worthlessness, in his personal failure, and he had been made to believe in it simply because he could not conform to the rules which had been set for him. Because he could not succeed in terms which were not his terms at all, the only terms allowed him had been those of utter failure. If this injustice was final, if nothing could be done to right it, then nothing was meaningful, nothing was worth while. Was that truly all there was to life, circuitous conversations, the fragments of gossip chapped into a pallid fleeting flame, people dying word by word, aimlessly, casually, in communal loneliness, while the canary chirped, and more coal was needed for the fire, and someone went out to the van for the wafers? Was there nothing more dynamic than this to connect those two images that haunted Charlies' imagination: the image of one man peeled of flesh and illusions, a skeleton of bitter hopelessness, lying in a lonely room; and the image of two people somewhere in another room living in quiet content? For he knew that for anything to matter these two images must be made to meet, must fuse to one.

For anything to be worth while, for all of their lives to have any meaning, there must be something more to connect those two images than casual trivia. Their lives were somehow insufficient. Something different was needed, something that would acknowledge what had happened and transform their trivial lives into an expression of it.

Somehow, he did not know how, it had to happen. And it had to happen through him. For where else had his father's suffering been registered except in himself? The mourners had come and gone, the obsequies were said and there had been no attempt to recognize the injustice his father had suffered. It might as well have been buried with him except that it had transmigrated to Charlie, now lived pent up in him as it had dwelt unrealized in his father. Only he could bring it into being.

He felt himself vaguely dangerous with its potential. As yet he could form no intention. The feeling was too vast and amorphous to admit of anything as finite as an aim.

He felt unknowingly that still desolation that each feels at some times in his life when he turns from pretending, evades the eyes of others and meets himself. It is as if you have passed through one of the strange concyclic circles of living, one of the secret doorways of the self, moss-grown with trivia so that the legend on the lintel is concealed and the chiselled enduring arch is hidden totally under the personal excrescences of your life so that you do not realize that this is a door through which all men must pass, a door made for all men to come to, mortared out of what all men are, and through which they may pass only one at a time. It may be much later before you realize that you are in a new place, have passed through many gates, and are come nearer to the final door behind which you wait with cup or knife to greet yourself. But from time to time in the press of hurrying intentions and talking friends and intermingling ambitions you glimpse yourself alone, fleshed in a private mystery, set out on a lonely road that none can travel with you. It is the same for all and different for each. In railway waiting-rooms, on late last buses, playing with their children, walking in the street, men find again the knowledge that was lost, hear news, come home to themselves alone. Commitments, demands, intentions, turn, grow, enfold, shut out the light, break suddenly and show, back-turned and deaf to your cries, the distant self, whose face you will only find at the final door. Voices of friend, brother, lover, call, here, there, near, far, this way, that, and suddenly fall silent. And you're alone, where one footstep makes thunder in the dark.

Chapter 7

MRS WHITMORE GLIMPSED HERSELF IN THE FULL-LENGTH mirror as she passed. She paused automatically, making the ritual gestures of arranging her hair while at the same time being careful not to disturb its lacquered elegance. She noticed a wrinkle in her stocking that was like an omen of age. Putting down the small folder she was carrying, she eased up her dress, held it with her elbows, deftly damped her fingertips, and smoothed her left leg back to nylon youth. She shimmied her dress back into order, strafed herself with a last expert glance, and was about to turn away when she suddenly stopped, staring.

Something about herself arrested her, something indefinable. It was a feeling comparable to knowing that there was something fractionally out of place in her appearance. But she knew that her make-up was immaculate, her clothes in good taste, her jewellery in keeping. Her eyes looked back at her, echoing their own question. Slowly, faced with herself, she came to face the feeling. It had been with her for some time now, prowling the edges of her consciousness, as if waiting for her to admit it. Doing her household duties, she had sensed its presence on the other side of each activity, and she had kept it at bay with preoccupation. But it haunted the small, still moments of her daily life like a patient ghost that longed to be incarnated. It constantly threatened to intrude more positively into her awareness. It was like something she had neglected to do or had mislaid, or like an unlatched window rattling quietly in the night. She might refuse to acknowledge it or to do anything about it, but she could not dismiss it.

Now, sensing its imminence again, she wavered on the verge of trying to force it into consciousness, to see if she could exorcize the ghost by giving it flesh. But she was a little frightened

53

of admitting it fully to herself because she knew that the substance of its shadow derived somehow from a lack in her life, and she dreaded the extent to which its acknowledgement might undermine her security. And yet, how could anything undermine her security? What was there that she lacked? She looked around the well-furnished bedroom, dwelling on the rich curtains, the plush carpet, the expensive furniture that reflected the light in polished patches. This was hers. And Peter's. This was their house. A bungalow. Her mind inventoried its rooms smugly, emphasizing special features as if for an advertisement, refrigerator, stainless steel sink-unit, garage with room for two cars. She was very fortunate. Peter was good to her. What cause did she have to feel dissatisfied? One closed door away, Peter was sitting in the lounge, talking with Raymond and Eleanor, their guests. What was there to trouble her? Unless it was the past.

She shied away from the thought. She had got over everything by now, she told herself. She had known that there were things she would miss terribly. She had known she would have to adjust. And she had adjusted. She had lived with herself for a long time by compromise, by a tacit and gentle self-deception, the studied exclusion of certain thoughts. She knew that you could only gain certain things by forfeiting others, that, where the achievement of one desire precluded another, you had to choose, that to possess was to relinquish. That had been her lesson, a hard lesson. Surely she had learned it by now. She had thought she had. She had tried, certainly. She owed Peter such an effort. It seemed unjust that old longings she had ascetically starved to death should resurrect their hunger in her heart. After so long. After so very long.

Yet something of those longings had survived. She knew it had. She knew that what troubled her was a gap that remained from the past, a need that the years between had not fulfilled. They had been good enough years and they had brought everything she had hoped for, except their own self-sufficiency. She had hoped that her life with Peter would absorb her entirely, leave nothing of her over to be a prey to

54

nostalgia or regret. There had been times when nostalgia had almost incapacitated her, like a recurring illness. Sometimes she had lived through a whole week in which every day seemed to focus exclusively on the past, and it was like being in a house which had windows at the back only. But she had learned to live with this, and she could cope with it when it came. She simply administered to herself gradually increasing doses of hard work and altruism until immunity had been re-established.

But the feeling as it affected her now no longer responded to such treatment. Perhaps it was just that her complaint had reached its secondary stage. It was more tenacious than it had been, and it had assumed a subtly different nature. Before, she had recognized it simply as an intensified form of the nostalgia that becomes a part of all people as they grow older and the past begins to outweigh the future. She had thought of her own feeling as merely a highly particularized species of that general tendency, intenser for her because it was localized in one particular place and personalized into a few particular people. But now that no longer adequately accounted for it. Now it was not properly nostalgia at all. It was not a retrospective look at an irrecoverable past, something made poignant by the very fact of its being irredeemable. It was no longer content to have that pittance of time with which the present pensions off the past. It seemed determined to encroach upon the future. She had found herself lately seriously considering the possibility of making some sort of vague undefined contact with that part of her past that she had foresworn. Every time the realization of what she was doing came upon her she felt shocked at herself and determined not to do it again. What did she hope to gain from it? Even if she did reopen that door, what did she expect to find there that belonged to her? There was nothing for her there. She had seen to that. This was where she belonged. In this house with Peter. Everything that she had any right to was here. There was nothing for her anywhere else. Then why was she not content? What was it that she wanted?

55

'Jane! Have you gone to bed or something?'

She started guiltily at Peter's voice. She hastily checked her appearance again in the mirror, as if afraid her mental disarray might have a physical extension. Putting out the bedroom light, she went through to the living-room, donning a smile at the door.

'I seem to have seen your face before,' Raymond said. 'We were nearly sending out a search-party for you there, Jane. You'd better take a compass next time.'

'Were you developing the photographs?' Peter's voice was just this side of annoyance and no more.

'Oh, the photographs!' Her hands went up in surrender to his reproach.

'Well, that was only what you went for, after all.'

'You'd better check that room through there, Peter,' Raymond said. 'And make sure there's not a lodger you don't know about.'

She went back through to the bedroom, mingling her laughter with that of the others to cover the furtive sense of guilt she felt. She tried to gear herself to their mood. This was where she belonged, she told herself again. She was going to enjoy this evening. But she couldn't overcome a vague feeling of strangeness as she re-entered the living-room.

'These had better be good after the time we've waited,' Raymond said. 'Malta, The Millionaire's Playground. A Pictorial Account of a Holiday on the George Cross Island. Golden beaches . . . Dusky maidens . . .'

'Here's one of Peter when his skin was just beginning to peel,' Mrs Whitmore said, passing the photograph to Eleanor.

'Ooh. Frying tonight.' Eleanor giggled. 'Mind you, Peter, you really suit blisters.'

'You mean blisters suit him,' Raymond emended.

'I mean exactly what I said,' Eleanor persisted.

'You can say it how you like. It's no skin off my nose.'

'It's not until the skin begins to peel that you get the full savour of your sunburn,' Peter continued, like a lecturer ignoring hecklers. 'The blisters are only a sort of apprenticeship

56

in agony. But once you get down to doing a striptease with your skin, you become a real veteran. It's like a Gipsy Rose Lee that doesn't know where to stop. You scratch and you scratch. And then you scratch. I could hardly wait for meals to finish so that I could go up to the room for my next performance. I used to invite Jane up to see my itchings.'

'This is one of the harbour at Valletta,' Mrs Whitmore said.

They settled down to a relay of snapshots, with Mrs Whitmore providing explanatory captions and Peter using the incidents they recalled as launching pads for sardonic commentary on Malta.

'It's lovely scenery,' Eleanor commented after some thought.

'God, I wish I had said that,' Raymond said, as he took the photograph from her. And went on at once, outrunning riposte, 'Especially in the foreground there. Wow! Where do you book for this place? I thought Maltese women were supposed to be very prim. Concealing the tempting flesh and all that.'

'Only the ones who've nothing to show,' Peter said. 'You do see some of them wearing long black dresses to go swimming right enough. Actually, they're a lot worse than bathing-suits once they've been in the water. The way they sag and cling. Typical Maltese Irishness. It's like the way you have to cover your upper arms in churches, isn't it, Jane? No sleeveless dresses allowed. But it doesn't matter how low the neckline is. Or how high you have the hemline.'

'This was taken just coming into Gozo,' Mrs Whitmore explained. 'That's the sister-island to Malta. It's only half-an-hour in the boat. We spent two days there.'

'Which was just about a day-and-a-half too much,' Peter said. 'It's strictly a poor relation. They play up everything, show you round any old bit of rubble they've got handy. They just about give you guided tours of the public conveniences. Remember the prehistoric temple? A ring of boulders with weeds . . .'

57

Mrs Whitmore was content to let him do the talking. It was all she could manage to take even a neutral factual part in the conversation. She found herself wondering what it had to do with Raymond and Eleanor. It was obvious that their interest was only token. They were more concerned with finding opportunities for needling each other. Why were they always like that? It wasn't the first time she had been at a loss to understand why they were still together. Surely it would have been more honest for them just to separate. Yet she couldn't help asking herself what right they had to inflict themselves on other people like this. On her. She felt a revulsion from them. What did she have in common with them? What was she doing sitting in their company?

'You see, I was trying to get him to tell us the price of the taxi before I got in. But he just kept saying, "Rambla beach, sor. Lovely for swim. I take you Rambla. No bother money. Later. Later".'

She was aware of Raymond's eyes on her legs. Like limpets. She didn't bother trying to distract them or to cover her legs more effectively, nor to stare him into emabrrassment. He would probably have taken any acknowledgement of his attention, no matter what form it was in, as a secret victory. He was always furtively intruding on her in this way. Sometimes when he was speaking to her he would stare very deliberately at her breasts as if it were with them that he was communicating. At other times he would engineer careful accidents and casual collisions. Sitting in at table, he would unavoidably brush against her thigh, pressing hard with his hand just as he touched her. Looking at something over her shoulder, he would lean on a little, his hand imprinting itself on her back. He always seemed to position his chair in such a way that when he faced towards her, his face was averted from Peter's. He didn't seem to mind about Eleanor. He probably wanted her to notice. Mrs Whitmore had mentioned his behaviour to Peter, but because of Peter's flippancy, she had not mentioned the subject to him again, for it hurt her too deeply. She was insulted that Raymond thought he could

58

take these trivial and casual liberties with her, and she was ashamed when it occurred to her what grounds he might have for thinking so. That was something else left over from the past. The present was riddled with the past. How did she think she could get over it? It had left her on the defensive about herself, inclined to sift the most trivial attitudes and remarks for concealed implications. The sort of perfunctory masculine examination that most women would construe as a personal compliment, she would distort into a personal insult, while it was nearly always no more than an impersonal instinct.

'And they were in process of building another one. They seemed to look on it as a sort of stake in heaven. And they had more churches than they knew what to do with already. Ludicrous. They'd rather have the sacrament than a bite of bread on the table. Building elaborate churches and some of them living in houses the size of outside toilets.'

She wondered how Peter could be so content in their company. He seemed to be enjoying himself, relating his traveller's tales. But then he liked an audience of any kind. He tended to adopt this cynical worldly-wise attitude to things when he was with them. They always seemed to bring out the worst in him. Listening to him, she could barely recognize the holiday. It was as if he had been with someone else. You would have thought it had been a penance to him. But it hadn't been like that at all. The things he mentioned were true to a degree. But he was taking them out of their context, distorting perspective. He was presenting them with isolated fragments, taken from angles that exaggerated their dimensions, and were jaundiced with cynicism. She felt betrayed in some small way that alienated her even further from the others. It made her realize again with a sudden familiar hollow feeling just how loosely she was anchored to her present life even after all this time. It only took one of these distant supercilious moods of Peter's to make her sense of security break its moorings and cast her adrift.

'It took me some time to realize what was missing in all the

59

rooms. Then it eventually got through to me. Fires. There wasn't a fireplace in any of the houses we saw.'

'That would suit Raymond,' Eleanor said. 'He hasn't quite mastered the art of getting one started yet. He uses newspapers, firelighters, and enough sticks for a Guy Fawkes bonfire. And he's still down on his knees blowing like a bellows.'

'How would you know about that?' Raymond spoke in the same pseudo-jocular tone that Eleanor was using. 'You're never out your bed till it's roaring up the chimney.'

'Well, it gives me an excuse for having a long lie.'

'You don't need any excuse for that. Talking of fires, though. Have you heard the one about the minister with the four sons? I heard it in the office yesterday.'

'All right, I'll buy it,' Peter said.

'Minister has four sons. David, Peter, Paul and James. Are you sure you haven't heard it now?'

'Let's all get down on our knees and plead with him,' Eleanor exclaimed brightly.

'No, but I hate getting told half-way through a joke that you've heard it. Or getting the punch-line stolen. Anyway. This minister has four sons. David, Peter, James and Paul. Three good ones. Follow in his footsteps. Become ministers. One prodigal. James. A right tearaway. Wine, women and song. Well, at breakfast this morning, the minister's down first. So he's standing in front of the fire. Warming his chorus and verse. Peter comes down next. "Good morning, Peter." "Good morning, Father." So Peter joins him, standing by the fire. Next one down is Paul. "Good morning, Paul." "Good morning, Father." And he joins the other two at the fire. That's three ministers standing in front of the fire. Right? The next one to come is the fourth minister. James. So –'

'James!' Eleanor struck like a cobra. 'You said James was the bad one. The black sheep.'

'Black sheep?' Raymond sparred for time, trying to gather his thoughts. 'Who the hell mentioned sheep? James. That's the third son that's a minister.'

'No. That's not what you said.' Eleanor mounted right-eousness and went into battle. 'You said James was the womanizer. I can remember *exactly* what you said, Smart Alec. You said the three sons who were ministers were Peter and Paul and . . .' she said, and slid indecorously from the saddle.

Raymond let her squirm in silence for a moment before he went on with devastating contempt, 'Thank you, Lesley Welsh. The Memory Woman. Well. As I was saying . . .

'So the father says, "Good morning, *James*." "Good morning, Father. Good morning, Peter. Good morning, David." '

'David?' Eleanor asked the ceiling, as if appealing for Jove's thunderbolt of justice.

'*David!*' Raymond ground out the name on a mill-wheel of determination that crushed all opposition, ' "Good morning, *David*." So that's the four ministers standing in front of the fire. They're all standing there. The four of them. In a line.' Raymond was playing for time, obviously rattled. His eyes had a hunted look. But he had to go on. 'They're all there. When Andrew comes in. "Good –" '

'God!' Eleanor exchanged martyrdom for denunciation. 'Andrew! Are you sure it wasn't Bathsheba? Or Uriah? Uriah the Heep.'

'Look!' Raymond threw words at her blindly, like stones from the rubble of his thoughts. 'Damnit. To hell. Who's telling the joke? What difference does it make? I'll call him what the hell I like. Admiral bloody Nelson if it suits me.'

'Fine, fine, that's right,' Eleanor soothed, like a nurse dealing with a fractious mental patient, rubbing him very gently the wrong way. 'That's a clever attitude. Keep that up and they'll give you a little padded cell where you can tell yourself jokes for the rest of your life. Because you'll be the only one who knows what they're all about. What's the point of telling a joke if you can't make sense of it? Why do you bother?'

'God knows why I bother!' Raymond's anger was more orderly now, having found a familiar flag under which to rally. 'When *you're* in the company, God knows why. Because

61

when did I ever get to finishing a bloody story? When? Smart Alexis has to butt in. Always has to throw a spanner in the works.'

'It's not a spanner I'm throwing. It's a life-belt.'

'Life-belt? You always manage to kill them, anyway.'

'It's what's called euthanasia.'

'It's a pity your mother didn't know about it.'

Peter got to his feet suddenly and pretended to do a soft-shoe shuffle.

'There will be a short intermission,' he announced. 'During which I will endeavour to entertain the company. Patrons are asked not to leave their seats. We are getting the fire under control.'

The sprinkling of forced laughter Peter elicited managed to dampen tempers down a little. He took the opportunity to pass round cigarettes like toys to soothe unruly children. There was an awkward pause, broken at last by Eleanor, who managed, by her air of saving a situation single-handed, to convey the impression that Raymond was alone responsible, although she was the one who bravely made amends.

'It must be wonderful, though,' she said in a false, determined voice, very deliberately ignoring Raymond, and leaving him to smoulder in the ruins of his self-esteem. 'I mean to be able just to go abroad like that. For a long holiday. That's where you're so fortunate, Jane. But then you don't have any children to worry about.'

Neither did she, as it happened. But every holiday-time, she acted as what she called 'foster-aunt' to a family of children from an orphanage. Just for a few days. To give them a taste of home-life, she said. Presumably to let them see that they weren't missing much. She had never had any children of her own. She compensated by playing at being maternal once or twice a year, but not long enough for it to become a nuisance. She made a great deal of it. Mrs Whitmore had wondered before if she only did it in order to give herself a certain conversational status. Certainly, she managed to get round to it at some point of every evening, and always with a remark that was directed at Mrs Whitmore. Mrs Whitmore felt that it might be a deliberate attempt to bait her, but she couldn't be sure. She had grown so touchy on that subject too that she could not be certain her own assiduity was not translating unthinking remarks into pre-determined insults. Either way, it wasn't the kind of remark calculated to make her feel any more at home with them. She had a depressing vision of growing old among people like this, with whom she had no real contact, for whom she had no real concern, strangers acquainted only with the surface of herself. It was a very sad and a very lonely feeling, from which the future seemed to stretch away like an empty echoing corridor, with only casual meetings to interrupt her progress towards the door at the end of it.

'I thought I was in hell there. This is what it must be like. A place where you can't see the fire for ministers.'

Everybody looked in an almost alarmed way at Raymond, as if he had gone quietly off his head. At least his words saved Mrs Whitmore the trouble of having to listen to Eleanor on the subject of part-time maternity.

'That's it,' Raymond said. 'The punch-line of the joke. For what it's worth. Although it's more like an epitaph now.'

There was a sound of something being dropped into the hall.

'That'll be your magazines, Peter,' Mrs Whitmore said, seizing the opportunity. 'I'll just bring them in.'

As she crossed the living-room, Peter laughed a consolatory laugh, and said, 'Oh yes. Very good.'

Mrs Whitmore closed the living-room door with a sense of tremendous relief. She stood for a moment, letting the sooth-ing insistence of the hall-clock massage some of the tension from herself. The magazines lay on the carpet, illumined dimly from the lamp above the door. She crossed and picked them up, riffling them automatically until she came to the local newspaper she still had sent to her, although the locality it served was no longer hers. She glanced at its front page absently and halted, staring in an action that echoed that

63

moment in the bedroom, her eyes held by a name in the deaths column. She closed the paper again at once, as if trying to shut out the thought it gave rise to in her mind. But she was too late. The thought was already there, emerging from a confused welter of sadness and regret and guilt and hope, riding them determinedly. It entered her mind fully realized, bringing her a kind of hope she had tried to live without, seeming to bear with it the answer to the alienation she felt with people like Raymond and Eleanor and sometimes even with Peter himself, seeming to offer her an alternative to that long bleak corridor. She was going to take it. This moment with the dim light striking across her in the darkened hall and with the magazines clutched in her hand was like a small miracle to her, the intervention of a benevolent fate. She was not going to let it pass from her. She knew what she was going to do. Yet she knew that she must achieve it by indirection, for it depended upon Peter's consent and assistance. She must first set about ensuring that and she would do it as circumspectly as she would go about obtaining money from him for an expensive dress. She stood a moment longer in the conspiratorial shadows before she concealed the newspaper carefully among the magazines and moved casually towards the living-room door.

Chapter 8

'AYE, IT'S A SAD BUSINESS RIGHT ENOUGH, CHARLIE,' MR
Atkinson was saying. 'He wisny an auld man by any manner
of means. An' there's a lot we could have done without before
yer feyther. But there it is, son. Facts are chiels that winna
ding. Ye've got tae cut your coat according to yer claith. It's
no' easy. But it maun be done.'

Charlie found himself wondering what he was doing here,
listening to these words of trite consolation. Atkinson's Book
of Proverbs for Everyday Use. Had he come here to be con-
soled? He felt a little ashamed that he should have inflicted
himself on Mr Atkinson. What right did he have to be standing in this office, letting himself be laved with sympathy?
Because Mr Atkinson knew his father and liked him? Because
he had worked here during the last university holidays and
Mr Atkinson had been nice to him, taking him out of the
cement factory and letting him work in the office?

While Mr Atkinson waxed philosophical on the vagaries of
fate, Charlie couldn't help feeling that his words were out of
place here, like a lectern in a washroom. He looked round the
familiar precincts of the poky office, with the teapot and the
blue-hooped cups filed under Z and the skewered invoices and
the bathing belle with the blood of a dead fly on her bosom,
epitaph on insect lechery, keeping her smile fixed through the
falling months. He remembered pleasant moments spent in
this place, making weak jokes and strong tea, doing cross-
words, reading prescribed texts and getting paid for it. Had
he come back here looking for the same uncomplicated
casualness? It was still here all right, in this sunlit little room,
in the sound of the kettle on the gas-ring, in Mr Atkinson's
even voice that made death a troublesome commonplace.

'Ye'll get over it all right, Charlie. Everybody does. It

65

comes to the best of us. Just give it time, son. There's nothing we canny take, just given time.'

Was that what he had wanted, kindly platitudes of consolation from the uninvolved? Why had he come here at all? The question was as familiar to him as his hand, seemed to be put by everything he did. So often in the past two or three weeks since he had stopped going up to university, he had gone to places that had pleasant nostalgic associations for him, to the pictures, to the library, to the café he used to go to with Mary, and now here to see Mr Atkinson. And every visit seemed to end in the same question mark. What was he doing here? What was he looking for? It was as if in each place he had been looking for something that would restore him to himself, a means to re-enter his old way of life. It was in a way a pathetic act of faith, a sort of romantic gesture, a search for the one accident of fable that resolves all problems and makes everything all right. Within himself he knew that he wasn't going to find it. But he had persisted in trying, because to do so had at least the negative virtue of postponing something else which he knew he would have to do. It was something seemingly trivial in itself and yet something he shrank from doing because of the implications it contained of binding him even more closely to the burden of his father's death. Every time he had left the house it had been with the intention of doing it, and every time he had allowed himself to be sidetracked into going somewhere else in the forlorn hope of finding there escape from what he feared was waiting in that other place. But there was no escape, and he would have to face it. His hand fingered the key that had lain unused in his pocket for so long.

'Everything'll sort itself out, though, Charlie. The mills of God grind slowly, but they do grind extra small.'

Some of the men were loading a lorry in the yard outside and their banter provided obscene interpolations to Mr Atkinson's text. Charlie had never heard him talking like this before. About the most personal things he had known about Mr Atkinson were that he was keen on the garden and his

66

wife suffered from migraine. There was something a little ridiculous about the sententious way he was talking, and Charlie felt guilty about it. What other way could you talk about somebody else's grief in which you were compelled to show some concern? It was Charlie's fault. He shouldn't have come here in the first place. How long was he going to go on trying to find a way out of his own commitments? This was his concern. He would have to cope with it himself instead of farming it out to people like Mr Atkinson. It was no use trying to atone for his father's death by proxy. His hand tightened round the key.

'Ah'd better get away now, Mr Atkinson,' he said. 'Ah just thought Ah'd drop in an' see ye.'

Mr Atkinson had crossed to where the kettle was, having rinsed out the teapot at the tap by the door.

'Hing on a minute, Charlie,' he said. 'We can have a cup o' tea. It's nearly ma dinner-time. But Ah can always squeeze in a mouthful o' tea.'

'Naw. Thanks all the same. But Ah'll be gettin' ma lunch directly, anyway.'

'Well. Ah've enjoyed seein' ye again, son. Look in any time ye're passin'. Look after yerself. An' see an' stick in at the college. Yer feyther wid have wanted ye tae dae that.'

'Right, Mr Atkinson. Thanks. Ah'll be seein' ye.'

'Cheerio, Charlie.'

Charlie emerged into the cold of the day and walked out through the big gate, seeing the loaded lorry parked just inside them, with the driver eating his lunch in the lofty cabin and drinking tea from a flask-cup. As Charlie passed, the driver nodded down to him, raising his cup.

'This is me having ma high tea,' he shouted indistinctly through the open door, and laughed a barrage of bread-crumbs at his own joke.

Charlie waved applause.

He came down the hill from the factory into the busier streets that were beginning to quicken with people having their lunch-hour. He ran his finger along the key as if it was a

67

memorandum. He would go today. But he would have lunch first. The clock on the Laigh Kirk said it was some time after twelve. He decided to go and eat in the café where he had lunched when he was working with Mr Atkinson. Another detour. But this would be his last.

The café was nearly full but he managed to get one of the small tables for two near the open fire. It was the same waitress who had always served him before.

'Hullo, stranger,' she said. 'Where've you been hiding yerself? Don't tell me ye've fallen for some other waitress?'

Charlie found himself answering in the same vein.

'Secret mission,' he mouthed. 'M.I.5. But keep it under yer apron.'

She chaffed him about it, and they kept it going, building it up as she moved back and forth to the tables. It turned out that it was Russia he had been to, and by the time she fetched his cake he had brought her back a pair of Cossack boots that laced up to the thighs and he was to get putting them on her himself. After that an elderly woman sat down opposite him at the table and her presence cut the line between them. She kept looking at Charlie every so often with a certain sus-picion, and then she would pull her open coat more closely round her body as if Charlie was too young to be enjoying such delights. As a cover for his embarrassment, Charlie took the letter out of his pocket again and read it, as he had done countless times. It was like one of those pieces of translation he used to do at school from Latin or French, when you knew what all the words meant and it still didn't have any meaning for you because the idiom was foreign to you. It had the same quality of irrelevant remoteness and as he looked through it he was more conscious of the meticulous script, up light and down heavy, than of the words it conveyed.

Darling,

It's here at last. You can stop worrying. Thank heaven. If it had gone on any longer I think my mother was bound to notice something. Something was bound to have

68

told her. And, just between you and I, it would probably have been me. I was getting more worried every day. It seems a bit silly now. But like my father says, women need worry the way a car needs petrol. I must have used gallons in the last few days. But that's it over, thank heaven.

Are you happy now? I can't wait to see you again. When are you coming back down? Write and tell me it's tomorrow. It seems like ages since you were down last. What has Shakespeare got that I haven't got? If you can come down for the week-end, Elspeth and Ted want to go to a dinner-dance with us. I think Elspeth has her eye on you. So if you come down, I'm going to keep a padlock on you. Give Shakespeare the blind for one night. Can you not?

I'll have to stop now. I'm writing this during my tea-break. I brought the writing-paper and stuff with me when I found out the good news this morning (and I don't mean about the dinner-dance). I just wanted to tell you everything was all right and to tell you that I love you. There, I've told you.

Come down this week-end. Will you?
I love you, darling,
Mary

It was like a dead letter to Charlie, one delivered too late to someone who had left no forwarding address. She obviously hadn't known about his father's death at the time of writing. The letter had been addressed to the flat in Glasgow and had been redirected by Jim and Andy. But somehow the person it was meant for had gone missing in the interim. All Charlie could get out of it was a sense of incredulity about the things he must have bothered about just a few weeks ago. Had he really been so distraught about that false alarm? It seemed so insignificant now. Mary's letter, with its archness and its exaggerated proclamation of relief, seemed to satirize what he had felt, so that its importance was deflated, banalized by a few grammatical errors. It was unbelievable that he could have been so worried about it. But perhaps you made your

69

own worries and it was all comparative. He could remember that even when he was a boy there always seemed to be some central worry occupying him at any given time. For a week or two it would be the darkness of his room at night. He would forget that and it would be the boy who lived at the corner of the street and whom he was afraid to pass. Vagrant worries came and went, stayed for a few minutes, for an hour, or for a day, like whether earwigs really went in your ear or not, or whether God could really see you anywhere you were, even under the bedclothes. But always there would be some official worry which he seemed to have in permanent residence. It never really proved to be the case that it was with him for good, but at the time it invariably seemed like that, and it never seemed to leave until another had arrived. And as he had grown older, he hadn't really changed. He had simply entertained a higher quality of worry, like whether he was going to pass his examinations or like this one about Mary. Now these too seemed utterly trivial, ousted as they had been by his involvement in his father's death. They had been no more than regents for this one, and now that it had assumed complete authority over him, it dismissed everything else from his mind as being irrelevant to its purpose. It precluded all other concerns. Everything else seemed trivial and point-less. He had not been in touch with Mary since receiving the letter, indeed, since first hearing of his father's illness. He couldn't bring himself to see her. He had nothing to say, no emotion left over to expend on her, and he felt guilty. He hoped she would simply allow the whole thing to peter out. It would be easier for both of them that way. He had intended to go and see her and explain, but he dreaded coming face to face with her anger or her hurt or whatever artillery she could bring against him, for he had nothing with which to oppose it, only a hollow where his feelings should have been. And he wasn't sure that he could trust himself yet to be honest enough to end it in her presence. He might accept the old relationship again as a means of hiding from the meaning of his father's death. As if to protect himself from any such temptation, he crumpled the letter in his hand, leaned across, and threw it into the fire glowing beside him. That small gesture was a symbolic act for him, and he watched the letter burn to nothing as if the fire were performing crude surgery on himself, obviating infection.

He left a tip under his saucer and excused himself from the elderly woman's eyes. Coming out, he told the waitress that she would find the usual few roubles under his plate, and she said, 'Thank you, comrade.'

Outside, the sun had upped a few degrees and managed to take the icicle out of the air. Spring was under rehearsal and Charlie had a sudden desire to look on for a little while. He decided he would take the roundabout way to his destination so that he could go through the park. On the way he bought a newspaper as if it were a ticket entitling him to sit in the park among other people. He felt the need of some badge of normalcy to hide behind.

The park was enjoying its first crop of tentative flowers and perennial people. A few groups of school-children were blowing about like puff-balls. Two of them were noisily taming the stone lions at the top of the steps. Four or five Indians stalked each other round the rhododendron bushes, discharging soundless arrows. Charlie found a bench about half-way up the slope, facing down into the central bowl of the park. Almost at once an old man came to sit at the other end of the bench. His rheumy eyes were veined like marble and they stared as impassively on the scene below him. Only the mouth that puffed at his pipe proclaimed life in thin wisps like smoke from a distant fire. Charlie made only a brief show of reading his paper before he rested it on his knees and let his attention drift over the park. The number of people about was surprising when you considered that the weather was still cool enough for a coat.

Below Charlie and near the bottom of the slope there was a group of factory girls sitting on the grass. They would be from the mill just across the river from the park. They sat wearing buttoned-up coats and head-squares, tonight's waves foretold

71

in curlers. They gestured freely, raucously dismembering reputations, blobs of primary colour against the pastel shades of the park. Some of the remarks they threw at each other splashed as far as Charlie.

'Aw her! A wee spew!'

'Thinks she's goat a catch wi' thon yin.'

'If ye skint 'im, ye widny get a poat o' soup oot 'im.'

'The wey she speaks tae!'

'Ah ken. Needin' her tongue scrapit.'

'Ah canny stick 'er! She's that bloody common!'

On the terrace above Charlie, a young woman was pushing a large new pram, airing her baby. She leaned forward frequently, mouthing into the raised hood and fussing with the covers. On a bench along from him, a schoolboy sat in pubescent conclave with a schoolgirl. They had grown together furtively. The boy's left arm was draped casually round her shoulder, innocent as a frond, but the hand to it disappeared under the collar of her blazer, rooted in something more serious. Her right arm was invisible beneath his blazer. Their heads touched fractionally and from time to time they kissed quickly when the park wasn't looking. Watching them tied in their secret love-knot, Charlie remembered the exquisite agony of adolescence as if he was as old as the man beside him. Condoning their conspiracy, he was careful to look away.

Down in the bowl of the park, some apprentices were playing football. The game had been going on for some time and was beginning to lose its impetus. It had reached the stage where one of them, having been beaten in a tackle, lay down, plucked himself a piece of grass, and started to barrack the others. One of his team-mates went over to try to hector him to his feet and was pulled down himself. They wrestled on the grass, a thresh of boilersuits and tackety boots. There were other signs of a certain lack of team spirit until somebody shouted, 'Next goal wins!' and the game was galvanized briefly into mock intensity. The wrestlers jumped to their feet. There was much shouting and running and pulling of overalls. Just when one team was running in for a certain goal, one of the opposing defenders brilliantly saved the day by running ahead to steal the jackets that served as goalposts. He re-established their goal a good thirty yards from the danger zone, and half-way up the hill. The game came to an end when somebody booted the ball out of distance of their energy. They sprawled in a sweating huddle on the grass, talking. One of them said something and they all looked towards the factory girls, laughing. There was a short consultation and two of them rose, stretching casually. They walked away to retrieve the ball and returned at a jog-trot, passing it between them. As they drew level with their friends, one of them kicked it very deliberately into the group of girls. They squawked and raised their legs as if there was a mouse among them. The apprentices, watching proceedings from ground-level, cheered. One of the girls jumped up, seized the ball angrily, and threw it away as far as she could, only to see it roll back down the hill to the feet of the boy who had kicked it, symbolizing how effective her indignation was. The apprentices cheered again. Then they struggled to their feet, disputed the ownership of jackets, and went off, throwing the ball among them and laughing at unheard comments.

Charlie watched them until they were out of the park. Something about their casual assurance fascinated him. Recently he had developed an almost awe-struck admiration for the trivial encounters between people that he witnessed. They seemed so certain about everything. On street corners, in cafés, in cinemas, he had become an onlooker, a hanger-around of places where people met, observing their poise. The past fortnight had taught him to savour other people's enjoyment, to be a connoisseur of ordinariness. The sort of flippant confidence that he had taken for granted in himself such a short time ago now filled him with wonder simply because he no longer possessed it. It had forsaken him completely and looked mockingly at him from other people. And what did he have in its place? A need that denied his right to be self-satisfied, an injustice that demanded utterance. A

73

dark insistence. And a key. He sat with his hand clenched round it, giving resolution time to muster. By the time he rose, the park had lost most of its people. The boy and girl had unravelled and were gone. The young woman had disappeared with her pram. The small boys had stabled their horses for the afternoon. The factory girls had returned to the mill, leaving a patch of flattened grass that the breeze, like a fussy housewife, was already fluffing back to shape. Only the old man remained, to lift Charlie's paper when he left and peer at it through his one-legged spectacles.

Charlie went over the bridge out of the park and crossed the empty lot. He had his key out as he reached the big double doors of the lock-up. But as he touched the half that held the lock, he found that it was open. The hinges hawked with rust as he pulled it ajar. Light infiltrated the gloom ineffectually, an unsuccessful assault. He went in and the door swung shut behind him, nudging him into the dark like the head of some docile animal. He stood waiting while his eyes came to terms with this contradiction of the sharp incisive sunlight outside. Gradually the amorphous darkness solidified into form. The walls drifted into shape and objects floated to the surface like men seven days drowned.

It seemed strange that he should have been almost frightened to come into this place. It was simply an old lock-up, very dusty, very overcrowded, but still completely commonplace. The central area was occupied by a van, single-coated with a maroon paint that did not quite obliterate the vague outlines of fruit beneath it. Near the door was a tool case with the fading initials J.A. on it. Jack Anyone. On top of the case sat a Gladstone bag with a broken handle. Beyond them and just visible round the van, the metal of a freezer showed dully, cancered with green mould. From a hook on the wall above it was draped an overall. One corner was divided into two sections by a couple of empty orange-boxes placed one on top of another. One section was heaped to overflowing with gas masks from which the metal had been removed. The other section was empty. Two treadless rubber tyres improvised

74

a seat at the side of the van and Charlie sat down on them.

It might seem quite unmoving, but Charlie knew why he had avoided it, and what he felt now justified his reluctance. The experience was as eerie as being alone in a dark sarcophagus. This place seemed as sombre and remote from what was going on outside as the vault of someone dead for centuries, whose only memorials were these ridiculous emblems of the materialism which he had served. It should have been thrown open to the public. Charlie could have labelled every object in it, each one representing a pathetic dream. These were the toys with which a man had been stunted, the means of preventing him from realizing his own manhood. They were what Charlie had not wanted to face, the utter shame of what his father had become, the pointless suffering he had been subjected to until he had capitulated and betrayed himself, recanting his faith in himself and accepting the identity they gave him. Everything here was a refined instrument of torture and, thinking of each one, Charlie relived his father's pain. He felt how considerable it must have been, because he knew that his father had been by nature sanguine and self-sufficient, and his despair must have been wrung from him with great difficulty. It must have been a truly difficult thing to achieve. But they had achieved it. They had done it with absolute thoroughness and commendable discretion. All that were left were these innocuous fragments that could be related to no one but himself. What was there here that could indict anyone else? Who was to be blamed for this? Who would pay for it? Who was guilty?

An accidental answer came in the scuffling of feet in the yard outside. The door opened and closed, and the dim figure of a man stood just inside the lock-up. He was swaying slightly and his breathing was noisy, with a hint of slaver in it. Small sounds of content came from him. 'Oh, aye,' he was saying to himself. 'Aye, aye. Right, then.' He was carrying a bottle and he crossed towards Charlie. He was almost on top of him when he suddenly halted, seeing him for the first time.

'Hullo, Mick,' Charlie said.

Mick blinked and looked at the bottle, as if he thought Charlie had emerged from it.

'Who the hell's that?' he asked himself, bending closer. 'Aw, it's yersel, Charlie.'

At once Mick seemed to sober a little, as if he had been douched with cold water. He straightened himself and his eyes came into focus, glinting warily in the gloom.

'Whit are ye doin' here, Charlie?' he asked, and his voice had become careful. He put down the bottle of cheap wine beside the van.

'Ah just thought Ah wid look in,' Charlie said, watching him steadily. He saw Mick's eyes flick towards the corner where the gas-masks lay. He suddenly understood the open door and the emptiness of one part of that corner. What he was thinking must have registered on his face, for Mick became belligerent.

'Whit's yer feyther been tellin' ye?' His voice crackled with aggression. 'If it's aboot the metal aff thae gas-masks, ye're not on. That wis a' mine. The lot. Ah stripped them all when yer auld man wis lyin'. He never struck a blow. They're sold. Ah've just been gettin' rid o' the rubber there. That's the last of it, there. The metal's delivered an' paid for. Tae me. Nobody's due anythin'. Not a coorie. Yer feyther had nothin' tae dae wi' it.'

'Ye're a liar,' Charlie said.

Mick leaned over, jabbing his finger in Charlie's face, seconded by the drink.

'Say that again an' Ah'll brek yer back. Think because ye're a college boy, we'll let ye aff wi' that? Ah'll learn ye a lesson right enough. Wan that ye'll no' get in yer books.' Holding up a mace of knuckles, 'Five-finger exercise. Is that no' whit they call it?' He paused, his breath like a blow-torch on Charlie's face. 'Now, Ah don't ken whit John's been tellin' ye – God rest 'is soul. But Ah ken whit Ah'm tellin' ye. Ah'm tellin' ye there's no' a brass farthin' o' that money comin' tae you or anybody like you. It's no' ma style tae speak ill o' the dead. Let them rest in peace. That's ma motto. Rest in peace.

Ah canny imagine that yer feyther wid try tae pull a fast yin like that. Ah fancy you're tryin' to paddle yer ain canoe here. Well, ye're up the creek. An' if it *wis* yer feyther that put ye up to this. An' if he did tell ye that some o' the money wis his, then he's a liar. A rotten liar an' a cheap-skate.'

Charlie rose under the impetus of his own blow. Mick blocked it and split Charlie's cheek with his counter, knocking him against the wooden wall of the lock-up. Before Charlie could recover, Mick had butted him with his head but made only partial connection, drawing a thread of blood from his nose. Blinded, Charlie caught Mick and closed with him. They grappled in a stalemate of strength for some seconds, heaving for vantage. Charlie's knee pistoned twice into Mick's groin, and he felt him sag. Feeling the deadlock break, Charlie slung him against the van and strung him up with punches, refusing to let him fall. His anger held Mick there desperately, keeping the valve open on itself until it should be exhausted. Charlie embedded his fists in Mick's stomach, following his buffeted body round the front of the van until a flurry of punches threw it against the door, which swung wide open, pitching Mick out into the day like a corpse thrown up from a grave, a portent in the sunlight.

Mick lay motionless for some time. Charlie stood watching him while the mist compounded of pain and anger cleared away from his eyes. Mick stirred painfully, groaning, and levered himself almost into a sitting position. His head turned and he was sick, on the ground and on himself. Then he sank back into his own vomit.

All at once Charlie felt overwhelmingly revolted. What was he doing venting his anger on a man who was pushing fifty and fuddled with drink? What did he care about a little scrap metal or who owned it? Why should he exact payment from this travesty of a man? He was as much a victim as Charlie's father had been, his life reduced to little windfalls like this one, small financial killings that bought a few glassfuls of oblivion, gave him the company of a bottle. The same thing that had made his father believe devoutly in his own

77

failure had made this man what he was, a scavenger, a gatherer of crumbs. He wore the same uniform as Charlie's father had, the livery of defeat. He was friend, not foe.

Mick groaned again on a rack of movement, striving to get up. Charlie went over and bent to help him.

'Come on, Mick,' he said. 'Come on.'

'Get away from me. Ya bastard,' Mick said, whimpering with pain and humiliation.

He rose unaided, with anguished dignity, biting on his pain. Hobbling over to the wall, he went off slowly, his hand propping him up against the stone.

Charlie felt terribly alone and the waste lot seemed to stretch indefinitely in all directions.

Chapter 9

SHE HELD HIS ARMS IMMOBILIZED IN A CASUAL LOCK, one of those courting holds that Nature forwards free with menstruation. It was a truce of the kind that punctuates such engagements, during which energies are restored in comparative stillness. Only his right hand made fitful, restricted movements around her breasts, like a bored sniper. She suffered no loss of calmness from it. The same campaign had been fought often enough before, strengths had been tested, tactics resolved into a pattern, and a measure of mutual understanding realized. It was more a matter of exhibiting honourable endeavour than of seeking complete success. The customary concessions had been granted towards the satisfaction of honour. Her blouse had been separated from her skirt and three of its five buttons had yielded. His left hand had gained the top of her thigh, but only outside her skirt. She was even relaxed enough to let the hem of her skirt remain turned up, a permissible laxity, like open gates in a city, the citadel of which has been proved impregnable. From past experience, she knew that no further ground would be lost. In any case, there wasn't time.

She tried to squint round his head, without moving her own, at the clock on the mantelpiece. She knew how offended he would become if he was aware that she was allowing such mundane considerations to come between her and his attentions. The tip of the minute hand appeared round the lobe of his ear like a diffident conspirator, pointing to four. He could stay barely ten minutes longer. It was a pity. Her neck relaxed back into communion with his cheek. With some surprise, she realized from the position of the clock in relation to herself that they were lying on the couch. Their running battle had started by the fireside. She tried to retrace the line of pursuit that had cornered her here. But it had been lost in

79

that blackout to external things that lust uses to focus concentration on itself. She wondered a little at her ability to forget everything so easily and it occurred to her that she should perhaps be ashamed of being able to forget so soon, even for a little while. She tried to feel guilty, but it was an empty gesture, carrying no conviction.

At eighteen she was still young enough to be subject frequently to the absolute authority of the moment. Her feelings had not yet fully evolved to that democracy which would establish their peaceful co-existence with each other. A strong emotion could still seize control of her despotically. She was still at that stage of emotional naïveté when an alien and impractical ambition might take possession of her for days at a time, like the desire to be a film actress or to marry a millionaire. It was hardly surprising, therefore, that an emotion able to overwhelm characters much less insecure than hers should compel her to discard for a time an identity that often sat but loosely on her. A few minutes ago, they had both been less individuals than representatives of the species, participants in a ritual that glorified body over brain, inhabiting feeling rather than time, kind rather than place. It was only now in the aftermath of calm when she divested the mask and resumed herself that the possibility of self-criticism returned with her surroundings. The room was waiting like an ostler to reharness her to herself, to put the present back between the twin shafts of past and future. It chafed familiarly against her consciousness in the curtains that would have to be washed soon, the fire that would soon be needing more coal, the spot in the carpet where she had spilled ink a long time ago – in the vague shape of an accidental flower now almost worn away, fading memorial to her carelessness. The clock tutted prissily on the mantelpiece and she took its brass-tongued shock to herself, once again feeling that there might be something irreverent in what they were doing. After all, it was only a few weeks since then. She recalled how this same room had rustled with people who shifted their feet and moved their hands awkwardly. Fragments of the scene washed back to mind, thrown up haphazardly, the self-conscious coughing that spread like a nervous contagion, the wetness of eyes, the small, saturated, lace handkerchiefs with which women strove ineffectually to wap the grief that overwhelmed them, the minister's voice, circling like a whaup above their desolation. Already such random pieces were all that remained of the total melancholy of that occasion. Could it really be forgotten so soon? Not forgotten, but endured. Even so soon it could be endured and lived with. It had to be lived with. Already this room, which then had been no more than the bare crossroads on which their griefs converged, had again resolved itself into home, the centre of a network of practical needs and relationships, and to go on living in it their grief had to become just as practical. Hers had become acclimatized, had adjusted to the practical demands that were made on it. The life which had gone on in this place for so long still had to go on and could only accept death as a temporary lodger, had no room for it as a permanent guest. This was not just the house where her father had died, but the house where he had lived and the house where they were to go on living. With the practical persistence of the furniture that needed to be dusted and the windows that needed to be cleaned and the floors that needed to be swept, the house was already reasserting on her its old familiar identity. It was resuming in her life its customary position, in which her father's death was no more than a part, and one that was beginning to be seen in perspective. It was true that her grief could still protrude awkwardly into the daily routine at the sight of a pair of her father's shoes placed neatly under the chair of his upstairs room – to be left until called for – or of one of his ties in the wardrobe, with the knot left in it that was his trademark. But these were temporary problems that she could cope with as they arose. She knew that she was over the worst of it. With patience and persistence, she would besom her sadness into order, find an appropriate place for it like an ornament. In the meantime, how could it be wrong just to kiss and cuddle on a couch? She writhed a little closer.

81

'Ah suppose Ah'll have tae be goin', Elizabeth,' Harry said, tickling her neck with his breath and making no attempt to move.

'Oh no, Harry.' Her arms resigned their defensive position as an additional enticement. 'Wait a wee while yet. Ye can always run for the bus. An athlete like you.'

'It's all right for you tae talk. It's no' you that'll get the varicose veins.'

But he stayed where he was, lipping her throat absently like a goldfish. She was glad to prolong the mesmerism of the moment a little longer. The evening ahead of her was a blank once Harry left, and she knew she would just have to doodle it away with some trivial activities. There was nothing in the house that she urgently required to do. The only thing was Charlie's tea. She had it made and it was being kept warm in the oven. She wondered why he hadn't come home for it. In a way it had proved to be a blessing. It wouldn't have been as convenient for Harry if Charlie had been here. That was an accidental connivance with their luck they hadn't expected. But the immediate advantage was more than outweighed by the long-term implications. This was typical of the way Charlie had been acting lately. She was worried about him. He seemed to have no further interest in university. He had become frighteningly withdrawn. He had spoken barely two consecutive sentences to her since their father died. She knew it was all somehow connected with their father's death, but whenever she tried to induce Charlie to talk about it, he became angry or completely quiet. It was frightening how close to him anger always seemed to be, following him everywhere like a dog at his heels, ready to snap at the slightest invasion of his privacy. He had become unexpectedly a mystery to her. The familiar brother she had known was lost behind strange broodings and inexplicable bursts of temper that excluded her from his confidence. She had no idea what he did or where he went during the day. She only knew him now by what was reflected in the reactions of others. She knew that he had avoided John for more than a week and that John was anxious to see him to talk to him about going back to university. She knew that he had not once seen Mary since coming down from Glasgow. She hadn't known what to say when Mary had called at the door earlier in the evening just after Harry had come in. She felt annoyed at not having asked Mary in, but it would have been awkward with Harry there. She still felt embarrassed for Mary as she recalled their conversation on the doorstep. Mary had been near to tears of puzzled humiliation, and out of pity Elizabeth had made a provisional arrangement for her to meet Charlie on Friday night, and she had said she would tell him about it. She didn't relish Charlie's reaction, but she had made the arrangement and she would have to do her best to see that he kept to it. As if for luck, she kissed Harry's cheek. He gnawed her ear in acknowledgement.

'Ah'll really need tae get away noo,' he said, coming out of his emotional hibernation.

His right cheek was red from contact with her shoulder and patterned with her blouse.

'Oh, no. Ye can skip the night school for one night.'

Her forefinger tobogganed down his nose on to his lips, and she eyed him with provocative petulance.

'Aye. But Ah canny skip the exam.'

'Ye don't really have to go, do ye?'

She knew that he did and she had no intention of trying to prevent him from doing so. Their relationship was firmly founded on practical considerations. It was already rather like a houseless marriage that had still to be consummated. They knew the financial preparations that were necessary. They were planning and saving with the acumen of two business enterprises due to be merged at some future date. Summer had been set as the time for their engagement. The following summer was the earliest possible date for their wedding. Meanwhile, life had become for them a sort of extended bottom drawer in which the future was being neatly laid out for their communal use. Attendance at night school was one of Harry's contributions, an investment that would earn them interest in terms of higher wages for himself. Elizabeth appreciated the advisability of the move. But she couldn't help teasing him about it now, playing off his allegiance to her future against his desertion of her present, in a jocular excess of that feminine logic which enables a woman to turn any compliment into an inverted insult.

'Ye're always so anxious to get away. Ah feel quite offended. Sometimes Ah wonder what goes on in that night class. Y're a wee bit too keen tae get there.'

Harry rose as delicately as a walrus to the subtle bait.

'Ah, wouldn't ye like tae know?'

'Confess,' she said, threatening him with a kiss.

'Well, actually Ah've got off ma mark wi' this wee textbook Ah met. Ye should see her. She's got a lovely set of diagrams.'

'What's her name?'

'Algie Bra. A sexy name, i'nt it? Ah think she's foreign.'

'If Ah get a hold of her Ah'll batter her.'

Love, like a studio audience, is easily amused. But the inspired fatuity of their conversation embarrassed even their indulgence and they transferred their mock dispute to the physical dimension. They wrestled briefly on the couch and then formed a last intense alliance of themselves before Harry would have to go. They became so engrossed that they did not hear the key turning in the outside door and by the time it swung shut, the living-room door was already opening. They struggled up blindly, Charlie's presence hitting them like the beam of a policeman's torch, sending their inhibitions scurrying for cover.

'Whit the hell goes on here?' Charlie said.

'Nothing, nothing,' Elizabeth said quickly, her hands trying to endorse her mouth by tucking her blouse inside her skirt and making nervous passes at the buttons.

Harry had stood up awkwardly, looking down and pulling at his suit as if he was getting a fitting for composure.

'Whit dae ye think this is?' Charlie was looking at Elizabeth, keeping his anger in the family. 'A bloody kip-shop?'

84

'Ah'd better be gettin' down now, Elizabeth,' Harry said.

'Aye, ye'd better.' Harry's voice drew Charlie's anger like a magnet. 'While ye still can, Valentino.'

'Who dae ye think you're speakin' to?' Having buttoned in her embarrassment, Elizabeth was ready to entertain other feelings besides shame, and the first one that came along was sheer indignation. 'The lord of the manor here. What does it have to do wi' you? You can go when it suits you, Harry. Not before.'

'It's all right, Elizabeth. Ah'm late as it is.' Harry picked up the coat that lay across a chair and put it on. He lifted the black attaché-case that was his passport to better things. 'We wereny doin' anything bad, Charlie.'

'Well, it wis a pretty advanced form of bloody tiddly-winks, then.'

'Never mind excusing yerself to him, Harry,' Elizabeth said, taking his arm.

Harry's lips puckered under the pressure of the anger they were holding in. He shrugged, and Elizabeth saw him to the door.

As she came back in, her anger hit Charlie from the hall.

'What do ye think ye're doin'? What was all that in aid of? You've got no right to speak like that to Harry. There must be something wrong with you.'

'Listen. Ye might gi'e the grass time to grow on ma feyther's grave before ye start bringin' yer boy friend into the hoose for wee sessions.'

'That's a filthy thing to say!' Elizabeth's anger gave way to self-pity. 'Why are ye sayin' that about me? Boy friends? Ah've been goin' with Harry for a year and a half. Ma feyther knew about him. He thought it was all right. Ah didn't mean any disrespect to ma feyther. Ah miss him as much as you do. But you're queer about it. Why are ye bein' like this? Charlie, there's something wrong with you. You're ill, Charlie. You're ill.'

Charlie looked at her bitterly, his eyes opaque with anger. 'If you want tae follow in the footsteps of your dear mother,

85

ye can do it some place else. Ye'll no' be doin' it here.'

It was an insult administered with brutal precision, the more painful because only those closest to her would have known where to hit. The desertion of their mother had scarred them all, but in Elizabeth the wound had gained extra depth because of implications of heredity that could not apply to her brothers. For her it had seemed that the natural sexual instincts that she felt might possibly be the first stirrings of her mother's shame manifesting itself in her. It had haunted her for a time. She had found it necessary to overcome them, to prove to herself that what she was experiencing was not her mother's guilt in embryo. It had been a bewildering and lonely time. The terrifying mystery of puberty had entered her body accompanied by her private multitude of vague, half-formed, whispering fears. The only person who could properly have helped her to understand the fearful quickening in her blood was present only as a sinister shadow, a prophetic whisper that had to be disproved. Alone Elizabeth had to try to find her way through a holocaust of conflicting feelings towards the simple state of being 'good', that rickety fire-escape down which people evade the complexity of moral problems. By consultation with other girls, by comparison and analysis, she had painstakingly evolved her sexual code, allowing nothing to anyone until she had done so, holding herself in careful isolation until she was ready to come down from her own minute Mount Sinai. The result was a naïve formula rigidly adhered to: only with the one she felt she wanted to marry would there be more than kissing, and with him there wouldn't be much more. The simple North of her home-made compass was virginity until marriage. Perhaps the caution with which she carved each hand-hold into the future was exaggerated, but then she dreaded falling into the past that had claimed her mother. If she let go, she did not know how far there was to fall, and she couldn't afford to find out. She had merely kept to her simple formula. And it had worked. Harry had fitted into it and with him she had unlearned her suspicions. Gradually she had ceased to associate

86

sex with guilt, enjoyed the limited expression of her feelings, and looked forward to their ultimate fulfilment. Now Charlie deliberately burst the closing tissues of time and reopened the wound. And the fact that his statement was utterly unfair only added salt to her suffering. Injustice only whets insult to a keener edge.

The noise of their two voices subsided into the single sound of Elizabeth crying. She was islanded in her misery, sitting with her hands covering her eyes as if Charlie wasn't there. Every so often she invoked her father helplessly. The scene, taking place in the same room, reminded Charlie of the funeral. It was as if one of the mourners had forgotten to go home, did not know that it was over. But he was the one who did not know, refused to accept that it was over. He was the one who wanted more. And was this what he wanted? A girl sobbing in a darkening room by a dying fire. Was this how to see justice done? By taking advantage of his sister's grief? What nobility of purpose! Charlie felt ashamed of himself. He had seen Elizabeth gradually coming to terms with the loss of her father and he had callously re-activated her grief. What was he trying to do? Her father had died of cancer and her mother of her own indifference, and he couldn't let her be happy for a little while with her boy friend. His own brutality sickened him. The fear he had felt on that waste lot after Mick had gone assailed him again. Why was he trying to make the victims of what had been happening endure the guilt of it? Why did he find it necessary to distribute the pain of it among other people? Did he want to see the suffering of his father acknowledged in other people, re-enacted in their own suffering? But why in people like Mick and Elizabeth? Because they were available and he could impose himself on them? That was only adding to the injustice. They were innocent bystanders. Then who was not? Who was guilty? Who was he looking for? He felt suddenly very frightened, frightened of himself, of what he might do. He realized how dangerous he was, to himself and to everyone else. He felt growing in himself an uncontrollable and indiscriminate

87

anger that could strike blindly, at any time and in any direction. Elizabeth was right. He was in some sense ill.

Was it just because his own small certainties were extinguished? The thought of it made him feel unbearably lonely. He *was* ill, he felt, and bore about him the smell of death, carrying it into their tidy lives. The terror of what might be ahead of him made him long for the small assurances he had lost himself, the security, the certainty of ordinary things. He felt a terrible need for help, for protection from himself in the company of others.

He crossed to Elizabeth and put his arm round her shoulders.

'Ah'm sorry, Elizabeth,' he said. 'Please forgive me. Ah'm sorry.'

She was hurt beyond the point of recrimination and was grateful even for the sympathy of her assailant. Her head sank against his chest, and in holding her he was not only giving but also taking comfort. It was the solace of mutual sadness, like the courage two children might gain from knowing that each other is afraid. They sat leaning protectively against each other, as pathetic as any babes in the wood, and more pathetic in that their proximity was illusory and each was lost in a private wood. For Elizabeth it was simply the confusion that Charlie had re-created in her world, the fears and doubts that overgrew the simplicity of things, shutting out understanding. Being not of her own invention, it was both as frightening and as easily escaped from as any wood in a fairytale. All it needed was the right reaction from Charlie, the magical resumption of his old identity, and everything would be all right again. If he would only revert to the person he had been before their father's death, her life could resume its old routes, laid by habit and surfaced with certainty. For Charlie the entanglement was greater, the shadows deeper, and escape seemed much more difficult. The thing that pursued him and from which he had to escape, was himself, and haunted him like his own shadow. He dreaded being trapped by his own anger round every corner.

They were content just to be still for the moment, damming sadness with their silence. But the ticking of the clock trickled insistently around them, breaching the feeling of security that immobility gave them. A coal, patiently hollowed out by flame, collapsed suddenly in the grate. The noise snapped Elizabeth out of her trance like the fingers of a hypnotist.

'Charlie,' she said. 'Charlie. What is it that's makin' you like this?'

The gentleness of Elizabeth's voice was soothing. The darkness deepening in the room made it as intimate as a confessional and Charlie felt anonymous enough to talk objectively.

'Ah don't know, Elizabeth,' he said. 'It's something Ah don't even understand maself. But Ah didn't mean what Ah said. Honest. Ah'm sorry.'

She sat away from him and rubbed at the tear-tracks round her eyes.

'It's all right,' she said. 'That's not what Ah meant. It's no' just that. It's everything. Why are ye no' going back up to the university?'

'Ah don't know. There just doesny seem to be any point to it any more. There's just no reason for goin' back.'

'Don't say that, Charlie. Don't say that. Of course there is. There's lots of reasons.'

It was a simple statement of faith, and one that she could not on the spot justify rationally. But she knew who could.

'Charlie. John wants to see you. He wants to have a talk with you.'

Her words sank into the silence of the room, across the surface of which the clock still fluttered its fly-wings of sound.

'Charlie. Will ye do it? Will ye go up an' see John? He wants to talk things over with you.'

Well, it was what he had wanted. The company of others. So here it was – a cordial invitation. Why not? He had learned already that what troubled him was not something it was easy to talk about, but perhaps talking with John would help him to see things more clearly. Perhaps this moment of

89

accidental objectivity that he had found with Elizabeth could be repeated with John.

'All right, Elizabeth,' he said. Something prompted him to commit himself more definitely while he was still in the mood. 'Ah'll go up the night. Right after ma tea.'

'Oh, good, Charlie. Thanks.' Elizabeth felt as if she had been granted a real favour, and the concession created an appetite for more. 'There's just wan other thing, Charlie. Mary was up the night.'

The statement masked a question. But Charlie's stillness in the dark suggested no answer.

'She was nearly greetin', Charlie. She wanted tae see ye.'

Somebody simulated maniacal laughter outside in the street and it was followed by a clatter of running feet and the whoops of mock pursuit.

'Ah had to do something, Charlie.'

Elizabeth was edging towards the point where she would have to just close her eyes and jump.

'Ah said ye would see her on Friday night. Seven o'clock. Outside McPartlin's.'

She had done it. She waited for the jar of landing. But still nothing happened. Charlie's first instinct was to refuse, but he paused. He remembered burning the letter and the finality he had meant that action to have. Yet it seemed to him now somehow a pathetic gesture, like sticking pins in a clay doll. Mary was present in his life. He couldn't efface her by destroying her verbal image. Anyway, the physical pleasure he couldn't help anticipating at the thought of being with her made him wonder if his anger at Elizabeth and Harry wasn't alloyed with jealousy. It would please Elizabeth if he accepted. He owed her some gesture of apology.

'Friday,' he said. 'Ah'll see her then.'

'That's great, Charlie.'

Elizabeth involuntarily touched his cheek and retracted her hand at once, joy in cryptogram. Intuitively, she kept her pleasure to herself, as if to reveal its location externally might make it possible for it to be taken from her.

She rose and switched on the light. The room, like everything else, was practical again. It was no longer ominous with shadows, but bright with mundanity – a fire whose embers were growing a fur of ash, a window that called for the decency of drawn curtains. She crossed and closed the curtains.

'What's happened to yer face, Charlie?' she asked, noticing the bruise for the first time.

Charlie fingered it self-consciously.

'Nothing,' he said.

'What is it? Were ye in a fight?'

'It's nothing, Ah said.'

She didn't want to disturb their new-found equilibrium with too many questions.

'Ah'd better mend the fire,' she said, lifting the pail. 'It's like Christmas day in the workhouse.'

'Ah'll get it,' Charlie said.

He took the pail from her and went out to the coal house, foraging in the dark for nuggets to get the fire going again. By the time he had finished and was washing his hands, Elizabeth had made fresh tea and his meal was on the table, with apologies for *hors d'oeuvres*.

'Ah'm sorry, Charlie. But it's a bit dry by now. It's been heatin' for that long.'

'That's all right,' he said. 'Ah like things done to a turn. Even if it's an ill yin.'

As he ate, Charlie enjoyed a sense of respite. The immediate future was at least filled in two places, like the spaces in a diary. Something was being done and that salved his conscience for the moment.

Through in the living-room, Elizabeth took pleasure in the small sounds that came from the kitchen. The house was being used as a house should be. Everything seemed normal again. She felt a temendous conviction that the worst of it was over. The rest would be a steady return to the old order of things. Charlie's anger had had the effect of bridging the separation that had been growing between them. Optimism enclosed her thoughts like a halo.

Suddenly she had an inspiration. Something that would make certainty even surer, turn the key another time on her happiness. She would have to hurry, before Charlie came back through. She went to the bookcase and took out writing-paper and envelopes. A search through the miscellany in the drawer revealed a biro. She felt almost mischievous, as if she were preparing a surprise birthday present for Charlie. After a brief consultation with what she remembered of form, she had her address in the right place. She wondered for a second about *their* address. But that was all right. It was the same as Charlie's had been, c/o Mrs Wright. 'Dear Andy and Jim,' she wrote. It seemed strange, writing two names like that, as if they were a comedy team, like Laurel and Hardy. But Charlie had always seemed to refer to them in that way, as if they weren't so much two people as one split personality. She would have to be careful what she wrote. She wouldn't say too much. Just hint at Charlie's moodiness and suggest that they might come down and see him. She felt quite daring, as if she was taking command of the whole situation.

She wondered how she should address it. Messrs. Layburn and Ellis? That sounded as if they were in business together. A. Layburn and J. Ellis. That would do.

She reinforced the comma after Jim's name and thought again of how easy it had been to get Charlie to see John and Mary. That was the most hopeful thing of all. His own willingness. The way he had grasped at the opportunity for the meetings endorsed the importance of them.

She did not realize that straws may look like logs to a man who is drowning.

Chapter 10

CHARLIE PRESSED THE BELL AND WAITED ON THE DOOR-step, as diffident as a collector for charity. He felt a little awkward about arriving at the door like this for a hand-out of elder wisdom.

A brief shower had fallen as he was coming up, and the street steamed slightly under the lamps. They weren't in any hurry to answer the door. He listened for a moment, but he could only hear vague indecipherable sounds drowned in a burst of gun fire from the television. He waited till the smoke cleared and rang again. This time a voice shouted something, incomprehensible as a newsvendor's cry, and a sudden thunder of hooves meant that the living-room door had been opened. The hooves reached crescendo as the outside door opened and John peered round it, holding himself in miniature under his arm.

'Aw, it's yerself, Charlie,' he said. 'Welcome tae the madhouse.'

'That's a sair oxter ye've got, John,' Charlie said, chucking wee John on the cheek.

'Aye. An' sometimes Ah canny get sleepin' for it at nights. Hang yer coat up there.'

The pegs, like everything else in the hall, were new. The house was a re-let and John was systematically obliterating the signs of former tenancy. He had finished decorating the hall and the living-room and was starting on the kitchen.

As they went into the living-room, Margaret shouted 'Hullo' from the kitchen. The room had that occupied air that the presence of a baby brings. Fender, chairs, and table were no more than improvised billets for the paraphernalia attendant on babyhood. Vests and a nightgown lay in neat array on the table. A pile of laundered nappies was on one

93

chair and on another, one nappy was laid out ready for use. Talcum and cream stood ready by the fire. A rubber mat lay on the hearth rug.

'Just wait till Ah fit Bronco wi' a silencer,' John said, crossing to turn down the volume of the television. The horses galloped on in silence.

'An' how's the Scarlet Pimpernel the night? Ye've been doin' yer invisible man lately, right enough.'

'Aye, Ah haven't been about much,' Charlie conceded.

'About much? Ah thought we were goin' tae have tae send out the police message. Whitehall 1212 stuff.'

John was preoccupied with completing the stripping of the baby that Charlie had interrupted. He laid him on the carpet and unpinned his nappy, averting his head from the contents.

'Oh, son. Ye'll need tae come fae a' that. That's inhuman. Ye'll no' make many friends that way. Ah've heard o' B.O., but that's goin' too far.'

The baby lay unconcernedly while he was wiped. Then John started to hold him above his head, raising and lowering him while he gurgled regularly like a mechanical toy.

'There he is. Look at 'im,' John said. 'Five months an' he hasn't struck a blow yet. They say they've got nothing for 'im at the Broo. He's still to say a word, too. Definitely backward. Spell "constipation". Ye can't, can ye? Well, if ye can't spell it, what about getting it? Eh? Before the hoose gets condemned.' A thread of saliva trailed from the baby's mouth. 'Ye can see the intelligence looking out 'im though, can't ye? See the witty way he's drooling at me there? Ye've got a great career ahead of ye, lad. Remember that. The sky's the limit for you. You could be slaverer to royalty if ye put yer mind to it. Hup, 2, 3, 4. Hup, 2, 3, 4.'

Margaret came in carrying a large basin steaming faintly with hot water.

'Stop it, John,' she said. 'You'll make 'im sick. An' how's Charlie? John. Ah've told ye already.'

She bustled out and back in again, bringing with her a yellow square of foam-rubber that she submerged in the basin.

Charlie realized how much she had changed since the baby was born. She had become much more defined as a person, had gained a new authority. The way she went about bathing John junior typified it.

'Ye're just in time for the big performance, Charlie,' she said. 'First house.'

She spread a towel on her knees, took the baby, and eased him into the water, cooing him into a sense of security. Conversation between John and Charlie was only incidental to the performance that was taking place in front of them. It had that natural rightness about it that makes people look at a flying bird or accord a few minutes' silent homage to the running of a river. Margaret was no more than an elemental extension of the baby, her hands providing the protection he couldn't yet give himself. He turned placidly this way and that in her grip, prismatically reflecting pleasure in whatever he was facing, the flames of the fire, his father, the edge of the basin, while the water was laved about him. Dry-docked on his mother's lap, he lay like an apprentice Michelin man, radiating with wrinkles, while John supplied Margaret with the required articles in turn, muttering tersely as he did so.

'Cream. Talcum. Nappy,' he said dramatically. 'Do you think the patient will live, Doctor? Look at it. Isn't it fantastic the amount of care that's lavished on the human bum? It's no' that it's a braw thing, either. But that's all weans are, when ye think of it. A pickle o' flesh round two openings. Entrance and exit. It's no' a human bein' we've got at a', Margaret. It's a one-way street for chuck.'

Margaret was unimpressed by John's philosophical insight.

'Never mind, son,' she said. 'It's just yer daft daddy talking.'

Now that he was nappied and nightgowned, hunger came on him like a conditioned reflex. It started as a preliminary wail and was maturing into a howl by the time Margaret had taken the bottle from the fireside, tested the heat of the milk on her wrist, and plugged his mouth with it. The yell transmuted to a gurgle and the gradual lowering of his eyelids

95

registered his progress to satiety. In the silence that ensued, muffled voices could be heard from the television.

'Ye might as well put that off, John,' Margaret said. 'There's no' much point in leavin' it like that.'

'Ah like tae get ma money's worth,' John said. But he went over and switched it off.

'He wid leave it on all night,' Margaret explained to Charlie. 'He forgets it's burnin' electricity. Because it's rented, he likes tae get every penny out it. Ah don't know why ye'll no' buy one outright, anyway.'

'Ah've telt ye till Ah'm Prussian blue in the face, woman. But ye've just got nae grasp of economics. Any repairs needed are done right away. No charge. Any new model that comes on the market, Ah can get it. When colour television comes in, Ah just get them tae install it. It's the best thing since bottled beer.'

It was an attitude that was typical of John. He was one of those people who like to surround themselves with very definite attitudes to everything, to whom manhood is a sort of masonic intimacy with practical things, discernible in the conviction with which you express yourself on the workings of a car or the way you talk about women. It could be recognized in revelatory flashes, code messages that could range from the telling of a joke to the stubbing of a cigarette, and it presupposed a common philosophy that knew what it was all about. John liked to feel that he knew the right way of everything, down to how to tie a parcel.

'It's no' the same as it bein' yer own,' Margaret said. 'Anyway, Ah'll need tae get yer heir to his cot. If ye wid make yerself useful for once.'

Charlie sat feeling superfluous while Margaret put the baby to his bed and John cleared up in the living-room. Their simple reoccupation mermerized Charlie. They epitomized themselves. Everything had its place. This night, like every other, was a series of small things to be done. Their lives were limited to themselves and the house and the baby. They needed nothing else. The world was reduced to these practical dimensions and nothing extraneous could come at them except via these routes. When Margaret came back, she lifted a pile of freshly washed clothes and excused herself to the kitchen to do her ironing. She was tactfully leaving John and Charlie free to talk. John came back in and closed the living-room door.

'Did ye notice the hall, Charlie?' John asked, settling back down by the fire.

'Aye, John. It's very smart.'

'Once Ah get the kitchen done, Ah can really get into the garden. There's always something. No rest for the wicked.'

He was pretending not to relish it, but that was really what he wanted to have, a kind of Forth Bridge of trivial household tasks, so that by the time he got to the end it would be necessary to start at the beginning again. It was like knowing that he could never become redundant as a person. He was going to be needed here as far as he could foresee. It was a good, safe feeling.

Charlie gave him a cigarette.

'Well then,' John said, giving him a light from a strip torn off a newspaper, a habit inherited from his father. 'An' when are ye goin' back up to the uni., Charlie?'

'Ah didn't know Ah was,' Charlie said.

'Aw, don't give us that, man. Can ye give me one reason why ye shouldn't?'

Charlie could think of a coffinful. But they weren't easy to articulate.

'If it's money,' John said, anticipating what to him was the most logical answer, 'ye'll surely get a bigger grant after whit's happened. An' ye could work spare time or something.'

'Aye. Ah suppose Ah could.'

'Well. What then?'

'Ah've just got no urge to do it any more.'

'Why no', Charlie? Why no'?'

For Charlie the question metamorphosed into another.

'What dae you think o' ma feyther's death, John?'

The question seemed somehow improper to the practical

little room. John saw how things were going. He remembered the scene at the graveside. He felt a bit embarrassed for Charlie. What did these things have to do with them?

'For God's sake, Charlie. Ah think it was sad. It was very sad. So what?'

'But that's all you think? Ah mean, it was just sad and that was it?'

'What else is there?'

'Ah don't know, John. But it seems tae me there must be something. Ye can't just leave it like this.'

'How not? What else can ye do? Go into mourning for the rest of yer life? What is it with you anyway, Charlie? What's getting you?'

'Ah just can't accept it, John. Ah can't accept it.'

John reflected momentarily on the hazards of going to university and spending too much time just thinking. It had isolated Charlie from his family. John had felt it before. Now it was as tangible as a wall between them.

'Ye just have to accept it,' John said. 'That's it. Everybody dies. What are you goin' to do about it? Dae ye think ma feyther wants ye tae go about lamenting 'im all yer life? Listen . . .'

Charlie listened, having to remind himself that this was his brother talking. It was only a few years ago that they had slept in the same bed, sometimes talking on through the night until the sparrows twittered that it was dawn. There had been a time when their thoughts and ideas had been so close that they had spoken in a kind of conversational shorthand. They had told each other so much, had shared experiences, had talked of girls and feelings and ambitions. They had helped to make each other, piecing together the fragments of themselves. Through the long summer holidays of boyhood, in games and in the wild prophetic vauntings that punctuated them, they formed a brotherhood of their own that was more intense than Nature's. At different stages of their development, the slight disparity in their ages had thrown their relationship out of joint. In childhood, Charlie had been only an embarrassment to John's freedom, like a tin can on a cat's tail, a hindrance at his heels when he wanted to play football or climb trees, a parental fifth column betraying the daring of boyhood to his mother, a teller of weepy tales. And again in the early teens, John was already apprenticed to manhood when Charlie was still a collector of skinned knees and preposterous facts, and to whom girls were no more than inadequate boys. But growing up is a cyclic process, and at other times when John lapped Charlie and they travelled some way abreast, they would find their old affinities reaffirmed. In their late teens they seemed to come more closely together than ever and it was like the meeting of old friends who had lost touch with each other. They found the same dreams still existing in each other, purified of their wilder impossibilities, but still reaching for fulfilment. Each restocked his faith in himself from the other's encouragement. The great things that they wanted were no clearer in outline, but much more imminent, and they were moving towards them together. Then almost casually, incidentally, it seemed, John had got married. And they lost any real contact with each other again.

Now as Charlie listened to him talking it seemed that they were just two people who had only this room in common. Not even this room. For Charlie didn't belong here. This was John's room. Not just in the furniture and the fittings, but in the certainty it represented, in the finality of shape it imparted to John. This was the very form John had imposed upon his life, the meaning he had given it. This was all the vague longings and the dreams, all the amorphous potential, actualized into a hard reality. He had found his own elusive grail. It was one that Charlie couldn't share. It seemed to him a terrible anticlimax, wine that had turned to water. Were all the huge ambitions, the racking progress into manhood, only to culminate in this? Was this a man's fulfilment? A steady job, a couple of mouths to feed, a wall to paint, a garden to dig, aimless talk to which death put an arbitrary period? Was this all there was to generate John's absolute assurance?

For he was so assured. Listening to him talk, Charlie was conscious most of all of that. His tremendous assurance. He spoke on and on so glibly, demonstrating the pointlessness of dwelling on death, pointing out that no son was obligated to perpetuate the morbid memory of a father, referring to his own child to illustrate the point. This was the assurance Charlie had wanted to borrow from. But it wasn't transferable. The peace John had made with things was a separate one and Charlie wasn't included in its charter. It was acceptable only if you were John. Otherwise, you were on your own. It was not contained in a neat phrase or a single idea that you could take like a pill. It was an idiosyncratic gesture of character, a subtle secretion of the glands of personality.

Charlie felt again that he had been stupid to expect anything from this visit. There were certain things you couldn't get from other people. You didn't go to your neighbour and borrow a cup of quiescence. It was never the brand you needed. With that simple realization, the conversation ceased to matter. John's voice continued in one dimension only, sound gutted of sense. It was not that Charlie disagreed with its conviction, but only that he was conscious of its reverse side, which was his own lack of certainty. All it meant to him was what he didn't have.

'Ah just wish Ah'd had your chance, Charlie. An' the brains tae go along wi' it. Don't be daft. Ye only get a chance like this once. Don't waste it. Go back up to the uni. An' stick in. That's what ma feyther wanted ye tae dae, anyway. Ye'll regret it for the rest of yer days if ye pack in now. Ah mean, you drop it now an' ye're worse off than a tradesman. What are ye goin' tae dae? Cairry the hod? Get a job as a labourer? Hump an' carry? There's a lotta years ahead, Charlie. Think about them. If ye don't go tae university again, what's the alternative? Think about that.'

That should have mattered, Charlie knew. But to him it didn't. There was no alternative. What he felt was separate altogether from policy, seemed somehow to preclude comparison or perspective. That was the trouble. There was no measurement of it, nothing that he could set it against and see it take on meaningful dimensions. He had no yardstick against which to comprehend what he felt. Nothing was adequate to it, not the grief of his family, the funeral, the talk, not anything they could do or say. These gave him a footrule with which to measure the magnitude of his father's death. This room could never contain the answers to his questions, it could only erase them. They simply could not exist for John or Margaret, were inadmissible here.

But they went on talking in preference to silence, each listening only to himself, until Margaret came back, having given them long enough for any problem to be settled. John immediately enlisted her support, explaining that Charlie was still undecided about going back to university.

'Don't you be daft, Charlie,' she said automatically as she went about tidying the room. 'You keep in at the college. Ye'll know the benefit afterwards. A collar-and-tie job, an' the heaviest thing ye have tae lift's a pencil. It's just no' tae be considered, anything else.'

She was right in her own terms. From her point of view there *was* nothing else to be considered. Charlie could almost envy her her bovine acceptance. The fireplace was the capital of her world, the shops its periphery. She might pretend concern in other things, but her son and her husband were all that really mattered to her. Family had become her private zodiac, determining her future. You could see what was ahead of her, the things that would amuse her and concern her. Young John would soon be at the stage of uttering his famous first words. There would be other children, and the small worries they brought with them, measles and cuts and disappointments. There would be days with the curtains drawn to protect a sick child's eyes, hours after tea when lessons would be considered, noisy outings to the seaside that were full of minor mishaps. There would be pride in small things, jackets straightened, admonitions given with bus money, reprimands at table. Each hour was ringed with practical concerns.

Reducing Charlie to one of them, she said she would go through and make a cup of tea, but Charlie said he would have to go. John told him to stay and Margaret said the kettle was already on. But it wasn't tea he had come for, and he got up to leave.

Margaret asked Charlie what had happened to his face. It was the first time she had really looked at him. Her conversations were always incidental to something she was doing, knitting or dusting or sewing. He explained again that he had bumped against something. In a way it was true. The fight had been no more than a pointless collision and the fact that Mick's hand had done the damage and not an inanimate object was by the way.

John was still obviously perturbed because Charlie had not reached any definite decision. At the door John touched his arm and said, 'Ah've got a headstane for ma feyther, Charlie. It should go up this week. It's no' a big yin. Ah canny afford much. But it's a marker.'

Charlie felt slightly ashamed. John had given his own memorial, in his own way, as best he could. Where was Charlie's?

John stood watching him walk away for a little while, looking puzzled, his hair blowing in the wind. Charlie looked back once at the bright square of the window. Then he went on, with his breath for company, through the cold streets where some houses echoed the brightness of laughter, others shrouded a conspiracy of silence. Above the roofs the sky was massed with white, as if each house had its private star. Somewhere, Charlie's had broken from its orbit.

Chapter 11

' "BE RESTRAINED AND TOLERANT WHATEVER THE PROVO-cation – you are inclined to fly off the handle." '

'Which, considering that you couldn't burst a paper poke, is hardly advisable.'

'A good week for kicking your friends' tripes in. Avoid people called Andy Layburn. "You must be especially careful not to upset elderly relatives." God, that means Ah'd better no' write a letter tae ma feyther. He'll just have learned tae live wi' the fact that Ah must be dead by now. Here's the best bit, though. Listen tae this. "You will receive a surprise invitation. Think carefully before accepting it." He will be six feet two and fifteen stones and desirous of giving you a mouthful of zodiacal headers. Be careful about accepting his invitation to go round the back. It could be detrimental to your health.'

Jim pulled the magazine he was reading over his head like a blanket and it heaved with his laughter as if he was making love to himself. Andy lay full-length on Mrs Wright's second-best settee, pen in hand, notepaper and a volume of Browning's collected verse in front of him. Their concentration had reached one of the intellectual lay-bys that mark an evening's study. All night Jim had been as restless as a class-bound child in summer. He had set out to revise *Richard III*, and only got as far as literally capering in a lady's chamber to the lascivious pleasing of his own imaginary lute before Andy had told him to shut up. He had then branched out into a textual commentary on the exact significance of 'lady's chamber', and what he called 'the difficulty of capering therein'. Now, as he lay sprawled in his chair in a self-inflicted agony of wit, one of his feet was bare because earlier he had been examining himself for what he termed 'Peruvian footrot'. His preliminary tests,

he claimed, had been positive and he would have to forward
the foot to the Central Laboratory to have new toes fitted.

The magazine slid down to his feet. Jim knuckled the tears
from his eyes and picked it up.

'Ah wonder who makes it up,' he said. 'He's a star turn,
anyway.'

'What about mine then?' Andy said.

'You'll be Virgo, Ah suppose?'

'Taurus. May the third. What is wrote in the stars for me,
O wise man?'

'Actually, yours is quite sensible. "Give all your money to a
friend," it says. "A safe period for emotional experiments."
You've never had it so good. In fact, you've never had it.'

'An' you're about to get it.'

'Naw. This is it. Gen. Straight from the bull's mouth.
"There will be a tendency to overspend on the one you love
most." '

'Ah wonder what Ah'm goin' to buy maself.'

' "Children's needs could be the cause of heavy expenses
this week" – i.e. twelve-and-six and a bag of coal. "Wednesday to Friday are the danger days." '

'What the hell does that mean? Danger days? This is
Wednesday the day tae. Ah've been crossing roads an' everything all day.'

'Aw, ye're all right, though. There's an astral P.S. here.
When Mars is in conjunction with Crookedholm, it will be
safe to go out without an overcoat. On Friday at ten past six
you may go out and enjoy yourself with an easy mind, provided you're back in by quarter past.'

'It's all right for you. But Ah'm the one that's walkin'
about tempting the fates.'

'Never mind. Ye can hole up here till Saturday. Ah'll get
Mrs Wright tae shove yer chuck under the door.'

They had played it out, and Andy resumed his reading.
But his concentration was gone, and Browning seemed to
echo Jim's nonsense.

Jim threw the magazine on to the chair opposite him.

'A load o' crap,' he said. 'Mrs Wright must be a severe case of arrested development. A tanner for that.'

He retrieved his sock and put on his shoes.

'Come on,' he said. 'We'll go down to Willie's café and abduct a coupla doughnuts.'

The suggestion was accepted at once by Andy. Since the evening was without perspective, immediacy was a fair substitute for urgency. While Andy got dressed, Jim rose and combed his hair down over his eyes. Stuffing one of Mrs Wright's scatter-cushions up the back of his pullover, he muttered, 'Richard's himself again', and started to hobble round the room. As he came back to the mirror, still mouthing, he stopped and lifted a letter from the mantelpiece.

'Here,' he said. 'Whit about Charlie's wee sister? Dae ye think we should answer her letter?'

'Naw,' Andy said. 'She'll no' be wantin' Charlie tae know she wrote tae us. We'll just drop in on him.'

'It can't be this week-end,' Jim said. 'We've got those dates fixed up for this week-end. First things first.'

'Aye.' Andy was putting on his jacket. 'It'll need tae be a week on Saturday, O Humphy One.'

'A week on Saturday it is,' Jim said. 'That's Charlie's horoscope fixed up, anyway. "Saturday is your day of danger, when you will meet a humphy stranger."'

They stood like grinning Gemini, Jim in the ascendant.

Chapter 12

THE WAITRESS, LOOKING UP FROM HER READING, COULD only see their bodies from the shoulders down, their hands loosely linked. Their faces were neatly blocked out by the white square of the menu-card that was pasted to the window. They looked like people in a newspaper photograph where anonymity has to be preserved. She hoped they would keep it that way and walk on past. Ralph and Paul were in the middle of a violent argument over Lorraine. It looked as if they would come to blows and she was anxious to see which would win. She hoped it would be Ralph because of the way Paul had treated Lorraine at the office party. But just as Ralph was standing over Paul and calling him a 'rotten coward', she felt the draught on her legs from the door being opened, and they were coming in.

Charlie held the door open for Mary. The air in the café came sudden and hot against his face, like someone breathing very close to him. The odours of old meals cooked and fried had been left to rot and moulder in the closed room until the atmosphere was a garbage of corroding smells, and breathing it made you feel as if your breath was bad. For a moment they stood paused at the door, plotting a course among the tables. Then they made their way to an empty one at the far wall, Mary sitting down at the side nearest the window, and Charlie instinctively sitting with his back against the wall, facing out into the room. The waitress gravitated slowly towards them, her eyebrows framing the question her mouth was too bored to ask.

'Coffee?'

Charlie deferred the unspoken question to Mary. She nodded without looking up.

'Two coffees, please,' Charlie told the waitress.

He looked round the café, a waxworks of people, a gallery of boredom. Over by the window, a fat man and woman were finishing a meal. The woman was huge, brooding over her chair, her body swallowing its hardest contours. Her arms overflowed her black crepe frock, elbowless and raw red. The man sitting with her was unmistakably her husband, and went with her so well that one of them in isolation would have been like a single book-end. They sat opposite each other like Gargantuan matching ornaments, and even the precisely timed way he lit her cigarette for her had a quality of clockwork in it. They stared placidly past each other, unspeaking. It was as if nothing new could ever occur between them. Time had filed and dovetailed them so well that every cog fitted. They didn't have to do anything else. The mechanism was complete. Wind it with sleep and it would run them till they died. In the far corner a little man sat with his coupon and a paper on the table. An old coupon was crumpled in front of him, an empty wrapper for used hope, and, with his head turned sideways to angle away his eyes from the smoke of a cigarette-butt burnt almost to his lips, he was drawing an extra dimension on his newspaper's headlines with his pen, seeking inspiration for tomorrow. In the middle of the café was a man who looked about thirty-five. He sat swaying things into focus through a distorting lens of liquor, ruminating visibly on some secret concern. Like strangers invited to the same funeral, Charlie thought. For the whole evening had had a sense of waiting like a wake. Everything about it had been enclosed in the same dark mood like a black border. They had gone as usual to the pictures, as if mere place and hallowed habit could restore them to each other. But nothing had happened. They had remained locked in their mutual uncertainty about each other. Perhaps Mary felt that Charlie should make the first move, that he owed her something for the way he had been towards her before. And Charlie himself moved blind in the darkness inside him, tapping his way with caution. Being unsure of what he felt, he kept silent. They had left early and walked aimlessly about the streets for a time and come in here because they needed somewhere, a place to try and meet and face whatever it was in each other they had to face, to try and find out what it was that had happened.

'One an' eight.'

The waitress rang up the price as detachedly as a cash-register, slopping their coffee on the table. Charlie paid her and shaved the bottom of his cup on the edge of the saucer and poured the surplus back into the cup. He watched her return barge-bottomed to her counter-stool, feeling the twinge of an absent reflex where his indignation should have been, like pain in an amputated limb. He saw the cover of the comic-book she lifted to read, bearing a face that was three-quarters manly chin and a title that stirred your very bowels – 'His love could conquer all.' He took as long as he could to sugar and stir his coffee, knowing what waited at the end of it – Mary and the need to explain to her what he didn't understand himself. He looked at her lifting the coffee cup two-handed to her mouth in a gesture that seemed to make her grow down. A strand of hair kept falling on her forehead and she blew it back up absently. It was strange to think of the inconsequential facts he knew about her. She didn't wear curlers at night. She had an aunt in Perth, Australia. She had been to Spain for a holiday. Her favourite song was 'Ramona'. She didn't like people who kept saying 'As a matter of fact . . .' There was something sad and forlorn about the small things people told each other, brief flashes of self exchanged across anonymous seas. As if in semaphoric answer to his thoughts, the persistent strand of hair drifted across her forehead, re-asserting her presence to his mind. Her face, familiar to him through all its common changes of mood, looked pathetically comic to him now, wearing as it did an expression of seriousness that seemed somehow too big for its features. He felt guilty that she should look like that. Outside, Friday night was going on and she should be a part of it. For her it should be going dancing and listening to records and just being happy. On *her* face that expression was ridiculously inappropriate, like widow's weeds on a virgin. And he

108

had put it there. The feeling that he was to blame brought him out of the lethargy that had held him all evening. The sense of terrible futility that had seemed to stretch aimless and diffuse ahead of him since his father's death narrowed to this momentary destination. He wanted to erase the sadness from her face, to make the features free to express the things they should be expressing, to let the eyes be casual and let the mouth put out talk the sound of which was its own justification. He wanted to make her laugh.

'Have you read any good palms lately?' he asked in a tone of professional interest.

The open hand she had been studying like a manual closed at the touch of his voice, became a clenched rebuff.

'It's chilly for June,' he said. 'We don't seem tae get the summers we used tae get. Ah think it's a' these atomic bombs they're dropping.'

It was a device he used commonly when they were quarrelling and she stopped speaking. She liked that sort of burlesque of small-talk and generally thawed to a smile in the face of it. But this time she remained unaffected. Charlie took out his cigarettes and offered her one. He wanted to make her shift her position, even slightly, to infiltrate just a small fifth column of movement behind her composure and undermine it. When she had accepted a cigarette, he held the match poised over the matchbox but didn't strike it, forcing her to give him at least a little of her attention.

'Ah died just yesterday,' he said. 'Ah just thought Ah'd mention it, in case it was of any interest.'

She stared doggedly at the match, but a muscle in her cheek twitched and the cigarette quivered fractionally in her lips, like a forked stick over water. Charlie divined laughter. He felt an almost childish delight in the thought that he could make her laugh and started to address some invisible companion over his shoulder.

'Ah've been going about fur quite a while with this wee dummy lassie here,' he said. 'She can't speak a word, ye ken. But Ah've learned the deaf-and-dummy alphabet from A to Z.

It's amazing how ye pick it up. Ah can talk away quite the thing to 'er.'

He proceeded to give a demonstration, leaning avuncularly into Mary's face. It was a digital extravaganza. His hand seemed to blossom with several extra fingers that assumed grotesque shapes and patterns that merged into a blur of movement, and all the time his mouth was benignly spelling out the verbal gloss, 'If-it-takes-a-man-a-week-to-walk-a-fortnight-how-many-oranges-in-a-barrel-of-grapes?' The cigarette was now bobbing frantically in her pursed lips and the swell of suppressed laughter was creasing the skin around her eyes. Charlie paused, happily triumphant, and struck the match. He made as if to offer it to Mary and then withdrew it. His other hand pointed like a painted direction-sign to her mouth.

'Danger,' he said. 'Unexploded Laugh.'

In that instant the cigarette fell like a stopper from her mouth on to the table and her laughter effervesced uncontrollably and Charlie was joining in, both of them suddenly laughing. And just as suddenly her breath seemed to catch and it was as if her laughter had fallen through that missed inhalation and sobbing came in to take its place. For she was crying and saying through her sobs, 'Damn you, damn you, Charlie. What are ye trying to do to me? What are ye trying to do?' And Charlie was staring open-mouthed at her and then glancing apprehensively round the café because emotion was playing havoc with her voice, raising and lowering it like someone twiddling the volume knob of a radio. And the match burned Charlie's forgotten fingers and they dropped it and it broke black and extinguished on the table. His brief sense of triumph and his foolish desire to make her laugh turned to recriminate with him now, and seemed to add their weight to everything she was saying.

'Is it something funny to you, Charlie? Is it?' Then it came, in gobbets of bemused pain that she couldn't hold in any longer. 'What's wrong, Charlie? What is it? Why wouldn't ye see me, Charlie? Ah came up to see ye. Why have ye avoided me?'

As she spoke she was shaking her head as if even now she wanted to deny the words that hissed from her mouth in sibilant pain. Charlie's face caught and held her anguish like a mirror. He saw that his attempt at flippancy was an insult to what she felt. He had been wrong to think that it was something that didn't properly belong on her features, was something inappropriate to her. The sadness and bewilderment expressed in her face were very real to her, written in her own calligraphy, and couldn't be erased with a little laughter. They meant more, and what they meant had to be faced. Charlie looked at her in the light of his own sudden understanding and the rest of the room subsided into darkness. Only Mary mattered, surrounded by his concentration like a patch of light with its ragged edges shading into the dimness of the café, the sounds of which occurred in the furthest distance, a tinkle of teacups coming as fine as needles clashing. Her grief was magnified in his close attention, loomed out at him as something very large. Unable to face it directly all at once, he came at her through a trivial kindness, lifting her cigarette for her, and striking another match and offering it to her like an apology. In the enclosed perspective of their confrontation with each other, the match seemed to burn as big as a candle in his fingers. At first she rejected the light with a preoccupied headshake, but he was gently insistent and finally she took it, sighing and exhaling simultaneously, so that the smoke hung a moment before her mouth, a visual measurement of what she felt, before it dissipated slowly.

'Ah mean, have Ah done something wrong, Charlie? What've I done?'

The pathetic inadequacy of that question, thrown despairingly like a fragile rope across an unbridgeable chasm, was a measure of the hopelessness of trying to tell her what had happened. How could he ever explain to her? How could he hope that she would begin to understand something which he couldn't understand himself? With how many questions had he himself tried to sound the strange depths of the despair that had possessed him since his father died? How many plumbline reasons had he dropped into it, only to find that they came nowhere near to touching the bottom of what he felt? He only knew that in the face of it nothing else seemed to matter. And how could he explain that to Mary? It was hopeless. All he could do was to try and make her see that none of it was her fault, to show her what weren't the reasons.

'Mary,' he said, shaking his head. 'Ye're no' tae think that. You did nothing wrong. Nothing. It isn't anything like that at all.'

'What is it like then, Charlie? You tell me. Tell me what it *is* like. It's been more than a year and we were goin' to get married and everything. And now ye've changed. Ye've just changed. Ah don't even know why, Charlie. Ah don't know why.'

'Ah don't know why maself, Mary. It's just nothin's the same any mair. Nothin'. But it's no' you, Mary. It's me. It's something wrong with me. What did *you* do?'

'Is it because your father's dead, Charlie?'

He saw her eyes alert with imminent sympathy, bright as a beagle's on the scent. For a moment he was tempted to submit to that explanation. He was tired of being hounded with questions and he had a sudden desire to accept that as the reason for the way he was and let Mary's sympathy overtake him and hold him. It would have been easy and pleasant to let her believe that. He had only to nod and she was ready to forget everything else, to minister sympathy to him. The nearness of her across the table made the prospect unbearably inviting. Perhaps if he just leaned on her now everything would be all right. She might help him to get over it and they could go on as they had been before. He could go back to university. He might look back on this time of his life as the time when he had 'taken his father's death badly'. He had heard other people say that sort of thing. Feelings were bearable if you could fit them into a common context. So why couldn't he make that one affirmative movement of his head that would naturalize this alien feeling in him, give Mary common ground with him and let her help him to overcome it? Surely in a sense she was right. It *was* because his father was dead. But only in a sense was she right. And not in his sense. That was the insurmountable difference. He knew what she meant when she asked that question. It emerged from an accepted background and in her terms it referred simply to the fact of bereavement. But for him his father's death had become something much more, straddling his life like a Colossus, and its shadow fell everywhere. It was not for him a self-contained fact. His feeling went beyond bereavement and left him no accepted terms in which he could express it. That was what separated him from everyone else. That was why he couldn't talk to John about it. Every word John said took meaning from a frame of reference that had no relevance to Charlie. The same words meant different things for both of them. And with Mary, too, that one question presented no more than a mirage of communication. Charlie saw the desperate loneliness of his position, where nothing could convey what he felt to anyone else. If he said yes to Mary's question his answer was translated into her own terms which had no relation to what he meant. If he said no, he was lying to himself.

'No,' he said into the silence that had followed Mary's question, and the word was like a door blowing irrevocably shut in his mind, keeping Mary out. He paused on the sound of it, feeling it close him finally inside himself. He felt that this was a terrible choice to make, to isolate himself, to reject the help that was being offered. But the help that was offered was help that he did not need. He couldn't use it. The help that he did need nothing could offer. Was there a choice? 'No, Mary. It isn't that. It's not because my father's dead.'

Mary took his answer. She did not realize how close she had come to reaching him. Something had shown for a second in his face that drew her attention like a sudden movement among foliage, but it was gone again almost at once and she assumed she had been wrong. She tried to come at him by another direction, moving unknowingly further from him.

'Charlie, what am Ah meant to do? We both made it this

way. You led me to believe. . . It's not just my fault that I feel this way. Am I supposed just tae stop feeling like this now?'

Charlie lifted the empty matchbox that lay in the ashtray and turned it in his fingers helplessly.

'Charlie!' Her voice tried desperately to reach him. 'Ah love you, Charlie. Ah mean I've got this feeling and it's just about all there is of me. What am I meant to do with it? Just forget it? Ah can't forget it. How much of me's goin' to be left? There'll be nothing of me left. And it's your fault, Charlie.'

Charlie looked at her through the dark bars of his own fingers.

'All right, Mary,' he said. 'Right. So it's my fault.'

'But why? Why are ye doing it? Don't you love me?'

Love. The letters writhed in his mind into an unintelligible hieroglyph.

'Ah don't even know what that means,' he said.

'Well *I* know, Charlie. I know what it means. And I'm stuck with it. What do ye want me to do? Wait till *you* find out? What's this been for a year if you don't know? Ah can't just wait, Charlie. Ah'm not doing it. You can't ask me to.'

'Nobody's asking you to wait, Mary,' he said. 'Ah know you can't wait. Ah know it, Mary.'

She waited for him to say more, but nothing came. He accepted the fact passively, had no reflex to it. He just sat looking at the table and holding the matchbox in his hand like a talisman.

'I didn't mean that, Charlie,' she said quietly. 'Ah just said it. Ah didn't mean it. Ah would wait. Could we not just go on the same as we've been doin', Charlie? Could we not? And see what happens? Ah'd rather do that than just let it stop. Ah don't want that to happen. It just can't happen. We'll just go on. Ah'm prepared to wait, Charlie. We'll just go on and we'll see. It'll be all right. Ah mean Ah can wait. . .'

'Mary . . .' Her name gave garrulity the bit, harnessed hope to reality and stopped it dead. 'You don't have tae say

114

that. Don't be like that. You don't have tae beg for anythin'. You don't have tae.'

'Don't Ah, Charlie?' Her eyes hinted at tears. 'What makes ye think Ah don't? Charlie, who would want me now?'

Her eyes were lowered as she said it and her face was veiled with shame like a yashmak. Charlie stared at her, trying to penetrate it. When he realized what she meant he had a strange chilly sensation as if tentacles were trying to enclose him and draw him in, and he wanted to shake them off in a frenzy of disgust.

The matchbox burst in his hand, a small explosion of wood.

'Jesus Christ,' he said. You draw the line nae-where, dae ye? That's the way isn't it? Every bastard's on the market for somethin'. An eye for an eye and a marriage for a maiden-head.

His anger rained words blindly around him and he could barely understand why. Since his father's death feeling had reduced itself to this eternal anger that ticked quietly inside him like a geiger counter, increasing in frequency without warning when certain words or situations crossed its path. Now it surged to an urgency that deafened reason, and all he could see to attach it to was Mary's hypocrisy.

'If Ah could give you back your stinking virginity Ah would. That's all it is for you, isn't it? Your own wee rotten set-up. It's like your mother wi' her bloody antimacassars. One oota place an' it's a tragedy. Whit dae ye think life is, somethin' ye knit tae a pattern oot the *Woman's Own*? Nae untidy edges. Listen, Mary. If you'd had it from everybody from Land's End tae John o' Groats it wouldny matter a damn. Things wouldny be any worse than they are. How can ye kid yerself on that you matter or Ah matter? Nobody matters. Nobody. Hoor or housewife, whit's the odds? Maybe yer mither or the neebors wid bother. But that's all. Nothin' about you matters. Nothin'.'

She sat clenched to the table, crying, her face averted as if by a blow. His anger treacherously subsided as suddenly as it had risen, leaving him stranded on the enormity of what he

115

had said. Her passive misery showed him how disproportionate and unjust his anger had been. He writhed in disgust that was a replica of what he had felt looking at Mick lying in his own vomit. Mary's tears became Elizabeth's.

'I'm sorry, Mary,' he said. 'Ach, I'm sorry.'

He started to break the matchbox methodically into fragments and set them carefully in the ashtray.

She continued to weep soundlessly, with her eyes closed. He looked down at himself, at the clumsy body and the pink hands that looked like malformed claws and he wondered how this ugly amalgam of bone and flesh could matter so much to anyone. He wondered how the lips could open and close and the teeth click and put forth sounds that could agonize another. How could these pieces of animated clay, happed in a few dreams and pretensions, move among their little lives, an exhalation away from death, and presume to think they mattered? But they did. They were stitched to life by a fraying thread of breath and beyond its breaking they knew nothing, but on it they hung hopes and plans and private certainties. Their assurance belied their nature. They found things to want and people to love and assumed an appearance of sufficiency. And when you took some of it from them, they fought or wept. He looked at Mary and thought that this was just someone sitting in a café. That was all it had been, two people talking in a café, on a Friday night. But Mary dignified it into something more just by feeling as she did about it. And he felt himself made something more significant because he mattered so much to another person. But to realize that was only to torture himself. To allow himself to be involved in it was to share the pretence of everybody else, and that was what he couldn't do. He couldn't sit with Mary and pretend to be communicating with her. He had been with her all evening and all they had conveyed to each other were mistakes, indifference and hypocrisy and anger. He respected what the anger had done. It had been misguided, but it had succeeded in cutting the knot that couldn't be unravelled. His separation from Mary had grown gradually in him, sifting like silt in his mind. Whether he could understand it rationally or not was not the point. It was there. All that had been lacking was their mutual acknowledgment of it. At least his anger had achieved that. To be with each other now was an exercise in masochism, the infliction of mutual pain. Nothing could be said or done to make any difference.

'Please go away, Mary,' he said. 'Please go home.'

She sat till she knew her tears were finished. She picked up her gloves and mechanically pushed back her hair. She paused for a moment as if expecting him to get up and see her home. But he knew the futility of prolonging the time that they were together. What he felt jammed the social reflex to escort her and he sat still. She got up and went out and he could see her for a second outside before the darkness swallowed her like jaws.

The action was somehow too simple. He had a sense of deceit, of mirage, as if where a moment ago there had been so much pain and grief and anger there was now nothing. He looked for signs of it. There was none, only a few pathetic emblems that couldn't convey what had happened, two crumpled cigarette stubs, the pieces of matchbox pyramidal in the ashtray, a memorial cairn of balsa-wood. He looked round the café, remembering the point when he might have turned the other way, towards Mary and the simple acceptance of things as they were. But that point was irrevocably past. Already the café itself was not the place they had come into. Subtle and unnoticed changes had taken place. The ruminating drunk was gone. The table where the man and woman had sat was empty, cleared of everything but the metal ashtray, anonymously clean. There was no small man or paper or coupon. Their absence seemed to erase the place where Mary and he had sat, to negate what had happened there. Charlie was aware of sitting in a strange place, given over to the preoccupied activities of others.

Opposite him sat a couple of doubtful age and intentions, looking as if they had been abstracted from a Breughel print. Drink had given their age a new lease of youth and they were

117

canoodling and ogling each other archly. They snuffled and simpered, pecked and withdrew. The woman wore no ring, but Charlie noticed bitterly that what her fingers lacked her eyes more than compensated. The only others were a group of young men who had commandeered the café like soldiers in an occupied country. They would go into a conspiratorial huddle and then break apart, sowing laughter all over the café before settling back into the positions that were the habits of an hour, postures they had reached through the secret and patient sculpture of restlessness. One was sitting with his feet up on a neighbouring chair and his arms around his legs, like 'The Boyhood of Raleigh', another was rubbing a coin to a desultory polish on his sleeve, a third was picking his nose with an air of dedication. The fourth one was going well, the way it happens sometimes, when the patter comes pat, and every joke rings the bell. He was generating his own atmosphere as he went along, like laughing-gas, so that it was the laughter which made things funny and not the other way round.

Sitting there in casual camaraderie and wearing their youth like a uniform, they made Charlie nostalgic for the past of a few weeks ago. He could recall like a distant memory when he had been like them. He understood exactly the sense of communal identity they drew from each other. It was not the identity you have from being a member of a family or living in a certain place, but that which, if you are young, you share with everyone else who is young with you. It was the superficial yet binding bond between people enlisted in the same rank of circumstance, when you form your own exclusive group with its own tricks of speech and passwords, and its habits of thought, and everyone else is just a civilian; when your personality has not yet been demobilized into that of a private individual and is still submerged in that of youth. He remembered the feeling. He remembered especially Saturday nights like that, when his behaviour must have corresponded to that of a million other young men and his actions seemed to take place in a sort of generic tense.

The pattern of so many such Saturdays came back to mind, a pattern that must have been obeyed by so many young men besides himself, automatically, unquestioningly, as if it had been coded through their blood, the orders of the day to which they responded en masse. Early in the evening, the compulsion came on you, like a distant bugle. You washed and shaved with special care and felt good with a fresh clean shirt against your skin.

When you got to the dance-hall, you checked in your coat and went to the toilets to comb your hair. There would be a group of young men there, talking gallous, already drunk on one part whisky and nine parts determination, exorcizing the timidity of John and Joe and instilling themselves with the fearless spirit of Johnnie Walker. When you came out the band would be at the stage of quiet perspiration and the drummer would be hunched in that professional attitude of ecstatic boredom that must be stipulated by the Drummers' Union. From then on you divided your time between the stag line and dancing. You learned to categorize your partners roughly. About the worst thing that could happen was that she might be a singer. 'I was waltzing one night in Kentucky ... ta-ra-ra-ra ... too sune ... and the bee-eutiful Kentucky mune.' Running this a close second in the Boredom Stakes, was a congenital hummer so that, dancing, you felt as if you had a hive on for a hat. You established contact in various places and tried to consolidate and assess during the evening, by the scouting pressure of a hand or the suave brush of lips on the forehead at the dance's end. And between sorties you returned to the peacock patter of the knots of apprentice men, talk puffed up with hyperbole and gaudy with swearwords.

'Hell! Talk about walk. She lives at the North Pole. Igloo-Strasse. Knock three times and ask for Chinook. An' fur whit? Ye winch her fur a year, and then maybe ye get tae put yer haun' on her left lug. A write-off, definitely.'

'Jist at that meenit her auld man comes out, ken? Doing his Willie Winkie, ken? Wearin' his stupit pyjamas. See aboot every two meenits efter that? He shoves his neb oot like a cuckoo-clock tae tell us the time. Ah politely puked an' left. Ah felt like askin' him whit he wanted tae be when he grew up, or givin' him a bob to lose himself.'

'Look. Ye're wrong! Ah know fur facts ye're wrong. Dempsey never seen Mickey Walker, never mind fighting him. Dempsey took the title off Lewis Firpo, an' he was a heavy-weight. Mickey Walker was a bloody middle-weight. Ten stone seven. An' Ah've got the books in the hoose tae prove it.'

'Ye shoulda been with us last night, boy. Fantabulous. One of the most best nights known to man. Ah don't remember a thing.'

So the night would pass, a hothouse of pleasant sensations, small seeds of fact blooming from inspired mouths into exotic fictions, mascara'd eyes ogling over shoulders, cigarette smoke veining dark corners, neat bottoms bobbing into sight, only to submerge again in a sea of bodies, artesian laughter suddenly unstopped, until you began to notice fewer people in the toilets and more room on the floor. And reading the signs of the night working to a close, with the body of dancers now in slower revolution like a wheel running down, and many stilled altogether, holding each other, swaying slightly like plants in a gently breathing wind, and girls with their heads drooped bouffant on their partners' shoulders like dying flowers, and the faint musk of perfumed sweat, and the drift beginning towards the door, couples leaving with collars up, the boys lean waiting, weaving minute silvered webs of cigarette smoke till their girls come clicking to them, swathed in raincoats and fresh powder, magnetizing the swivelling attention of the lobby-loungers with a whiff of perfumed promise that says 'Don't you wish it was you?' and then mounting the stairs hand-in-hand until the big door is un-barred and swung open and with the sputter of a cigarette-stub in a puddle and a clack of eager heels they are gone.

You would walk with her, enjoying the tingle of strange-ness, the first fumbling verbal contacts, making conversation out of a puddle you had to skirt or a drunk man coming to-wards you, steering her subtly towards one of the familiar parts of the geography of your relationships with girls, where you felt more confident – the archway leading to disused stables where when it rained you stood in a dry arch of darkness with a beaded curtain of rain on each side of you, or the Burns Monument in the park, a building deft at darknesses, giving sudden black shadows, shallow but deep, which shut behind you like a door, so that someone standing a yard away couldn't tell you from the brick, a building sworn into the freemasonry of courters, that mushroomed lovers in its shadows after dark, under stairways, in clefts and corners, while above them the Bard stood in stone, conniving with the moon, his hand raised in apparent benediction of their efforts, smiling, and, when the sun rose, revealing nothing to the respectful visitors who came to do obeisance to a dozen dusty, illegible books and a score of faded prints.

Once there, you might talk a while. Sometimes talk wasn't very necessary. But sometimes it was and wouldn't come, and the situation would freeze on you. At other times sudden intimacies sprang up in the crevices of darkness like tropical flowers, the sweeter for their transcience, the richer because you felt you wouldn't always be capable of such sudden depth of contact with a girl. You could talk about pictures, people, places, anything, and what you said seemed to matter entirely. Nothing was trivial. Things you had done or known were rediscovered in her reaction to them, and you were surprised to find how interesting they were.

You would talk and kiss and go off into a twin trance, lost in each other, grown together like statues shaped from a single piece of clay, until the chaperoning owl hooted the night and the trees back into your awareness and the poplared avenue beneath you laid with moonlight, down which you would be able to see the lake ringed with lamps whose lights were elongated, wavering in the water like tapers of cold fire, and you would embrace and kiss and become industriously involved in each other again, happy in the collisions of your flesh and the feel of wall on hand and the smell of hair and the taste of mouths, and would break off from time to time to talk or smoke or just stand happy, and would start again and stop, continuing and leaving off casually and deliciously, with conversation growing in the interstices of your activity.

You continued, wrestling pleasantly, resting between rounds, and the decision would vary from girl to girl. You would walk her home, usually in the region of midnight, and wait at her door until an irate mother or father, depending on whether the household was matriarchal or patriarchal, called or appeared. Then you came up home alone with most of the town asleep and a pleasant taste of morning in your mouth.

He let the memory of it leave him, dissipate like a dream, facing him with the café. The waitress had started to stack chairs on the cleared tables with a noise that was a reprimand in its loudness. Only he and the young men remained as small islands of vanishing Friday in an encroaching sea of Saturday. Tomorrow no doubt they would be following the same pattern as always. But he didn't have any pattern to follow, no ready-made means of expressing himself. Saturday meant nothing to him. It used to mean Mary. But he had put an end to that.

He sat feeling as if more than one Friday was ending in the café clock telling the time invisibly behind its steamed face, a burst of laughter and a jabber of Italian from the back-shop, and he had the feeling of having put dust covers on so many areas of his life and of having isolated himself from many people. It was as if he was deliberately preparing himself for something he knew was going to happen. But what it was, he didn't know.

Chapter 13

FROM HER TABLE IN THE CORNER OF THE TEA-ROOM, Mrs Whitmore was watching the door intently, with a nervousness that was almost adolescent. She wanted to see Peter's expression as soon as he entered the room. She became irritated by an unidentified stickiness somewhere in her right hand. Giving it a detachment of her attention, she found it was a fragment of the cream cake she had eaten, and extradited it to the ashtray. It reminded her that she hadn't washed her hands or renewed her make-up, and she wondered if she still had time. She checked her watch. The football would have been over for twenty minutes. Allowing Peter half an hour to get here, she still had ten minutes. The doorway was still empty. Leaving her umbrella hooked on the chair to deputize for a 'reserved' sign, she went out into the side corridor and along to the ladies' room.

It was a bit scruffy, but it would do. She hurriedly bathed her face and dried it and applied fresh make-up. She had to keep moving her head back and forth because the mirror was badly scuffed and gave her only a piecemeal reflection of herself. She took a lot of trouble with her lipstick and when she was finished her eyes scouted anxiously from the smooth mask she had created. In the dull, stale room, she made a small moment of pathos that had no witness as she advanced on and receded from her careful image, mouthing and pouting, in the glass whose scruffiness was like an ironic prophecy, a mercury preaching. Her vanity, too desperate to be damning, contained its own punishment, being overshadowed by its own futility like fatalism. The importance she attached to every pore of her face was juvenile in its morbidity. To her, age was a personal and avoidable misfortune, like pimples. She beat back nature with a powder-puff. Against those inroads of age to which most people capitulate imperceptibly, and often casually, she fought a desperate rearguard action, simply because it was all that she had left to defend. No frontal defence was necessary. When she had married Peter, she had left behind not just a house and furniture and some people, but much that was less tangible and more significant. She had left behind almost everything that had been herself. Peter's attraction to her had been physical and, in responding to it, she had fostered a spurious allegiance, one which was not natural to her life as she had known it and which, like a cuckoo, excluded all others, abiding none besides itself. Indulging her senses in an Indian summer, she had allowed herself to be carried away by an emotion that she couldn't control and the motive power of which must soon die under her. All she could do was try to prolong it as long as possible. The pivot of her relationship with Peter was purely physical and, in the absence of much else, she could only maintain it. No matter where she might go, or how many things she might do, or how much she might have, she would always be forlorn and displaced, a very temporary person. All she had was the body she stood in, her physical desirability. She couldn't face the thought of losing that. That was why for the past week or so the hope of something more had filled her with the sort of restless expectancy that is usually the monopoly of children. If Peter agreed, it could make her more than an errant body, give her a bulwark against the encroaching emptiness. If Peter agreed. She had broached it to him more than once already, showing him the idea from time to time, letting him become familiar with its strangeness before asking him to decide. He hadn't seemed very agreeable. But tonight would tell.

Back in the tea-room, she found that Peter still hadn't arrived. She sat down to wait. She hoped that the football team had won, knowing the importance of accidental trivia to any plan. Her tea-cup had not been cleared away, and she tilted it mechanically in her hand, looking at the dregs like a spae-wife trying to foretell a surprise visit from which happiness will come.

Like a happy omen, Peter came into the room, announcing his mood with a smile.

Coming up to the table, he said, 'Come on, Cleopatra. Tonight we eat the big dinner. Your barge is waiting.'

'To what do we owe this?' she said, laughing. 'Did your team win?'

'And that's the least of it. A double up at Catterick, that's worth a good fifty quid. And I just had it from Ritchie Evans there . . . You remember Ritchie? At Bert's party the other week. The one that played the piano – a real case. I saw him at the football there. He has it on the bush telegraph that they're polishing Carruthers' shoes for me to step into. Seems just about a certainty. Ritchie's never been wrong yet. I knew Carruthers had just about done the old hara-kiri with the hash he made of that last contract. But I didn't know the funeral would be so soon. But that's the way it goes. And I'm not complaining.'

Her congratulations were drowned in his own talk and hustling activity as he conducted her out into the street. Her reaction didn't matter too much, anyway. All he needed was her presence, like a dictaphone into which he could tell his urgent happiness, someone with whom to talk his feelings into shape. He was away ahead of her, making conjectural memos and dusting the seat of office, speaking to various people from his new status. Any contribution she could make to the enthusiasm he was generating was necessarily so indefinite as to be insignificant beside his own.

'This is my night. Keep with me and I'll give you some,' he said, stepping aside to let people pass with a proprietary smile, as if he was leasing them the pavement.

When they reached the car, he was still talking, throwing words about like baw siller. Driving, he showed none of the usual impatience that seemed to be set in motion with the engine. Normally, he was an extreme sufferer from driver's disease, that jaundiced disillusion with humanity that afflicts those who observe the world through a windscreen. But tonight the car seemed to run on solicitude. He smiled at people overtaking him, he slowed down to wave cars out of side roads, he treated jay-walkers like amusingly mischievous children, and the horn was redundant. It was a lot more than Mrs Whitmore had hoped for. The omens were very favourable. She was tempted to put her suggestions to him there and then, in the intimacy of the car. But she decided against it. Better to wait and let his thoughts come to terms with one another before introducing a stranger to them. He was so taken up with himself at the moment that the mention of anything extraneous to his imminent promotion would be like an insult.

'It's nothing short of the "Royal" for us tonight,' he had said, and that was where he took her.

They had a long apéritif in the lounge bar before making an expansive entrance in the dining-room, a bowing waiter preceding them like a red carpet. Peter enjoyed ordering the meal and choosing the wine, a Beaujolais. All through the meal they talked about the promotion. It was a very happy and successful hour and a half, in which the food and the drink and the talk supplemented each other perfectly, words adding savour to meat and being washed down with wine. It was an inspired and sustained orchestration of enjoyment, the first movement of which ended when she came back to the simple repetition of how wonderful it was that he should get the job, a remark which had been the motif of the entire meal. But Peter brought that motif to an end when he said that they mustn't be too presumptuous, because he hadn't actually been given the job yet. Having infected her with his own enthusiasm, he was now schooling her in how it should be cured. That was the frame of mind he was in, a one-man-band of a mood in which he couldn't help wanting to play all the parts. And he struck the chord that gave the evening its second movement with his next remark, spoken after he had finished the wine.

'My God, Jane, you look wonderful tonight,' he said, seeing her through three rose-tinted glasses.

The opening theme of the second movement had had as

126

prelude the warmth and stimulation of the meal and the wine, and had been hinted at in glances and moist lips and eyes that sent mute familiar signals of what was ahead. It did not have to be articulated. It was the more effective for not being articulated. But it continued and grew in certainty when they moved from the dining-room back into the lounge. They found a table in a quiet part of the room and, talking and sipping a few more drinks, they gradually brought the feeling in them to a higher pitch. It wasn't so often now that their physical attraction for each other reached such a spontaneous mutual expression. At first it had frequently hit them with electric immediacy, stunning them into unconsciousness of what was going on around them in restaurant or living-room. Then everything else tended to be an unbearable obstruction between them and the consummation of what they felt. Now, with the adeptness with which every relationship leavens the flatness of its own custom, they savoured the interim, making it contribute positively to what lay beyond it. They did not attempt to hurry the evening towards its culmination. Rather they deliberately side-tracked themselves, seemed to lose sight altogether of the tacit tryst they had made between them, tantalizing their own desire. They detoured down comments on current news, dawdled in irrelevant discussions of their friends, disappeared behind short silences, leaving here and there small sensual clues, a long promissory look through an ineffectual veil of small-talk, laughter that was there before the cause for it, a languid stretching, the secret markings that only they understood. And all the time Mrs Whitmore was pleasantly biding her time, preparing her small, affectionate ambush.

She waited till they had about three-quarters of an hour remaining to them in the lounge. She had wanted to put it off as long as possible and at the same time to have the atmosphere of the lounge as an ally in case she was forced to discuss it at length. Conversation drifted for a moment into silence. Having grown sufficiently accustomed to his new image of himself, Peter had been busy being gallant to her, making her feel at home in his happiness. He had just been joking with the waiter, giving her an oblique compliment. When the waiter had brought the drinks and left them, she decided to speak.

'Peter,' she said, 'remember we discussed going down to Kilmarnock? Well, what about it? Could we? I would like to see them.'

He prevaricated with a sip of whisky.

'Not now, Jane,' he said. 'Don't let's talk about it tonight, eh? We'll just keep tonight for celebrating. This is a night for Whitmores only. Exclusive lease.'

'But we've put it off already. Please, Peter. It would just complete the night perfectly for me. Just say we can go down. That's all.'

Peter took another sip of whisky and waited vaguely for the reaction of his stomach as if thinking was a gastronomic process.

'All right,' he said. 'We'll go down to Kilmarnock. Soon. All right? We don't have to name the day, just yet, do we?'

But concession is tutor to demand, and reading his mood correctly, she had no intention of leaving it at that.

'No, of course not,' she said. 'But I've been thinking. Well, since the football team goes down to Kilmarnock next Saturday . . .' She gave him a minute to turn the fact over before she proceeded to planting. 'Well. I could come down with you. You could go to the match in the afternoon. And I could do some shopping. And at night . . .'

Too late, he realized what was happening. The loophole of the indefinite future became a lasso on the present.

'It's ideal really,' she said, pulling it tight.

'But right out the blue like that? They won't even know we're coming.'

'But they wouldn't know anyway, would they?'

'They might not be in.'

'They might not be in any other time as well. That's a chance we're taking any time.'

'But . . . I just don't fancy it, Jane. I don't even know them. And I'm quite sure they don't want to know me.'

'They will once they've seen you.'

'I wish my bookie was laying odds on that.'

'Come on, Peter. For my sake. Please. Just give it a chance. That's all I'm asking. Just come down with me and see. That's all. Please, Peter.'

Peter shook his head, not sure whether it was in refusal or resignation. There should have been objections, but he had mislaid them somewhere in his immense feeling of well-being. All he could find was a vague and inexpressible misgiving, an incommunicable fragment of the reasons against it that he should have been able to provide. He was too happy to argue vehemently and he couldn't bring himself to spoil the conclusion to the night that he had been looking forward to. But he couldn't escape a sense of treachery in the bright warmth and the murmur of soft voices and the gentle, molten passage of the whisky. He might have known there would be something like this at the end of such a day, the pay-off of pleasure. It had all been just too good. So here was the evening presenting him with the bill. Yet he still felt too generous to quibble.

'Right,' he said. 'All right,' and an incipient huff surrendered to her smile.

Mrs Whitmore's happiness was complete. The room froze into a reflection of her joy and everything and everyone in it seemed to be employed on her behalf. She was so happy that she felt a little guilty. Pleasure of such intensity seemed somehow forbidden. She felt its physical luxury enclose her like a net. But its meshes were silken, silken. Slowly, they were drawing curtains on the evening, and 'bed' flashed like neon in the warm darkness of her mind. All that remained was to find some words to fill the interval, some mundanities of conversation, the more ridiculous the better, so that they didn't disturb her anticipation by involving her interest.

'Tell me about the football, Peter,' she said. 'What happened?'

Part Two

Chapter 14

'THEN MITCHELL GOT HOLD O' THIS LOOSE BALL. AH mean it looked as if there was nae danger. He'd hardly had a shove at it up to then, as well. That's the thing aboot Mitchell, though. He can lie out a game for eighty-five minutes. But if ye just get 'im on it for the ither five, you're home to tea. Anyway, this ball broke to 'im, ye know? He was standin' facin' his own goal too. He trapped it and turned in the wan movement. An' then without stoppin' he brought it right past the back, just as if he wisny there. Ye woulda thought the ball was fixed to his foot wi' elastic. He moved in to about the corner o' the box, an' the centre-half cut right across. Then it was just a blur. Mitchell kinda juggled the ball over the centre-half's foot. His right foot. An then, still in the same position. . . . Ah mean ye woulda thought he would shove it in tae Cairns. But naw. His right foot was still in line wi' the centre-half an' he blutered it wi' his left. Really low an' right inside the post. Inch perfect. Travellin' like a train. The goalie was naewhere. No chance. It was like somethin' out the *Rover*. Wasn't it, Jim?'

'Apart from the questionable literary allusion,' Jim said in his professorial voice, 'your account may be considered more or less accurate. It was a great game, though, Charlie. You shoulda been there. The boys was glorious. They really was.'

'We were standin' at the usual place too,' Andy said. 'We thought we would see ye there. Wee Alex Andrews was there. Shoutin' like a daft yin.'

'Naw. Ah don't know,' Charlie hedged. 'Ah just didn't fancy it. Couldn't be bothered.'

He was still recovering from the surprise of Jim and Andy visiting him like this. Lately he had lost any sense of the phases of the week. The focus of his life had so shifted that time lost all perspective, ceased to be ordered into a series of habits that promised to recur indefinitely into the future. Now suddenly into his mapless despairing thinking had come Jim and Andy, proclaiming Saturday night. With their smart suits and Italian shoes and their bright complementary appearances, they were like a vaudeville team. Their conversation too was sustained cross-talk, with catch-phrases and cross-references. They often told things in duet, finishing each other's remarks. Mutual acquaintance had so worked on them that when they were together they seemed to speak parts written by habit. Listening to them, Charlie felt a response to their glib patter and easy acceptance quicken in himself. Because of the sense of dispossession of himself that he felt, the ease with which they seemed to inhabit their identities impressed him as something much finer than in truth it was. Its effect on him was almost apocalyptic. Sometimes when you think too deeply into the reasons of your life, uprooting every habit and blighting instinct with questions, your being becomes so barren that all you can do is let it lie fallow for a while and wait for any seeds of chance to blow in and take root. To Charlie this seemed such a moment. He had thought himself into limbo and now suddenly into it had happened these two people who were their own reasons. They seemed effortlessly to contradict Charlie's despair. Being with them, he couldn't help wondering if they didn't have the right of it after all, being content just to go on from day to day being themselves. He had painfully left behind him everything he had accepted before and taken up his lonely position, entrenched in his own despair. And now Jim and Andy had caught him off his guard and infiltrated their fifth column of spontaneous enjoyment and made him wonder if his position was tenable at all.

'That's us second tap o' the League,' Jim said. 'After that it's the European Cup. We'll take Real Madrid tae the cleaners. Scotia, the rickety cradle of soccer, will oncet again lead the van.'

'Ah'll have a penny poke of mixed metaphors, please.'

Andy said. 'But we didn't come here for to do wur roving reporter, did we now? Shall we tell the man?'

Jim volleyed his eyebrows up and down, pouting sexily.

'We bring you news, O Master,' Andy said solemnly.

He clapped his hands like a Grand Vizier and Jim went into his own version of an eastern dance, swivelling his hips and peering enticingly over his downturned hands.

'Behold,' intoned Charlie. 'We know of a place, O Great One, where the V.P. flows like wine and the women are soft and yielding to the touch. Umpteen of them. Yea, a veritable harem.'

'And each of them partial to a wee bit harum-scarum,' leered Jim, dancing over to nudge Charlie.

'There are all things for a man's delight. Women beauteous as the dawn.'

'And game as they come.'

'Unlimited supplies of the sacred weed.'

'An' ye get free fags as well.'

'Sweet music.'

'The pick of the pops and the popsies. Can you beat it?'

'Whit he means is we've been invited tae a pairty,' Jim explained.

'My crude compatriot would make a fairy-tale sound like a shopping list. But Ah suppose ye could put it that way. An' not only that. But by public demand you are invited also as well. So get on yer hunting hat and let's go.'

'Naw, no' me,' Charlie said. 'Ah'm no in the mood, Andy. Ye can tell me about it.'

'Let us not talk mutiny, Charles,' Jim said. 'Since when did crumpet become a matter of mood. It's a matter of principle man. We have an obligation to our fans. Are ye goin' tae let all these women go to waste? Think of your responsibilities.'

'Ah'll let you worry about that, Jim. Ah know ye've got a fine sense of public duty. Whose pairty is it, anyway?'

'Eddie Gibson's,' Andy said. 'His folks're away for a week-end somewhere. So Eddie's got the fambly mansion to him-self. It's quite a house too. Plenty o' rooms tae get lost in.' Jim interpolated caddish laughter. 'And he has invited a formidable array of cuff. Everything's laid on, man. Booze. Talent. Record-player. Snuggery with room for as many couples as you care to mention. What a set-up, Charlie. Carpets will be rolled up and hair will be let down. Morals will be left at the door. Trousers optional. Cost of admission: one bottle of nothing in particular. Cold tea, if you're stuck. How can ye refuse, man? How can ye refuse?'

'You canny, Charlie,' Jim said. 'You just canny. How can ye sit here in preference to that? It's like turning down Hawaii for a week-end in Arran.'

'Aye, just you wade in there then, Jim,' Charlie said. 'An' good fishing. But it's no' for me. The way Ah feel the noo, Ah don't think Ah could muster enough patter tae last me through a sentence. Ah just don't feel like all that merry chiff-chaff an' casual talk.'

'Who said anything about talk?' Andy's hands spread in appeal. 'If it's taciturn you feel, that's the way you play it, boy. Tight as a clam. A man of mystery. Ah can just see it. Ye come in wi' a fag hangin' out yer mouth. Ye give the company a friendly sneer. All eyes are on you. Then it's just a matter of pickin' out the one ye fancy an' noddin' towards the bedroom. It always works in the pictures.'

'No' in the ones Ah've seen. Naw, thanks all the same, boys. But Ah'd feel like the proverbial spare one at a wedding. You go an' have a few for me.'

'Now, now,' Jim said in a tone of brusque competence. 'Just a minute.'

He made a great show of restraining Andy, took out an invisible stethoscope and proceeded to sound Charlie methodically.

'Hm. Uh-huh.' He nodded sagely to himself.

'Just as I thought. The so-and-so's deid.'

'I demand a second opinion,' Charlie said.

'All right then.' Andy supplied it. 'Ye're damn near deid. But we're givin' ye a chance tae get back to life. Lazarus, I say, git up off yer hunkers an' walk. With us down to this place here an' see whit life really is. Come on, Charlie. Whit dae ye say?'

'Ach, Ah'd just be a drag on the rations, Andy.'

'Such modesty,' Jim said. 'Listen, friend. Nobody who brings a bottle with him is ever a drag on the rations. Anyway if ye just leave one o' yer heads at the door, nobody'll be any the wiser. An' ye can tuck that third leg o' yours out of sight. An' as for yer leprosy, Ah've told ye often enough before – whit's that among friends?'

'Ye know, Jim,' Andy said, 'Ah don't think this man fully appreciates yet the chance he's getting. Do ye know some of the people who're going to be there?'

Andy proceeded to rhyme off a series of girls' names, accompanying each with a brief biographical note, touching upon appearance, past history, and potential. Charlie listened amusedly. He wasn't unwilling to be persuaded. Already he had fallen into the same idiom as Andy and Jim, feeling again its old familiarity. It was reassuring just to listen to them and to fall in with their mood, to concern yourself with football matches and parties and girls without worrying too much about anything. In this company Charlie could almost believe that the only thing that was wrong with him was that he had lost touch with these casual aspects of his life, and that this loss was the cause and not a symptom of the way he felt. And after all, you needed these trivial concerns, these parts of your life that you could take for granted and be jocular about. They were the essential ballast of your everyday life that kept you sane, saved you from becoming too introvert. This was the law of levity that governed your existence.

'There you are then, Charlie,' Andy said. 'The riches of the Indies. At your disposal. Just stretch out yer hand, man. And watch ye don't get it cut off. Or better still, just get yer jacket on and come down with us.'

'Ah must admit Ah'm tempted, boys,' Charlie said uncertainly. 'But Ah don't know.'

For the first time for a while Charlie seemed to see light at the end of the dark warren of circuitous thought in which he had lost himself since his father's death. He relished the prospect of going out with Andy and Jim. For the moment everything suddenly seemed simplified and he could not readily bring to mind the reasons for not going with them, except that in the past weeks impassivity and isolation had become almost habitual with him. And it was this instinct which now made him reluctant to be ferreted out of his inactivity.

'What gives with ye, Charlie?' Jim was obviously baffled. 'Ye're no' still goin' wi' Mary, are ye? Ah thought Ah'd heard . . .'

'Naw, naw,' Charlie helped him out. 'We packed it in. The other week there.'

'Do I detect the rattle of a broken heart, fond lover?'

'Ye'll detect a rattle on the side of the heid just directly,' Charlie said. 'Naw, Ah think Ah'll survive.'

'No' at this rate ye'll no'.' Andy shook his head gravely. 'Speaking in my professional capacity as your physician, Sir Charles, I must warn you of the danger of letting your fractured ego set in its present position. I recommend strenuous exercise of the libido.'

'Come on, Charlie,' Jim said. 'Don't let it get you. It happens to everybody. Come on out and forget it.'

That was all Charlie needed to sway him. By the easy way in which they categorized his feelings, they made it seem perfectly normal, a commonplace state of mind. He was the traditional disappointed lover, trying to forget his disappointment. He had a convenient peg on which to hang his troubles for the moment, leaving him free to enjoy the evening for its own sake.

'Fair enough, then,' he said. 'But Ah'd have to change an' give maself a shave.'

'Well, it'll be a come-as-you-please sort of caper, Ah fancy,' Andy said. 'But suit yourself.'

Charlie went through to the kitchen and put on a kettle. He washed and shaved carefully, going through all the familiar actions like a ritual that evoked his old self. Everything he did seemed to normalize the situation further. He savoured the cool contact of the clean white shirt against his skin, chose his tie as carefully as a politician chooses his policy, and then spent time on the exact tying of it, as if he was putting the knot on his rediscovered assurance. He did it all methodically and deftly, feeling himself firmly buckled in the armour of normalcy.

Left in the living-room together, Andy and Jim exchanged a significant glance like a password. Jim gave a congratulatory wink that included both of them. He lifted a newspaper and spoke from behind it in low tones in case Charlie should come in.

'Ay, Charlie's no' that far gone, anyway,' he said, 'that he canny hear the call of the crumpet.'

'But just take it easy,' Andy said. 'Let's not push our luck. Phase Two doesn't come into operation until we've all had a wee bit drink. Fair enough?'

'Roger. Over and out,' Jim said. 'Here. When did Charlie say Elizabeth and her boy friend would be in from the pictures? It's nearly half-six the noo.'

'Well, they went to the late afternoon house. Probably no' be in till after seven.'

'By which time the birds will have flew. We'll nip down to Gowdie's and have a few jugs of aphrodisiac. Hey, Charlie. Get a jildy on man. There'll no' be a virgin left.'

Chapter 15

GOWDIE'S WAS A BIG PLACE, A SORT OF ARCHITECTURAL
Siamese twin. The bar, where Charlie and Andy and Jim
were, was the original building, but with the shift of the social
bias towards the acceptance of women drinkers, it had grown
a more refined extension. Gowdie had bought out the seed-
store next door and now it blossomed with plush furniture and
bright fittings. The large cocktail lounge was Gowdie's ambush laid for the latest clientele, a conspiracy of soft lights and
tasteful décor. Lush leather chairs beckoned the more bureau-
cratic bums, wooed the soft flanks of women in smart suits,
whose rings flashed casual wealth as they lifted long-stemmed
glasses in the amber glow of wall-lights. Fish swam back and
forth along the walls in the inset aquaria, weaving through
pseudo seaweed, looking phantasmal and goggle-eyed through
the coloured glass. Waiters in smart white jackets bent politely towards men who ordered particular brands of particular
drinks. The lounge was connoisseur country where men were
impressive and women were impressed, and didn't need a
purse. Voices were seldom raised, unless the remark was
clever. The small groups talked together quietly and drinks
were incidental to other things. A hand would touch a knee.
Two heads would come close. These activities continued
suavely and restrainedly, oblivious to the rowdier enjoyment
in the bar, except that occasionally the sliding-door to the
latter regions would be pushed open, and someone would
head for the lounge toilet with the polite 'Excuse me. But
they're queuin' up through-bye.'

The bar itself had undergone some modification due to its
offshoot, so that its old robust identity was somewhat compromised. Patrons swore in a lower key. New formica tables
had been introduced to various parts of the room, making it

look like the lounge's poor relation. They had installed a television set in which grey figures gestured mutely behind a barricade of beery voices. The dart board had been relegated to a symbolically tight corner, just one remove from the window. And behind the extended bar was displayed a new cosmopolitan hierarchy of exotic drinks, venerable whiskies of ancient ancestry standing beside parvenu vodkas and alien brandies, while the wines and liqueurs ranged above them jostled for precedence. But most of these drinks were for transportation to the lounge. In the bar the most popular drink was still, as it had always been, the draught beer, pulled up manfully on the pumps in cloudy pints. It imparted to those who drank it its ancient secret brand of expletive philosophy and wet-mouthed argument, so that the bar still retained some of its old earthy vigour.

And this was especially true at week-ends. During the rest of the week, the lounge seemed to succeed in imposing its atmosphere of restraint upon the bar. But on Fridays and Saturdays, the air was so laden with exhaled spirits, alcoholic and merely human, was so thick with the smoke of cigarettes and obscure argument, that nothing could have properly subdued it, not even the presence of Gowdie himself. And on such nights Gowdie was not anxious to subdue it. Gowdie was a big-boned and bluff man, body and limbs put together roughly in powerful slabs. He was by nature choleric. The air of camaraderie he assumed was strictly professional, as formal as a buttonhole and liable to wilt at the first whiff of trouble. He measured people according to their pockets. You rated as high with him as your rate of exchange and your friendship ended with your money. But on this night, since it was Saturday, the spendthrift of the week, three figures in the credit column, he was playing mine jovial host, hail-fellow-well-spent, and his laughter rang out regularly like a cash register. He walked amiably about the place, dropping remarks like receipts on this group and that, supervising expenditure, and keeping an eye to the waiters who scurried back and forth to the lounge with trays that brimmed with liquid money.

His face clenched as if he was wrestling with a thrombosis when a young man stood up suddenly in the path of one of these waiters and nearly spilled a couple of quid on to the floor.

'Ah'm sorry, Mac,' Jim said to the waiter. 'Ah nearly made ye swallow yer tray.'

The waiter nodded brusquely and went past. Gowdie's face relaxed into a spurious smile.

'Ah better watch that,' Jim said to Charlie and Andy. 'That stuff's too valuable to baptize the floor wi'. Well then, gents? Same again?'

'Thanks, Jim,' Charlie said.

'Wait a minute now,' Andy said. 'Ah'm thinking we'll be after haffing a drap o' the dimple forbye, Jamie my lad. Just for to whet whur whistles, you understand.'

'Aye,' said Jim. 'An' I'm thinking you'll be after halfing me with the bill, Andrew my friend.'

'All right, all right.' Andy dropped his Highland accent under pressure. 'Three doubles an' we'll split the damage.' Jim returned with the whiskies in a few moments, but had to go back to supervise the drawing of the pints.

Charlie drank off what was left of his pint and gave the glass to Jim to take back with him. The beer was winning all right. The first couple of pints had seemed to be absorbed almost at once into his porous sadness. But now his thoughts were beginning to drift aimlessly in a gentle wash of beer, tugged lazily back and forth by the talk of Andy and Jim and the other activities in the bar. He was seeing things with a cool and casual clarity, and his mind was lazily treading water like a swimmer in a sheltered moonlit bay where every landmark is familiar and the winking lights ashore are each one known to him and signal that he is safe. He saw Gowdie, a constant presence in the bar, his attention sweeping the room at regular intervals like a lighthouse beam. He saw Jim easing his way towards them, holding aloft two pints.

'Dinna ye hear it, dinna ye hear it?' Jim said. 'The pipes at Lucknow sound.'

When Jim had brought across the third pint and sat down, Andy raised his whisky glass.

'A toast,' he said. 'To such natives as prove friendly tonight.'

'May they also prove good-looking,' Jim added.

'Hell, you want jam on both sides of yer toast, right enough,' Andy said.

Charlie and Jim downed their whiskies in a oner, while Andy sipped and savoured, holding his glass like a yellow nugget to the light.

'Please, dear proles,' he said. 'Don't gulp. Your palates could sue you for assault and battery. You've got to woo each taste bud individually, not rape the bleeders en masse. That's the worst o' the Union Bar up at university. No spirits. Beer, lager, and cider. Ye jist canny achieve the full symphonic inebriation on that lot. Ye need the contrapuntal thingamijig of the more subtler spirits. Ye just canny do it wi' beer on its Todd. It's like tryin' to play the 'cello without a bow.'

'Aye,' Jim agreed. He was consciously attempting to regain sobriety because he sensed the direction in which Andy was heading and he knew the need to be serious was at hand. 'This is better. It's just no' the same in the Union. No wonder the clients is going elsebit. The place is gettin' derelict.'

'Aye, aye,' said Andy. 'What wi' the absence o' spirits and then the absence o' Charlie. Times is bad.'

'Aw leave ma heart in one bit, Andy,' Charlie said. 'Ye'll have me watering ma beer. Gowdie'll report me tae the Brewers' Union.'

'No, but jokin' and kiddin' aside, Charlie.' Jim was doing his hazy best to put on his 'fidus Achates' expression. 'When are ye comin' back up, man? Ah mean it's no' the same without ye.'

'Aye right, Jim,' Charlie said. 'My gums bleed for you. Naw, Ah've got no plans in that direction.'

'But why no', Charlie?' Andy leaned forward concernedly, beer sketching the gesture into caricature, so that he looked like a doctor in an advertisement. All he needed was a pair of glasses in his hand with which to tap knowledgeably. 'Why do ye say that? What do ye have against it?'

'Ah've got nothing against *it*.' Charlie shrugged, contemplating his beer. 'Ah just don't have any notion o' goin' back up, that's all.'

'Is it because o' the money side of it?' Jim asked. 'Because if ye see about it, ye must be due for a bigger grant because of, ye know, what happened.'

'Naw, naw. Ah'm no' exactly neck-an'-neck wi' Aristotle Onassis right enough. But Ah haven't really thought about it from that angle at all.'

Andy was nodding, wise in years and hops, waiting his chance to proceed with the diagnosis.

'Is it because of – what happened to yer father, Charlie?' he asked gently. His expression was expectant as a doctor's probing a pain, and his eyes asked, 'Does that hurt?'

Charlie shuffled slightly in his chair – as if he was skewered uncomfortably on the remark.

'Well,' he said. 'Ah suppose it is. Aye.'

Andy paused on the kerb of his next remark, like someone letting a cortege go past, before he took a deep breath of philosophy and went on.

'Well, Ah suppose Ah know how ye must feel, Charlie,' he said. 'Ah mean it must be quite a thing to have to take. Especially wi' somebody like yer father or mother. Ye live that close to them all the time. It's the kind of relationship that's tacit. Ye just grow into it. Ah mean there's no time when ye have to work at it consciously. Ye get to feel as if it's always goin' to be there. But it isn't. That's the way it is, Charlie. Ah mean ye just can't spite yerself because of it. It may be corny, Charlie, but, after all, what's happened to yer father happens to everybody.'

'Naw, but it's no' just that he died, Andy. There's a bit more than biology involved. Fair enough. So he died. But it was the way he died an' everything about it. Ah don't know. But it shouldny have been like that. Ah mean ye've no way of realizin' what he musta felt like before he died. Nobody

144

could ever know what that man musta felt. Ah mean, *me*. Ah'm his son, an' Ah just didn't know 'im. What a waste it was! The good things in 'im that were wasted. That's what gets me when Ah think of 'im. . . .'

Suddenly Charlie was talking fluently about his father. Mysteriously it had happened. A series of things, his mood, the night, the beer, the place, the talk of Andy and Jim, had all come together in the right million-to-one sequence, and it was as if someone should fiddle long and futilely with a safe and then for no apparent reason should hit the combination. Without warning and without Charlie's understanding why or how, the click came and it swung open. He was bringing out many things about his father and showing them to Andy and Jim. He was talking about incidents from the past, some serious, some humorous, about the things his father talked of, about how he remembered his uncle Sanny, about the great egg-breaking contest, about habitual sayings his father had. He ranged from the serious to the comic, was nostalgic and thoughtful and laughing by turns, and Andy and Jim listened well, put in appropriate comments and seemed to appreciate the things he was saying. They formed their own closed circuit of conversation and attention, oblivious to the rest of the bar. They made a little private moment among them, and Charlie found an ease and naturalness in it that he hadn't known for a long time. He talked at length and bought another round of beers and whiskies and talked some more. And while he talked the pain and bewilderment seemed to ease out of him like pus.

When he had got it out of himself, they let a pleasant and unstrained silence rest for a time like a poultice on his revelations and Andy bought another round and they all talked sensibly round the situation, comparing attitudes. Jim's mother had died when he was very young and he explained how he had really been too young to understand fully what was going on. He remembered mainly the oppressive need for quietness that had preceded her dying and in his memory the images of his relatives' eyes, watery with sympathy, suddenly overtaking him at his self-absorbed activities, alternated with those of forefingers being put to lips. He said that even after her death he had for a long time moved about the house on perpetual tip-toe, especially in the dusty rooms upstairs, as if he was frightened to waken her from a sleep. But he admitted it wasn't the same as losing a parent when you were old enough to appreciate what was happening and feel just what it meant.

Both of Andy's parents were alive, but he made up for this deficiency by talking of how his feelings might be similar to Charlie's in the same circumstances. He tried to explain what his relationship with his father meant to him and the things about him he would miss most if he died, as if he was making out a blue-print of prospective grief.

The situation was to some extent ridiculous. Beer had so clouded that mirror of self-consciousness in-built in everyone that they couldn't see their own ludicrousness. Here they sat like a panel appointed to draw up the definitive attitudes to grief, The Handbook of Filial Piety. They were somehow like boys telling each other secrets momentously trivial. But alcohol was not the only component in the situation, nor was the ludicrous its only dimension.

Sentiment and beer and indulgence might have gone into its composition but out of them had grown something genuine. The feeling of community they had among them was real, so that in their mouths dead clichés vibrated for a moment into life, were reaffirmed instantly by their exact correspondence to the thoughts of those who heard them. They met together on common ground, and Charlie continued to feel a genuine affinity that counteracted his sense of isolation, his sense that he was someone alone with a private problem. They were three young men on a Saturday night, talking to each other. The feeling of identity was so strong among them that when the conversation came round again under Andy's direction to university, Charlie was able to join in and at least talk about his reasons for not going back. The only excuse he could think of was that he had already missed too much work.

As soon as he had made that admission, Andy became more animated.

'Ah, but ye don't have to worry about that, Charlie,' he said.

'Ah don't see how ye arrive at that, Andy, Charlie countered. 'It wid be pretty well impossible just to take up where Ah left off. It's no' just a matter o' missin' a few weeks' work. Ah've missed a coupla class exams in the time Ah've been off as well.'

'Calm yerself, youth,' Andy said. 'You are reckoning without yours truly, the poor man's Clarence Darrow. I have been arguing your case for you. Only this week Ah dropped a bug in the esteemed lug of your august tutor –'

'Ye spoke to Ramsey?'

'How did ye guess? Ye must have secret information. Naw, but Ah did, Charlie. Ah told 'im the circumstances. An' Ah quizzed 'im about the class exams. He's definitely on your side, Charlie. He reckons he can virtually guarantee ye your class ticket in English. Yer first term exam was good enough on its Todd. He says he wid also put in a word for ye wi' the history department as well. He wants to see ye, himself. How about that, Charlie? Fair enough?'

'Pretty good, right enough.'

'Well how about it, Charlie?' Jim was insistent. 'What about Monday? Get right in there.'

'Are ye gemme?' Andy asked.

Charlie was hesitant. But the eager optimism reflected in the faces of Andy and Jim made it seem churlish to refuse. And the beer was prompting him to share their optimism.

'Right,' he said. 'Monday it is.'

Andy and Jim cackled triumphantly, slapping Charlie's shoulders. The mood created by Charlie's answer completed the work of the beer. Drunkenness was now in order. Jim was the first to fall. Delight unclicked the safety-catch and seven pints and three doubles seemed to explode in him simultaneously. He banged the table obstreperously and blew an invisible hunting-horn. Gowdie materialized beside the table, his face forcing itself into a constipated smile. Jim nearly swallowed his hunting-horn. Andy nodded reassuringly to Gowdie and he hovered off.

'Aye, come on,' Charlie said. 'Let's get out before Gowdie goes for his six guns.'

They all rose noisily and were heading for the door when Jim suddenly stopped them.

'Wait a minute, though,' he said. 'We have forgot the traditional cairry-oot. The entrance-fee to Eddie's is a bottle.'

'Jeez aye,' Andy said.

They crowded round the bar, jostling their way in to make their choice. Now Gowdie appeared behind the bar, with a smile as wide as his wallet.

'Yes, gentlemen. Can I help you?'

They looked at the glittering array of bottles.

'Have ye anything for a penny?' Jim said.

'Ye've got to choose carefully here,' Andy said. 'It all depends on how dishonourable yer intentions are. Sherry for a wee bit slap-and-tickle. Liqueur for the heavy necking. An' whisky if ye really mean business.'

'Ah'll have a case o' whisky,' Jim said. 'A half-bottle o' Bell's please.'

'Here, Andy,' Charlie said. 'Ah'll get your bottle. You got an extra round of drinks there. Ye're throwin' yer money about like a man wi' nae arms.'

'Think nothin' of it,' Andy said. 'Ah'll get it. The old man had the fixed odds up the day. An' he slipped me a coupla quid on the strength of it. Then Jim an' me had a wee double up with our turf accountant. You are hobbing and also nobbing with men of some substance.'

Charlie bought whisky too and Andy took vodka.

'Now,' said Andy. 'If youse will accompany me to the toilet, I will show youse something to your advantage.'

'Right,' Jim said. 'We'll go to the lounge one as being more sedater and more suited to men of our calibre.'

In the lounge toilet Andy supplied each of them with a small square packet.

'I trust, gentlemen,' he said, debonairly arching one eyebrow, 'that you are fully cognizant of the wee contrivances that is contained in these packages? And that I need not instruct you as to their application to the human anatomy?'

'Not at all,' Jim said. 'The only thing is, Ah have an exceptionally big forefinger. Ah just hope this fits it.'

They went out through the lounge with a lot of laughing and jostling. Jim lagged behind in the toilet, so that Andy and Charlie were out in the street before he came through the lounge. On the way out, he brushed against a man at one of the tables and went on without an apology.

The man looked after him briefly. When he turned back round, the woman with him was smiling at him.

'Temper, temper,' she said.

'No, no,' he said. 'I was just thinking it's an awkward age. Don't you think it's about time we went up?'

'In a minute,' she said, thoughtfully sipping her drink.

He watched her for a moment, then took out a monogrammed cigarette-case and lit a cigarette with a monogrammed lighter. He fidgeted for a second. He lifted his empty glass and drained the last bead of whisky from it.

'Look,' he said. 'I'll bring the car round to here for you. You can powder your nose while you're waiting. If we're going up, we'd better go now.'

She nodded, lifting her handbag.

Chapter 16

'COULD I SEE YOUR CREDENTIALS PLEASE, GENTLEMEN?'
The voice came through the letter-box. Three bottles were
held up, and the door swung open.

'Come in,' Eddie said to them. 'And bring your three
friends with you.'

They took off their coats in the hall. The sitting-room was a
medley of sounds, several simultaneous remarks, a stutter of
raucous laughter, a shouted name, 'The Shadows' plangent
in the background, all shaken together into a confused
cacophony.

'Listen to the noise,' Eddie said. 'You would think they
were having a party to listen to them. You've arrived in good
time, boys. We've got so many wall-flowers in here, it's beginning to look like a conservatory. Forward. To the front line.'

He ushered them into a room where his command didn't
seem out of place. Backslaps and waving hands and thumbs-
up signs and faces smiling in recognition exploded all around
them and they were bombarded with phrases like 'guests of
honour' and 'Charlie himself' and 'the three must-get-beers.'

'No autographs please,' Jim said, bowing all round the
room. 'Buttons from my jacket may be had on request.'

'Only from your jacket?' somebody shouted, but it was
buried in a ruck of remarks.

Eddie filled out three generous glassfuls from random
bottles and opened three cans of beer.

'Here, you can try to catch up,' he said. 'We're a bit short
on the glassware. One each. That's your issue for the night. If
you want to try a different drink, you can lick the glass clean
first. I think somebody must be eating them. Beer is drunk à
la can.'

Amid a lot of laughter and cross-talk and mock toasts, the

three of them were merged with the rest of the company. Gradually, through nods and repetitive smiles and shouted comments, they began to get their bearings in the room, to see who was where and what the signs were. They were helped by Willie McQueen. When 'The Shadows' had twanged to a halt, Willie took over the gramophone for a couple of records. He had brought along a few records from his collection. Willie's records were a bit like Mary's lamb. They were what he had instead of a party piece. Every chance he got, he took his records with him and played them to the company. So for a little while conversation dropped a couple of keys while they all more or less listened to Bechet being played by the clarinet and the menacing monotony of Don Ewell, like water on dead leaves.

In the comparative lull, Charlie and Andy and Jim were able to get the feel of the party. Eddie hadn't been quite right about the 'wall-flowers'. The proportion of male to female was about right. It was just that the ingredients hadn't mixed to the full effect as yet. The boys were still stalking, circling tentatively, scenting possibilities, testing terrain with witticism and too loud comment. The girls were opening out slowly, petal by provocative petal, a knee showing here, a lingering smile there, and bright attention in many places. A general merger was imminent, could be foretold in a hand resting casually on a shoulder, a shared drink, the intimacy of eyes. Already a few had anticipated the trend, especially among those couples who had come to the party together and could curtail the preliminaries.

And Jim, assessing the opposition, couldn't help thinking that they increased his chances. He wondered where Eddie had got hold of so many non-starters. He watched Tom Quigley trying to prize his way into one group with his customary crowbar of uninentionally sarcastic humour. The others in the group went awkwardly quiet for a few moments. Poor old Quigley. He was a born fuse, with his wrists always showing two inches under his sleeves like naked filament, short-circuiting every conversation he entered. He noticed

Sam Harris embarrassedly footing the bill for another laugh. Somebody had made another joke at his expense. That was the way it was with Sam. The next round of jokes is on me. He was positively philanthropic about it. He was the tongue in everybody else's cheek. He saw Jimmy Adams padding about with his tongue hanging out, like a newly-appointed eunuch to a harem. He was drifting unobtrusively from group to group with his eyes crawling like ants all over girls. His was a severe case of galloping pornography.

Andy, talking now in an off-hand way to Bert Thomas, was giving himself a running commentary on the talent on hand. In some back room of his mind, observations were being fed in like ticker-tape and were checked off against past information. Agnes Semple seemed still unattached. Looking most trim in a blue sheath, but somehow uninviting. A bit like Elizabeth Taylor, but definitely a bowdlerized edition. Alice Evans. Oasis in Sahara, topcoat in winter. Some smile. Like a Christmas tree lit up, filling you with corny thoughts of firesides and slippers and protective instincts. Terrific in a dangerous sort of way. Sally. Very nice. And a very smart talker. Sometimes too smart. When she was in the mood, the noise of deflating egos was deafening. But she could be very coy when she wanted it that way. Jessie. Engaged on one of her epic anecdotes. By appointment Romancer to the late King. The usual elaborate gestures and expressions. Like an amateur production of 'East Lynne'. Out into the snow with her. Celia Meldrum. Strange. No sign of Faithful Fred the watchdog. Might be a chance there. Correction. Fred appearing with recharged glass, all twelve-and-a-half stones of him. Let interest cease. A choice of two, really. Put them both in the hat and let the evening pick one out. One other very attractive nameless one. Somebody new. Very dark, very interesting. But preoccupied in sending out strong signals to Charlie. Get tuned in, Charlie.

Talking with Eddie and Frank Rogers, Charlie was enjoying the feeling the party gave him. The room was full of that atmosphere that only young people can create, that comes from an ability to take things purely for themselves at this moment, without question or interpretation or complication. Space and time hung in a void of alcohol and high spirits. For the moment, obligations, responsibilities, commitments did not exist. There were just people together. Charlie let his senses lackey to him. He enjoyed the feel of the glass in his hand, the taste of the whisky on his tongue. He listened to the talk of Eddie and Frank and joined in himself, and words were an enjoyable physical experience in themselves beyond anything they might mean or achieve. He watched a pretty, dark-haired girl who was looking at him and it was pleasant to meet and hold her eyes from time to time. And everything was enveloped in a sensation of well-being. These things revolved round him like planets round a sun, fulfilling a natural law that was self-sufficient. They would follow their own course, whatever it was. He might just go on talking to Eddie and Frank. He might go over and talk to the dark-haired girl and see what came of it. He might just sit and have another drink. Whatever he did, he would enjoy it. For the moment he was content to let these things pass pleasantly around him, pulling him in whatever direction they chose, bringing things about.

When Willie McQueen's recital by remote control was finished, there were stirrings throughout the room as if the party was stretching itself for action. Bert Thomas came over to Eddie suddenly and asked him for two milk bottles, as if it was the most natural thing to ask for, like two halfpennies for a penny. When he got the bottles, he proceeded to demonstrate how far he could travel on them, using them like stilts for his hands, until his body came close to being parallel with the floor and someone callously kicked away one of his bottles. News of his prowess travelled even to the most isolated neckers and soon pilgrimages were being made from the four corners of the room to see the wonder. Others tried to outdistance him. Voices were raised in encouragement and accusation. Demarcation disputes arose. Only gradually did they manage to evolve the rules for travelling on milk bottles. The interest it aroused lasted for some time, and it brought out the circus performer in all of them, so that by the time its popularity had waned they were searching insatiably for substitutes. They tried lifting matchboxes with their lips, kneeling on the floor like strange devotees with their hands clasped behind their backs. They tried putting matchboxes on the floor beside their feet and lifting them by roundabout routes with their arms curled round their legs. Charlie suggested an egg-breaking contest and was volubly supported by Jim and Andy. But it was immediately vetoed by Eddie as being too messy. Fred Aitken announced that an egg could be thrown over a house and would not break as long as it landed on grass. Cynicism hissed like a hydra around him. In his more sober moments Fred might have let it pass. But riding the crest of the beer, he was adamant.

'I,' he enunciated defiantly, 'will throw an egg *over* a house – over the *roof* of *this* house – and it will *not* break. Provided it lands on grass.'

It became evident that the honour of Fred and eggs was so far compromised that only a contest could redeem it. Eddie said that he had only two eggs in the house and they were for his breakfast tomorrow. Under pressure, however, he nobly agreed to sacrifice one. The gauntlet was down.

With his tormentors trailing him, Fred went forth into the darkness of the front garden, his standard a lion rampant on an egg. Fred was taken round to the back of the house and shown the lawn where the egg must land. He walked about testing the grass with his feet, and found it satisfactory. A detachment was left on the back lawn to follow the egg's flight and check its condition on arrival. The rest came round to the front with Fred.

Fred went out on to the roadway in front of the house. The lighted windows in the quiet street behind him proclaimed families at their mundane activities of television and talk. Fred gave the invisible waiters a preparatory halloo and set about the throwing of the egg. His arm looped backwards and whipped forward.

'One away!' somebody shouted.

There was a small sound in the expectant stillness, such as an egg might make alighting on a roof. Baffled silence was audible from the other side of the house, giving way to discontented mutterings. In the front garden people were leaning on each other, dancing minuets of wheezy laughter. Alone on the roadway, Fred snapped his fingers in irritation and remonstrated silently with himself. A scout came round from the back to see how things were progressing.

'Where's the egg?' he asked innocently.

Jim pointed upwards.

'It's having a night on the tiles,' he said.

When the others followed him to find out what was going on, Fred was subjected to an ignominious barracking. But many still maintained that he should have a second chance to prove himself. Their motives were dubious, but Fred was agreeable. Only Eddie was not. It was put to him that one egg on his plate would be no more than a bitter reminder of that other on the roof, and he was eventually persuaded.

Act Two: the scene as before. In the middle of the road, Fred holding egg, juggling it in his hand like a fateful die. Others offering sarcastic encouragement. 'The world awaits, Fred.' 'Throw, man, throw.' The night holding its breath as the moment comes. The egg is cast. Loud cheering as the egg vanishes over the roof. Ejaculations all round, congratulations following.

'Ye did it, Fred.'

'Your country is proud of you.'

'It's a civic reception you should get. The first egg into space is a Briton, sir.'

'Come on. We'll join the reception committee.'

They stampeded round the house to find the others deployed across the garden, quarrelling good-naturedly and striking matches. 'It definitely musta went to the right. I saw it and then lost sight o' it.' 'Naw. It came straight over.' 'Where is it, then?' 'Have ye no got a torch in the house, Eddie?' The search continued for a time, refreshing itself with intermittent laughter. But Fred's fate remained sealed in darkness.

People started to drift back into the house. Somebody put on records and dancing became general. Nonsense was done with and business was under way. The place became partitioned with intimacy and conversations occurred in private booths. The party had come of age. The dancers drifted round, a mobile suggestion-box. The dark-haired girl danced past Charlie. Her eyes said S.O.S. At the end of the record, he cut in.

'Thank goodness for that,' she said, fitting into his arms as if she was made to measure.

'Just call me Penicillin,' Charlie said. 'I've saved so many lives.'

'I've listened to so many commercials about how good he is, I feel like I.T.V.'

'I thought he was your boy friend.'

'So does he.'

A verbal handkerchief has just been dropped. It is only polite to pick it up.

'You have been chosen, madam, to have demonstrated to you our new Lovermatic. The latest thing in love. No longer need you endure the tedious boredom of wishday. The pointless conversation. The clumsy overtures. It quips as it fascinates as it sweeps you off your feet.'

'Not another commercial.'

'With a difference. My card.'

A gentle kiss. Very suave. The latest thing in human relationships, right enough. Start in top gear and just keep going till you hit a wall. Any minute now.

'Just my luck. From a bore to a madman. You're stone mad.'

Your shock is pure pretence, my sweeting. Your mouth votes noisily. Your eyes abstain.

'A family characteristic. Goes back to my grandfather. Came over from Ireland in a tattie famine – and a boat. With clouts on his feet. Married my grandmother because she had a shebeen in the back door. Had a squatter of weans. Never did a day's work in his life. Drunk every day God sent and a few he didn't. They all said he was mad. But he died laughing.'

'And you take after him?'

'I take after the world. The whole thing's mad. Admit it now. Isn't it? A Saturday night. A few drinks. A roomful of people. A strange house. And us two gyrating in a clinch, with nothing more in common than Adam and Eve. Yet here we are. And I can feel your body against mine.'

'So what do we do?'

'Well, it's very simple really.'

'And matched, you hope, by my own simplicity.'

'Aye. That's right. You learn fast. You see. We forget all about who we usually are. Obligations. Commitments. The lot. And we just take each other as we are for the night. To have and to hold. A kind of pagan marriage ceremony. The marriage of moments. We have the bodies. All we need are the names. You give me your name. I give you mine. And that's us. And nobody's your uncle. Or your brother. Or your father. We're just two people.'

A pause. What now! A call for the constabulary? A hurried withdrawal? A moment spinning like a coin. Heads or tails? 'Jane Leighton.'

'Charlie Grant.'

Two names inscribed on a blank moment like a marriage certificate.

'I now pronounce us you and me.'

'That's it? A simple marriage.'

'We pagans are a simple people.'

'Just what does this sort of pagan marriage involve?'

'Ah, never mind these practicalities.'

'As your wife, I think I have a right to know.'

'Don't nag me already. Fear not. Nobody said it had to be consummated. Let's just enjoy our new status.'

Dancing very close. Hands, do thy duty. Her hair smelling pleasant. Keep your head up so that you don't knock off the laurel wreath. Confused images of the party bursting all around like fireworks to celebrate a victory. Dancers with closed eyes. Industrious neckers in corners. You would think they were on bonus. Jim winking like a satyr over a shoulder. Dance over towards the door. It's ajar. The hall is dark. Shut the door from the outside. Dark as a villain's moustache.

'Heh. Where are we going?'

'I'm looking for a place to spend the honeymoon.'

A cabal of giggles. Love in a forest of coats. Teeth parting to admit a tongue. Breasts tauten in their harness. Belly shivers. A handful of silk skin. A mouthful of cold crombie.

'Hell! I thought you had grown a beard.'

Sweet tenuous moment collapsed with a gust of laughter. Let clowning resume.

'The case of the bearded lady. It's a very sexy coat that all the same. I could really go for that. My love she's but a crombie yet.'

Pulling her towards him in the dark. A grey glint of eyes. Delicious collision.

'Let me show you the rest of the premises. I hope you're going to like them. I'm afraid the butler's on holiday. Now this here is a real innovation. We call these things stairs. You put one foot on them like that. That's right. And your other foot there. My, you do catch on. That's it. And you find yourself going up.'

Going up the stairs like Siamese twins. The boundaries of bodies blurring, merging. Sweet progress in unison. Back to nature. The good old fundamentals. Just walking can be wonderful; if you know how to do it. Behind a camouflage of patter, a left hand running quietly amuck.

'And this here is the upper hall. Or in coamming parlance, ra landing. Aha. I nearly forgot. I must carry you over the threshold.'

Surprisingly difficult to find the right position for the hands.

'And this we call a bedroom. It gets its quaint name from that object over there. The uses of which can be demonstrated at your request. Sometimes even without your request. Its softness is its predominant feature. I'm going to let you fall on it now. Just to show you. And don't worry. This won't hurt at all.'

The rustle of springs. A soft spinnet, whispering of past moments, distant rooms in darkness. This room half-lit from a street-lamp outside. A tumble of bodies. A romp of love. A confetti of giggles. The mirror watching with one cataracted eye. A slap-and-tickle of voices. Laughter. Talk. 'We should be getting back.' Rise up from the bed. Stand at the window. Let her prod and push at her hair in the mirror. What a caper! Do I wake or sleep? Who gives a damn? I like it. What was she doing now?

She went over and sat heavily on the bed again, leaning back on her arms, laughing.

'Phew. My life with a pagan.'

Her skirt rode right up her legs, exposing a lush expanse of thigh above her stocking. He let his eyes graze on it. The smile dwindled on her face, thinned into the distance of her eyes. A stillness fell across their jocularity like an adult shadow at a nursery door. Leave your toys and come into the dark. You are summoned.

Their bodies met in spate. Thoughts churning, eddying together to the drop. The room subsides. A welter of broken pictures. A curtain blown. Soft flesh. Spinning mirror. Cataracted into one submergence. Tidal throb. Words are blown like water-bubbles to the surface. Words of sweet despair. Fists clench. At last relax. Turn, borne by a gentle current. Drift slowly to the surface, wash to land. Lie stranded there. Thoughts unopen slowly. Images bloom like water-lilies on the eye. Window. Hair-brush. Ceiling stain.

Easy breathing. Sated words. Clothes reassembled in case of intrusion. Find something to fill the vacuum. Cigarettes. The match illumines intimate strangers. Good evening. Who are you? An ornament for an ashtray. A flight of madness ending here, at the glowing end of a cigarette. The evening ends in a cul-de-sac. What now? All right, funny man. Where's your sense of humour? Levity turns to lead. And what are you going to do? Because she's crying. Another success for the bringer of tears.

'What are you crying for?'

159

The words come sterilized with hopelessness, cold as surgical instruments in the dark.

Tears fall. Like millstones. Each one a megalith. Other people's grief can crush you to death. So this is it, funny man. The illegal marriage produces its offspring. One bastard of a situation. Who is she, anyway? On a bed beside you, crying? How the hell can you help? You don't know her. What makes Jane Leighton cry? Who the hell's Jane Leighton?

'Tell me what it is.'

What difference will it make? Words rattle like buttons in a blind man's cup. The noise is reassuring.

'It's just this. Oh, how could I do it?'

By lying on your back. That's the conventional way. There are others, of course. But perhaps you wouldn't be interested.

'I suppose you think that's pretty hypocritical.'

'It's pretty hypocritical.'

'I knew you would think that. I knew you would.'

'You have great foresight.'

Fresh eruption of tears. Handkerchief aswim. How did you think you could escape down a maze of inconsequential action and talk? It follows you. When you think you are running away you are running towards it. Always you meet with people. They're alive. They have to be accounted to and for. Everyone has rights. And each one matters.

'How can you be so cruel? You would think you hated me.'

'I don't hate you. I hate the way we have to pretend that we aren't anyone. I don't mean the stupid game we played tonight. I mean all of it. I mean we're trained to be slick and glib, to laugh things off. "Don't take yourself too seriously". "It's the way of the world." "Take it with a smile." Christ! People are rotting away all over the world. They're nailed to nothing. And no bastard cares. They're chained to their posts. And for what? There's only one rule left. No open wounds in public please. Haemorrhage quietly to yourself and die.'

'I can't understand how it's happened. I mean I came to this party with Tom. That's my boy friend. And then I just came up here and . . . This happened. I mean I wouldn't even let Tom. . . . And if something happens. My parents. Oh my God! I'm so ashamed.'

You go your grief, I'll go mine. We talk in monologues, madam. Our griefs and worries are crossed by the infinite, payable only to our secret selves. Not transferable. For you a boy friend's rage, a broken taboo, a mother's shock. Stoned with gossip. For me, a father murdered with a yawn. Society stirs for a moment in its stinking bed. The glib pretence goes on. A dream of idiots. And life narrows to nothing, shrined in a pinewood box. With six feet of earth to hold putrescence down. We part here. I wish you luck with yours, as terrible no doubt to you as mine to me. But I envy you a little. You can fill a handkerchief with yours. You can be sorry and the pain may ease. You want a little forgiveness. It may come. I want a resurrection. But from where? How do you make life mean? I don't know. But you can't help me just as I can't help you. In you I can see only a mirror. Your grief reflects my own, reminds me that it's real. We see only ourselves. Our divorce is consummated.

'My God! What can I do?'

'You can blow your nose.'

'Why are you being so horrible?'

'I'm not. Believe me, I'm perfectly serious. Make it into wee physical actions. It'll help. Do practical things. Dry your eyes. Get some make-up on. Powder your nose. Reduce it all to conformity.'

'It'll take more than make-up.'

'Not much more. Once you've got the technique. Tell yourself it was the drink. Tell yourself anything. Say it was rape. It doesn't matter what you tell yourself. Just keep repeating it and you'll come to believe it. That's how it's done. Everybody does it. It's a nice arrangement. That way nobody's to blame for anything. Things just happen.'

'You're really horrible.'

'That's it. You're getting the idea already. Soon you'll not be able to think of yourself for hating me. I'll leave you to practise bright faces in the mirror.'

'Where are you going?'

'Look. I'm going downstairs and out. And I won't be back. Nobody will know anything. You wait a wee while and compose yourself. And then drift in. Nobody will be any the wiser. They'll all be too busy at their own wee ploys.'

Outside the door he made a final check on his appearance and went downstairs slowly. Hercules descending. To the nether gloom. To the place where shadows gibber, pretending to be alive. Where transparent falsehoods pose as truth and pretence is exhaled by the very earth, a convenient mist that hides them from each other. The infernal regions. Where Dis presides. Dis, the negative prefix that attaches to all our living. But how did you overcome it? How could you force things up into the light to acknowledge their own falsity? They were so well protected. By the three-headed Cerberus. Convention, Conformity, Connivance. They all bayed terribly, so that you were afraid to go beyond them. Instead, you always threw them the sop, the small futile action of acceptance.

As he was getting his coat in the hall, a shadow shaped itself into Andy standing with a girl.

'Here, Charlie. Where are ye goin', man?' Andy said.

'To hell outa this.'

'Okay. Just hold on a minute an' Ah'll be with you. We'd better tell Jim we're goin'.'

Andy turned back to the girl. Her hands hadn't left his neck.

'You'd better go back in now, Celia. Before Fred comes back in. Ah don't want him to find out this way. Ah'd rather tell him.'

'I'm going to tell him tonight, Andrew,' Celia said.

'Do ye want me to come in with you?'

'No. I'll tell him at the house. But I'll see you tomorrow, at the café? I mean, that's definite?'

'Ah'll be there. Waitin' for it opening.'

She was fixing herself up and, using Andy as a screen, she reached back surreptitiously to hook up her brassière.

'I must look a mess,' she said, smoothing her hair.

'You look terrific.'

'Oh, darling,' she said, snuggling into him again.

Charlie stood impassively staring at the coats in the hall. Andy prised her gently away and kissed her forehead.

'Go on in, now,' Andy said. 'Ah'll give you a coupla minutes before Ah come in to see Jim.'

'I don't care,' she said at the door. 'They'll all know about it by tomorrow, anyway. And I'll be glad.'

When she had gone in, Andy looked for his coat and put it on.

'Hell,' he said. 'Ah feel such a crummy chancer. A room full o' them, an' Ah have to pick somebody that's attached. The thing is Ah like Big Fred, too. But, Ah just can't help it. How did *you* make out, Charlie?'

'Ah had a ball. Look, Andy, Ah'm goin'. If ye want to tell Jim, ye'd better do it now.'

'Fair enough. We've just got time for one before they shut. Ah'll tip Eddie the wink as well.'

In the living-room, Andy couldn't see Jim. The room was pretty confused. Something had happened to the party. It had aged prematurely. Conviviality had gone sour too soon. Eddie was not to be seen and, looking around, Andy wouldn't have blamed him if he had gone to bed. A group of boys were sprawled untidily on the floor, moving some matches back and forth, arguing about cannibals and white men. They bickered leadenly, their arms waving as if they were clearing away clouds of smoke from their eyes. Mouths lolled. Their eyes stared dully past each other. They were solemnly passing a whisky bottle among them.

'Burrifyedorat,' one of them said, 'ye've got two cannobals to the one white man. An' they'll eat 'im.'

Bert Thomas had Jimmy Adams pinned against the wall, threatening him with destruction. Two others were trying to pacify him. A couple were dancing to nothing in a corner. Somebody had sat on Willie McQueen's records and Bechet lay quartered on the carpet. Willie sat like Ezekiel, forlornly putting him together. Andy saw Celia talking with Alice Evans, and she looked at him soulfully. There was still no sign of Fred. It was rumoured he was looking for his egg.

Suddenly there was a distinct slapping sound and, following it to the far corner, Andy saw a crimson patch bloom like a late rose on Jim's left cheek. Andy reached Jim just as Esther Anderson swept past him and across the room, with the eyes of the others following her like train-bearers.

'Heh, Jim,' Andy said. 'Charlie an' me's leavin'. Ah think ye'd better join us.'

'Ye'll no' have to twist ma arm,' Jim said, and was already crossing the room, leaning on his dignity like a walking-stick. He picked up a whisky bottle from the sideboard on his way out.

In the hall, Charlie was sitting on the stairs. Esther Anderson had retired to the toilet. But the sound that came from there was not one of weeping.

'See's ma coat,' Jim said, grabbing it.

He struggled into it and opened the door in one movement. He turned on the top step, cupping his hands.

'Hoors and comic singers!' he managed to shout before Andy pushed him and they all clattered outside, closing the door.

The night air came to their brows like a cold compress on a hangover.

Chapter 17

THEY STOOD AT THE BUS STOP LIKE LONELINESS IN triplicate. They did not speak to each other. It was a moment set aside for private masochism and each stood tightening his personal thumbscrew. Charlie was hunched in his coat as if it was a protective shell. Andy stamped his feet absently like a horse impatient to be saddled with tomorrow. Jim stood shaking the pole of the bus stop as if it were Esther Anderson. He was the only one who talked. But he was not speaking to the others. He was simply making sounds of pain towards a cruel cosmos.

'Hell,' he said. 'What is it with me, anyway? When Ah'm around, the only thing they bare is their bloody teeth.'

Andy was retracing the contours of Celia's body.

'What an effect to have, eh? Ah'm better than a John Knox sermon. They should make me President of the Society for the Prevention of Unmarried Mothers. Lord Jim, the Prude Maker.'

In Charlie's mind the night was a kaleidoscope of fragments that formed grotesque meaningless patterns.

'Ah could do somebody out of a job wi' this. Sell my secret to eager millions. Be your own contraceptive. Don't get near enough to them to cause any trouble.'

Andy saw Fred and himself walking towards one another down the long empty street of their rivalry.

In the cold air their breaths rose faintly like the smoke from three extinguished candles.

'Stuff yese all!' Jim suddenly bellowed. 'Stuff yese all!'

'For God's sake, Jim,' Andy said, coming out of tomorrow to see what the noise was. 'It's the Black Maria we'll get a seat in, no' the bus. What the hell did ye do in there anyway. to make Big Esther do her nut like that?'

The question was thrown out absently, like a bone to a barking dog, and Jim slavered on it bitterly, sharpening his anger.

'Whit did Ah do? Whit do Ah do? Ah'll tell ye what Ah did. Ah was the perfect gentleman. Ah made Cary Grant look like a corner boy. There we were, necking away like champions. An' she was lappin' it up. That's the bit. An' then, not surprisingly, a certain part of my anatomy commences to get up to see what's going on. Well, Ah mean, whose fault's that? What the hell! Ye canny buck biology. Anyway, Ah senses her going very stiff, as if a stranger had come into the company. So Ah decides Ah'll have to put her at her ease. Do the introductions sorta thing. "You'll have to excuse my friend," I whispered politely in her ear, smooth as honey. "It's just that he's so polite. Always stands up in the presence of a lady." Wouf! A bunch of five right across the chops. Ah mean, why? She must be subject to fits or something. Could Ah have been nicer? But that's what ye get. Ah'm a bloody martyr.'

The bus cut across Jim's careering train of thought like a level-crossing. It was so surprisingly busy that they had to stand downstairs. At this time of night they should have had it pretty much to themselves. They couldn't understand it at first until they realized from the talk (about prizes and who had won what and how long somebody had gone without winning anything) that they were all coming back from the bingo. There was a popular bingo hall in the village two miles along the road. Half of its clients must have been on the bus. Charlie hung from his rail, watching them bitterly.

Some swayed back and forth from their straps further up the bus. Like carcases in a butcher's shop. Only these ones were alive. Alive? Well, euphemistically speaking. For the moment, more or less. Let us say that they are, as it were, en route for the butcher's shop. And this is a cattle cart. Forward. To the knacker's yard. Communal euthanasia awaits us. Outside, people walk and talk, look and point, single, in twos, in threes, in groups, bending and leaning, holding and letting go, lying on beds, doing things in houses, screaming, laughing,

166

cutting their fingernails, being sad, being sorry, feeling anger, feeling love, stirring tea in cups. Little boys dreaming virility. Old men spitting rheum. Being born. Dying. And someone dismissing the universe in a hiccough. The newsreels running in silent cinemas, lighting the dumb upturned faces. Television sets shining in darkened rooms. Fingers writing a letter, exuding sweat on to the page. And a woman in the bus sits chewing on her gossip, wearing on her head a hat made from feathers presumably plucked from the living dodo. They might as well have been. Their source is dead. Just as the source of everything we do and have is dead. Where is the point of meaning found? Nowhere. Lost. We simply accept it all like an aimless nursery rhyme we learn as children. This is the house that Jack built. Falling down. Falling down. What can survive it? Nothing. Death means more than we do. We bow down to a dead man. He supersedes us. He is our destination. We hurry towards him. Home is the belly of a worm. An announcement for my people. Friends, we hasten towards nothing. People on this bus, the driver is dead. We travel on time's driverless bus, zigzagging into the empty dark. The driver is dead. Even if the conductor isn't. He's here, with his hand out. They still charge you, just the same. Even when your only destination is No. 1, Narrow Place.

'Fares, please.' The conductor had edged his way towards them, running out tickets and talk. 'Make a bit o' room there. Ye wid need a tin-opener tae get into yese. An' get yer donations ready. Whit dae ye think Ah am? A public servant?'

Jim reached into his pocket to pay, but Andy had his money out first and got three tickets. As Jim brought his hand out of his pocket, the package Andy had given him in Gowdie's came out with it and fell on the floor of the bus. Jim picked it up and looked at it wryly.

'Look at that then. Aye, friend,' he said to it. 'Ah've got about as much use for you as the Venus de Milo has for a pair o' gloves. Ah think Ah'll blaw it up an' give it to ma wee brother for a balloon. Cut ma losses. Or rather cut yours, Andy.'

As he was putting it back in his pocket, he grimaced and hissed with pain.

'Oh,' the small man next to him said. 'Was that your foot Ah stepped on?'

Jim looked at him incredulously.

'Not at all,' he said. 'It's really ma brother's. Ah'm just wearin' it in for him.'

'Ye don't need tae get narky,' the small man said, bridling slightly.

'Ah'm no' narkin', Mac,' Jim said. 'Ah enjoyed it. Anyway, Ah've got another one in the hoose. Ah just use this one for walkin' wi'.'

'A funny man, eh?'

'They have been known to die laughing, friend.'

'Look. It wis an accident.'

'An accident? More of an atrocity, Ah wid say maself.'

'Anybody could step on your foot.'

'It just wouldny be the same, some way. You've got that professional touch. What are ye to trade? A foot-powderer?'

'Now, listen, you,' the small man said, anxious to get back to first principles. 'Ah just asked ye a civil question. If it was your foot Ah stepped on. All right?'

'Whose bloody foot is it likely to bloody be on the end of my bloody leg?'

'Ah've just about had a bellyful of you.'

'An' Ah've had a footful of you, friend.'

The small man was beginning to dance slightly, like a ferret on fire. He was thrusting his face as near to Jim's as he could get it. Jim put his hand flat on the small man's chest.

'Keep back,' he said. 'Ye're standin' so close Ah can see the reds of yer eyes. Get away from me. Before Ah do yer dentist out of a job!'

Their argument had begun to assert itself on the other people in the bus and an insidious silence came just as Jim spoke, so that the volume turned up even further on his remark. The little man looked as if Jim had been trying to crucify him.

'D'ye hear that?' he said to a jury of strap-hangers.

Their eyes put Jim in the dock.

'Did you hear him threatenin' me?' The little man appointed someone with a paper as foreman. 'Did ye?'

The other man almost ate his paper with embarrassment. But someone further along the bus took up the cry, smelling blood.

'Ah heard him all right, Sam,' he said loudly. 'It's the polis ye want for that kind.'

There was a round of ominous murmurs on Jim.

'Ah'll go quietly!' Jim said dramatically.

His jest was not appreciated. Mutters of 'Enough o' that!' and 'Who does he think he is?' and 'No' safe in yer ain house any mair!' were spat at him like poisoned arrows.

'Ya buncha mugs!' Jim stood nobly defiant, Rome surrounded by Huns. 'Morons. All you can count up to is "Bingo!" Dae ye want me to stand here an' let this wee runt do a tango on ma taes?'

'Right, Jim. Here's our stop,' Andy said hurriedly.

They were a stop too early. But Andy decided a diplomatic withdrawal was called for. They managed to get Jim hustled off before he realized it. A woman sitting on one of the side seats by the door snarled at him like a maenad. Sneers and angry voices pursued them.

Outside, Jim ran to the front of the bus. He stood to attention at the kerb as the bus pulled away and gave all the inmates the fingers with both hands, bowing when they mouthed out at him.

'Come on, ya half-wit,' Andy said. 'You're definitely buckin' for a pair o' handcuffs the night.'

'Not at all,' Jim said. 'An' what did ye get off there for anyway? That's no' our stop. Ah was enjoyin' it fine.'

'Aye, that's right,' Andy said, catching up with Charlie. 'Ah heard ye laughin'. Ah just didny fancy goin' up to yer father the night an' handin' in a paira shoes an' a coupla fingernails. "Hello, Mr Ellis. Here's Jim. Divide him out among the weans." You want to watch yer mouth, man.'

'Me? Me? Ah want to watch? What would ye make o'
that, Charlie?'

Charlie said nothing.

'Me?' As they cut through the side streets, Jim expostulated
with the world. 'It's no' me. It's all a bloody plot. Ah'm
tellin' ye. Ah mean, don't think this is anything new. Ah'm
hardened to it. If Ah go into the pictures just, they're waitin'
for me. Somebody there is goin' to pick me out. Specially.
Some sixteen-stoner is goin' to decide to use ma head for a
footstool. Or else the smoke from ma fag is definitely goin' to
go into someone's eyes.'

The door of 'The Hub' came like a hyphen in Jim's dia-
tribe, introducing a smoky parenthesis of brightness and
noise.

'Look at them,' Jim continued, crossing to the bar. 'They've
got the word already. He's here. Have your insults ready.
Will you have first nark, Cedric? Or shall I? Have a little
mercy, friends. Ah, lead me to the malmsey-butt. Ah'm goin'
to do ma Clarence. Drown ma persecution complex in its
depths.'

'Three pints, please,' Andy said. 'Heavy.'

'Very heavy,' Jim added.

Andy repeated the order a couple of times because the
place was still quite busy. Elbows were working against the
minute-hand. 'The Hub' was purely utilitarian, as cramped
and functional as a W.C. It afforded little more than room to
stand and manipulate your arm, plus a small adjoining cubi-
cle in which to make way for more beer. The only concessions
to *la dolce vita* were a draughtsboard without draughts and a
set of veteran dominoes, showing the hollows of missing pips
like empty eyes. The bar had been named from its position at
the centre of the town. But time had made it a misnomer in
any but the shallowest physical sense. 'The Hub' had been
the centre of a town where 'wheel' connoted stage-coach and
penny-farthing. Inside, the past was preserved, pickled in
alcohol. The steel bar-rail glowed dully, scuffed with several
fashions of footwear. In the dim prints on the walls horses

contested a forgotten handicap and dogs chased an eternal fox across dun fields. Outside, the town had reorientated, making this place as peripheral as a barnacle. But both the bar and 'auld Simpsy', who stood behind it, were too old for change. Cornered in the present, 'The Hub' clung like an arthritic hand to the past.

'Three pints of heavy over here.' Andy was touching his forelock like someone at an auction.

Simpsy relayed the order to his assistant.

'Aye, in a minute,' the younger man called over. 'Ye can see how we're placed.'

Hands were reaching out all over the bar, a Briareus of orders. A young man bumped Charlie roughly as he pushed towards the bar. Charlie found himself pivoted on his own anger and his hand shot out to clamp on the young man's arm, an automatic extension of his mood. Acting without thought, he forced the young man back, aware distantly of a faceful of amazement at the end of his arm, an expression that was undefined and smudged with beer, that receded steadily until it merged into a background of others, a press of lurid faces, each one wearing its preoccupation like a mask. Distended mouths. Blank eyes. Gargoyles pouring out words like water. Was this all people were meant to be? Begetters of aimless actions? Celebrators of nothing? He looked round the vivid faces. All worshipping their private totems. Frenzied dancers round a fire that fed on their own flesh. Faces and voices fading inconspicuously into the dark. Unnoticed. Others took their place. No questions asked. Just be yourself. Don't impinge on anybody else. And don't let them impinge on you. Be casual. The password to manhood. Don't care about things. Pretend that nothing is happening. Let each one die in lonely innocence. Never seek to know who lives behind the ridiculous pot-belly, the operational scar, the balding hair. It was all an extended joke. This was the refined way to die. Decorate the void with pointless little actions and concerns. Like his father's grave. A hole covered with flowers. How long can you go on shutting out the smell of death with the scent of flowers? The flowers withered too. How long could you conceal meaninglessness behind clusters of little actions that stemmed only from their own purpose? How long could conviction last that was rooted in error? How long could you feed on lies before you were mortally sick? Some time you had to say 'Enough!' There had to be a time when you threw them back in their faces, when you said no to the easy smiles and the calm assurance and the unquestioning acceptance and the laughing intoxicated faces and Andy being sad and Jim being elaborately funny.

Suddenly he blundered from the bar and into the toilet. Almost before the door swung shut behind him, he vomited. An old man wavered on the edge of his awareness, seeming as distant as a tree on the horizon. While Charlie spewed, the old man buttoned his trousers and looked on philosophically.

"To much bad beer, son. Ah doot ye've been gettin' the bottom o' the barrel,' he said, and went back into the bar.

In the bar Andy was drinking thoughtfully. Jim was apostrophizing his pint.

'Aye,' he said intimately, using his pint-glass like a microphone. 'Ah've got it. A sudden inspiration. The Ellis Plan. How to turn failure to your advantage.'

Andy stood impassively beside him. He felt the night dim depressingly to boredom, like someone putting off street-lights in his head. They were swigging from the whisky bottle Jim had salvaged from the party's wreck, shoving it to and fro along the counter. At last complete drunkenness, following them all night like a patient footpad, waiting for the right moment, had relieved them of sobriety.

'I have called this press conference,' Jim said into what was left of his pint, 'to inform youse of my latest venture. Everything to date in my life has only been a sort of preface to . . . Where the hell is Charlie?'

They faced each other across the question as if it was a misted pane of glass. The talk of the others in the bar ran out around them like water from an abandoned hose. Andy peered at Jim, like someone trying to remember where he had seen him before. His hand waved vaguely.

'Ah thought he went for a pee.'

'But his pint's no' touched.'

Andy's eyes detoured towards the counter to corroborate the statement. Understanding staggered after sight. The pint glass was full and losing its ruff of froth.

'His pint's no' touched,' Andy informed Jim.

'He hasny touched it,' Jim relayed to the upper air.

A few moments were consecrated to the interment of the news.

'He must be in the toilet.'

'Must be.'

They straggled towards the toilet. Andy pushed open the door. It was empty.

'Somebody's spewed their ring up,' Jim observed.

'Charlie!' Andy shouted. 'Heh, Charlie!'

Jim crossed over and began to pummel the door of the W.C.

'Open up in the name of the law,' he bellowed. 'I have a warrant for your arrest. The crime is arson.'

Muffled oaths took place behind the door like underground explosions. The jacket hanging there was pushed aside and a face was pressed against the frosted glass, peppered with transparent boils. Jim's face met it on the other side of the glass, peering in an attempt to identify it.

'Father!' Jim shouted, throwing up his arms. 'I've found you at last.'

There was the sound of a bolt being drawn. The door was edged open. A leg appeared round it, the trousers precariously clutched above the knee. A face, red and angry, followed at a higher level.

'Whit the hell dae ye think ye're on, Jock?'

'Now, now, sir. Address me through the chair. Ye're out of ordure,' Jim said and gave a stillborn cackle.

Then at once they were both shouting, 'Charlie'. They came back out into the bar, still shouting. Others in the bar turned to look at them. After watching them in amazement for a moment, a few others took up the cry in heavy irony, until soon almost everyone in the bar was shouting in mocking unison.

'Charlie! Charlie!' they chanted, a ludicrous chorus of loud and beery voices, while the pint still stood untouched on the counter. 'Where are you, Charlie? Charlie! Charlie! Where are you?'

Chapter 18

HE WAS NOWHERE WHERE ANYONE COULD REACH HIM
It was as if an avalanche had happened in his mind and he
was trapped inside himself. Beyond the impenetrable rubble
were other people and their lives. But he could not pass
through to them. He had to turn back alone and find his
way.

His mind spun like a broken compass. The buildings rising
sheer around him were no more than vague hieroglyphs to
him, the dim configurations of his thinking. The traffic and
passing people tore at his consciousness like burrs or thorns,
and with everything that touched his senses he bled. He wandered aimlessly and his feet made a desert of every place he
passed through. Despair was like the millennium in his mind,
crowning time triumphant, so that everything came to him
ground to anonymous dust that sifted aimlessly back and
forth. The crowds moving in the streets were no more pur-
poseful than blowing sand. Faces drifted past him like fallen
leaves. Voices blew in gusts about his head, sounding hollow
as sea-shells. He was surrounded by a trackless waste in which
there was no landmark of himself. But above his barren consciousness protruded one thought like a stunted tree on an
empty horizon. It lay on his mind as if it was the last thing
that was left of himself, recalcitrant against oblivion, like a
hollow skull beneath an empty sky. He wanted to look at his
father's grave. He wanted to go there and see the headstone
that had been erected. Using that thought as a landmark, he
started to move himself towards the graveyard as if it were his
home. That one intention seemed all that was left of him and
it pushed him on towards the grave as if he would find himself there.

His progress was blind and instinctive. He was not aware of

how the light and noise modified as he approached the out-skirts, how country infiltrated gradually into town, how trees became more frequent, streets grew quieter, and the parentheses of darkness between the street-lamps lengthened. His hands slipped twice on the low moss-grown wall before he scaled it and dropped, his fall gagged by the green turf of a grave. The shock of his landing jarred his still senses into action for a moment, as a shaken watch may tick into life for a few seconds. It was long enough for him to observe the lighted window of the attendant's house some fifty yards away, fenced in from the rest of the cemetery. The door opened, cutting a swathe of light out of the dark, and a misshapen ball bounced out into it, coming to rest as a dog sniffing the ground. A man appeared in the doorway, smoking a meditative cigarette. The dog wagged into the darkness. Some minutes passed like a cortège. The man took a few proprietary paces back and forth, looking around. Night watchman to the dead. Satisfied, he flicked the stub of his cigarette into the darkness. Ten o'clock and all's well. As he turned back into the house, he whistled once, throwing the sound casually over his shoulder and pulling the dog in on it like a leash. The door banged shut.

Charlie stepped quietly on to the gravel path, like an uncertain thief who did not know what he was here to take. The moon disclosed a confused network of graves, a garden of tangled stone. Charlie moved among it, away from the lighted house. It was difficult to locate his father's grave. Around him stone reared, blossoming into strange shapes in the moonlight. In many places stood pitchers draped with cloth. Miniature angels petitioned heaven, faces set in marble beatitude. Huge ornate stones dwarfed smaller ones, but signified the same. Above the earth vanity made its last flourish and individuality sought its final perpetuation in desperate stone. Beneath the earth were the impartial worms.

Charlie passed the shed where the workmen's tools were kept. Outside it, a tap dripped water into a trough, near which stood a couple of lemonade bottles for carrying fresh water to the vases on the graves. A waste-basket was stuffed with withered flowers that rustled and sighed sorrowfully in the wind.

Charlie continued to walk slowly round the graveyard, patient as a prayer-wheel, until his persistence was answered. He saw the place on the small hill where only grass grew and the ground was unbroken. He walked on a little way down the incline until he came to the first headstone. Crossing over the newly turfed ground, he bent down and struck a match. The headstone was small and simple, hewn carefully as it was from John's small wages. In the momentary flare of the match, Charlie made out his father's name and the two dates under it before the wind peremptorily drew the darkness over them again. So closely did the carvings on the stone coincide with Charlie's mood that it was as if only his coming to this place had put them there, as if his journey had culminated in a profound revelation. For this was truly all they could give his father for epitaph. This was the ultimate meaning he had for them. Here was their final pronouncement on his father. And Charlie, like his father's only prophet, felt that he alone could interpret the true meaning of these hieroglyphs. For him they were written in fire, illumined by his experience, their significance entrusted to him, as surely as the tablets had been to Moses on the mountain. He understood their meaning. For what had his father's life been but a hyphen between two dates? It had no place or meaning in the life that went on outside these walls. They gave it no acknowledgement. For them it was a pointless parenthesis. That was the meaning of the hieroglyphs. But what was their commandment?

Charlie crouched huddled over the grave, a pilgrim at the end of a strange pilgrimage. His mind was unnaturally still. And his body, like a restless servant, occupied itself mechanically in taking out cigarettes and lighting one. The wind honed itself on his face, ruffling his hair, and he was as insensate to it as the marble around him, transfixed as if in some strange ritual. He crouched over the grave as if he could exorcize its contents and conjure the chiselled dead out of their stone.

His hand, abandoned by the mind, moved restlessly and nervously of its own accord, as if frightened by what was being devised for it. A finger tapped dementedly on his cigarette as if it were a morse key that spelt out S.O.S. S.O.S. S.O.S.

Chapter 19

THE MAIN STREET SHOWED SATURDAY NIGHT IN THE last stages of decomposition. There were only a few twitching remains of the vitality that had been. The night had had its brief chronology. There had been the twilight time when the main street was suddenly in spate with people from the tributary lanes that led from the football ground until these washed home, leaving some isolated in picture queues that sifted grain by grain into cinemas, measuring time like an hourglass. There had been the dull flat time when newspapersellers shouted, melancholy as muezzins, and the streets were peopled strangely by those who followed private purposes. There had been the time when the steeples struck curfew for the prim, and the pubs scaled their drunks, spilling them bawdy and singing on the streets to trickle fitfully home to fireside philosophy and beery reminiscence. There had been the brief still time before the dance-halls launched their separate invasions of the young, and couples entered parks and shadowed places.

Now it was carrion time. The two cinemas on the main street were shuttered and dated for next week. A few papers and tickets littered the pavement like skeletal pleasure. The only people left were a few groups of young men, like pariahs, casually distributed at street corners, talking fast and interrupting each other, grabbing their share of what was left of Saturday. In the awning of shadow from a shop doorway a policeman stood, quietly smoking an illicit cigarette. In the empty bus-station a small capped man in wellingtons was hosing it out, oblivious of everything except the jet of water he controlled, holding the nozzle close into his side so that he looked like some monster of virility.

These activities gently ruffled the subconscious of the town

179

like an eyelid's flicker in a sleeper's face, and across them
Charlie passed like a troubled moment in a dream. He had no
consciousness of walking or of the physical presence of the
town. His body inhabited a separate world that followed its
own laws, so that his legs obeyed their nature and led him
home, as a horse might return to its stable, dragging its dead
master hooked in a stirrup. But within the body's automatism
he lived in another place, without geography, that could not
take its identity from the town, that had no home. He was
given over to a force that denied the demands of time and
place, the ties of home, that took possession of him darkly and
swallowed his personal identity. Alien, it did not correspond
to anything around him, had no reflection there. It did not
obey the cause and effect of ordinary feeling, was not provoked by anything around it. It did not partake of ordinary
life, did not belong to the world where desire and fulfilment
co-exist, where wishes presuppose the possibility of their ac-
complishment. It had no finite origin and no predestined
end. Cause and result, beginning and end, were all alike nowhere, and it was here, having begot itself upon itself. It
resided in him like a dark divinity of feeling, unrelated to the
finite world, superseding his identity, supplanting his very self.

What was happening in Charlie was barely thought. He
was not thinking of any particularity. He did not think of his
father dead. He did not think of that bitter room, nor of his
mother's desertion, nor of Mary's thumbscrew of sadness, nor
of the girl laughing on the bed, nor of the fleeting faces in the
pub, nor of the windy graveyard. All of these things he had
taken into himself, had allowed them to take possession of him
and convulse him, until they emitted him now into what he
was, the result of their interaction upon him. They were not
his thoughts. He had become their physical agent. A series of
finite situations and thoughts and wonderings had so worked
upon him that they had brought him to a state of mind
beyond themselves, a consciousness that transcended finite
reasons and intentions, existing in its own right.

As his body brought him nearer to the house, his mind was

not engaged in consecutive thought. The motive power of his brain had run to a halt. Reason had guttered, doused, gone out. Thoughts had stilled like icicles. In the void they had left, his consciousness was a slow vertigo, a gently rotating darkness whose blank progress insistently recorded a fixed point ahead like radar oscillations. The point was unseen, unknown, but it was towards this that the feeling in him moved and sought to come. Only this unseen point, whatever it was, mattered, and nothing else registered, so that the familiar markings of his route seemed to bring him on without his awareness. The car parked at the kerb outside the house went unnoticed by him, with its sleek outline and shining chrome and the small flag on the bonnet furled in midnight calm. The path led him up to the door with a key in the lock, and the key took his hand and turned and the house took him in.

He was alone in the hall, the bland darkness of which showed a scar of light along the bottom of the living-room door. He took off his coat and hung it up, making the familiar sounds with the precision of someone making flag-points on a map, charting his position in time and place. He handled his way from contact to contact across the hall, fingering for the little table until it found his hand. The darkness seemed to absorb movement like a porous surface. He tilted on the crutch of his hand upon the table as he untied his laces, which were damp and impacted with walking. His body maintained the steady ripple of these sounds and contacts like a rope running through his hands, leading him blindly. Like an experienced valet it performed its habitual tasks without prompting. His jacket slid from his shoulders and was held in his hand. Then suddenly the automatic actions of his body were interrupted by an unfamiliar sound, startling in its unexpectedness, a bright flare of conversation, the simultaneous sound of several voices. Without thought, without anticipation, he blundered towards the sound like a moth to light, and pushed open the door of the living-room.

The scene came to him fragmented, like a torn photograph.

There were Elizabeth and Harry, their faces made familiar in the turning of a head, nose, mouth and eyes sketched swiftly into the patterns he knew. Harry acknowledged him with a facial cliché of recognition. But made separate from them by unfamiliarity were two others, a man and woman. The man exuded well-being, was like an advertisement for success from the well-groomed hair to the dark suede shoes. He sat with one leg resting on his other knee in a posture of cultivated youthfulness. The grey hair that flecked his temples looked more an affectation than an effect of age, a decorative addition to his toilette. The left hand resting across his leg, blazoned with gold ring and wrist-watch, held a half-burned cigarette between well-manicured fingernails. His face, like a calendar someone has forgotten to change, still showed a smile that antedated Charlie's entry. The woman at first glance seemed to come from a page of the same magazine. She wore a smart green fitting suit that carried on one lapel a glittering brooch like a badge of membership to an exclusive club. The total effect, upwards from the trim legs sheathed in nylon, coincided with that of the man, was one of the arrest of the years. The clothes covered her like preservatives, so that an immediate assessment of her age was difficult. But something distinguished her from uniformity with the man. There was a subtle diffidence in her appearance, as if all of her had not been able to subscribe to it fully, but part of her somehow remained aloof from it. It could be seen especially in the face, set in its frame of lacquered hair. It had been carefully made up, but behind the cosmetic mask of assurance the features were set in a habitual expression of uncertainty like a tic. And now, as Charlie looked at her, this tic became intensified. Her expression changed like a broken barometer, worry extinguishing an incipient smile, rue supplanting gladness, each returning to apprehension. It was this uncertainty that enabled Charlie to penetrate the smart appearance and see the person within it. The realization of who she was struck him with guilt, as if he had been betrayed into a moment of cerebral incest. And it made the two halves of the scene all the more incompatible, especially since his understanding was obliged to link them in the improbable connection that the tea-things on the table meant that they had been having tea together. Elizabeth could not have been taking tea with her.

'Hullo, Charlie,' his mother said quietly.

His hand dropped the jacket he was holding on to a chair and it slid unnoticed to the floor, assuming an attitude of anguish.

'Hullo, Charlie,' the man said nicely.

'We've just been waiting for you coming in, Charlie,' his mother went on. 'We wanted to see you and get a chance to talk to you –'

'Look,' Charlie heard his own voice saying urgently. 'You'd better go. Now, on ye go. Just go away. Please. Please go away.'

He heard his voice acting as intermediary between them and the feeling that was mounting inside him, trying to fore-warn them, to keep them away from it. He was aware of a twin consciousness in himself, a strange duality in which a dark part of him, who seemed to welcome the presence of these people here and sought to come at them, existed in con-flict with his customary self, that part of his nature which recognized the dangerous provocation of their presence and was concerned to evade the danger. He felt himself locked between these two forces, the latter of which held the upper hand for the moment, strengthened as it was by habit, but how long it could keep its hold he did not know.

'Charlie, Charlie,' his mother said. 'Please don't be like that. Please. I know how you must feel. But at least give us a chance to talk.'

'Talk!' Listening to her induced in him a series of minor irritations, against her strangeness, her complacence, her politeness of speech. They affected him like an acne and he wanted to scratch them, to counteract their annoyance, so that he spoke with deliberate broadness, interpolating swear-words.

'Whit the hell dae we huv tae talk aboot? Whit the hell did
183

ye come here for, anyway? You've nae bloody right tae be in this room.'

'All right, Charlie, all right. I'll tell you why we came. We came to see you and Elizabeth. Oh, I know what you're going to say. I should have thought of that a long time ago. Perhaps you're right. But you know the way things were. What happened between your father and me's in the past. And it's better to leave it there. You think I was the villain. All right, maybe I was. But it wasn't all as black and white as you seem to think. There were reasons for what I did. Reasons you can't imagine. But I didn't come here to talk about that. It's over and done with. Long ago. Charlie, Peter and I want to help you. We've talked it over. Peter's very kind about it and he understands how I feel. He wants to help as well. We could do an awful lot for you. I mean we could help you with the university. You could finish your studies. And we would see that you didn't have any money worries. And then it's not good for Elizabeth being herself in the house like this. I mean I don't see why we should all go on living separate lives like this, as if we'd never heard of each other. You won't know it, but I tried to send money and things for you before, only your father wouldn't hear of it. I'm not blaming him. But it was hard for me not knowing how you were getting on, although I always tried to find out as much as I could about you. But after that – what happened – I could never get seeing you. But I don't see why we can't all try to understand each other a bit better now. Probably even your father would have wanted it that way. We just want to help you, Charlie. That's all.'

She had started talking very quickly to prevent Charlie from interrupting her before she had a chance to explain things properly to him, and then when she had been given a hearing and Charlie surprisingly made no attempt to cut her short, she had continued in a desperate effort to break through his impassivity, casting around her for the phrase that would evoke the response she was hoping for. But when she had talked herself to silence, Charlie still stood silent too.

184

The unreality of the situation was too much for him. Too many strangenesses surrounded him, overgrew this familiar room like foliage, so that he could not see where he was nor what was happening. Here was Elizabeth sitting taking tea with his mother, in this room where she had not set foot for so many years. Here was this man who before this had only existed in his mind as a sort of expletive asterisk, now suddenly created in person for him, daring to appear in complacent flesh in this house. Here was his mother talking to him and explaining why they should all simply carry on together and forget the past. The whole situation was so incredible that he could not answer his mother directly, could not participate in it until he had slowed it all down to his pace, had pruned it to fit his comprehension. He ignored his mother and looked round the room.

'This is very nice,' he said, like giving a commentary, supplying his laggard understanding with the necessary intelligence. 'Awfu' nice. A tea-party. Just a nice wee family group. Daughter and boy friend. Mother and . . . husband. Ye've just been sittin' here havin' a cup of tea and a talk. Very sociable. An' ye've been waitin' for the son tae come in tae tell 'im the good news. We're all tae become one big happy family again.'

He paused, as if waiting for the full realization of it to catch up with him.

'Well then, Elizabeth,' he went on quietly. 'You seem tae be easily won over, don't ye, hen? Whit did they promise *you*? Nice frocks and drives in their big car?' Elizabeth was near to tears, and Harry was looking down at his hands in embarrassment. Elizabeth's reaction to her mother's coming here had developed from a simple incompetence to deal with the situation. The tea and the talk had merely been improvisations on an awkward circumstance, delaying tactics until things should resolve themselves into some established form or other. She always tried to act according to the dictates of a straightforward social ethos. But no clause in these ethics covered this eventuality, the arrival of a divorced mother with her second husband. 'Very nice. That's more than yer feyther could ever give ye, isn't it? All he ever did for ye was keep ye alive when yer mither ran away an' left ye. All he ever did was work an' scrimp an' save till they dug 'im under, just tae see that we didny miss onything. But that's easy tae forget, isn't it? Ye can forget aboot that when Mother comes back with her car and a brand new man. Ye've really got tae be nice tae her. So ye sit them doon an' give them their tea. Ah hope ye attended tae them with proper care.'

Inevitably, Mr Whitmore cut Charlie short. If Charlie had been allowed to talk on to himself, it might have given the anger in him a safety-valve. But Mr Whitmore couldn't listen any longer to his ludicrous monologue.

'All right. Right.' He almost shouted, on the point of rising. 'I didn't come here to listen to your stupid insolence. Now, listen to me –'

His anger touched off Charlie's own like igniting gas.

'Naw. You listen, stud bull. You listen to me, fancy man. An' you, "Mother". An' you, Elizabeth. Dae ye no' see whit they want, Elizabeth? Dae ye no' see? Oh, they wid like it right enough. They wid like tae help us, all right. That wid make everything fine. Because we wid be condoning whit they did. There wid be naebody left tae say whit they had done, or whit they are. They wid be makin' up for it. But ye canny make up for it. Ye canny hide whit ye did tae ma feyther. Ye destroyed a man that wis worth baith o' ye put thegither. Ye destroyed him.'

'Charlie!' His mother was crying. 'How can ye talk like that? How can ye?'

'Because Ah see you. Whit ye are. Ah ken why ye come here. An' it's no' wi' the divine spirit of giving. You're here tae take. That's why ye're here. You want tae get back whit ye lost when ye left us.'

'I don't see anything here that Jane would miss,' Mr Whitmore said angrily. 'Not a thing.'

'Naw, you widny. You don't see anythin' unless it's got a price on it. Ah don't mean the place. Ah don't mean us. Ah'm quite sure your good woman managed tae overcome her maternal instincts without too big a struggle. But even she must've felt since just whit she did. Have ye no'? You've had a long time tae think noo. An' ye don't have tae be a deep thinker tae understand you, tae see whit ye did or arrive at why ye did it. You just milked a man until he had nothin' and then ye left him. With nothin'! Ye waited until he had used himself up and then you turned round and told him it was worth nothin'. An' ye went tae this! Whit is he? Look at 'im. My God, how could ye dae it? Ah hope ye think it's worth it. Ah hope the fancy clothes an' the bungalow an' the car make up for it. For don't kid yerself. Ye as good as killed a man tae get them.'

'Charlie, how can you talk like this? It wasn't like that at all. And I don't believe what you're saying. I don't believe it.'

'You'd better no'! For if you ever turn round by mistake an' catch yerself when ye're not lookin', if you ever really see whit ye are . . . you'll bloody well vomit. You'd better go back among yer cars an' yer bank balance. An' never look back. Never even think o' whit ye left ahint ye in this hoose. Don't think o' it. For that's the only way you could live wi' yerself. An' never come back here. Never come back expectin' tae get told it's all right. A few bloody pennies for the poor. Did ye think that wis all it took? Ah hell. Ye're known fur whit ye are here. It's written all over this hoose. An' whit you are Ah don't even want tae put ma tongue on. It's too dirty! Jist take yer boy friend an' go away. The two of ye jist go away somewhere else an' play at bein' human beings there. Just go away. Go away.'

The scene had disintegrated completely. The centrifugal force of Charlie's anger had thrown the others to the edge of what was happening and held them pinned there helplessly. He raged in the room, a fanatic hurricane, leaving them bereft of their social composure, isolated in their own emotions. Elizabeth was crying quietly to herself and Harry was attempting to console her from his position of non-involvement in the whole thing. Charlie's mother was weeping

187

terribly, shaking her head in disbelief, and at the same time
holding out her hand to Mr Whitmore to restrain him,
coiled as he was with fury.

'No, Peter, no.' She shouted as if he was a long way away
from her. 'Please don't do anything. Please don't.'

In the centre stood Charlie. He leant on the sideboard, his
left hand covering his eyes. Conflicting emotions harangued
for a hearing in his head. He was aware that this was his
mother he had spoken to in this way. He was aware of how
pleasant the scene had seemed when he entered. He was
aware of Elizabeth crying. He hoped that it was finished, that
somehow enough had happened to appease the anger in him.
He wanted them to leave before he lost control of himself
completely.

Mr Whitmore stood up, staring at Charlie, gathering his
bile. As he made towards him, Charlie's mother moved to
intervene. She attempted to compose herself so that she would
lessen her husband's motive for anger.

'Peter,' she said. 'Let's just leave. Please come on out now.
Please.'

But she was too late. Mr Whitmore was already standing
over Charlie. And the realization of what was going to happen suddenly flashed on her like lightning and she could only
wait helplessly for the physical confirmation that would follow
as inevitably as thunder.

'No,' Mr Whitmore said. 'We'll leave when I've told this
upstart one or two home-truths. You scum!'

Charlie gestured with his hand, not looking round.

'You'd better go away,' he said.

'You filthy, rotten scum!'

'For God's sake now,' Charlie said. 'You'd better go
away.'

'You know what your trouble is?' Mr Whitmore was
sneering. 'You're the same as your father was. I've heard
enough about him to know. You just can't bear to see somebody successful and making a go of things, can you? You just
can't face up to reality. All this talk about your father. What

188

happened to your father was his own fault. He failed just because he was a failure. That was all.' Having found his range, Mr Whitmore regained his composure. 'He didn't deserve to have your mother. He wasn't good enough. Do you understand? He just wasn't good enough.'

The face seemed to enlarge before Charlie's eyes, to bloat until it filled the room, like the huge head of some malign idol. It was not like a human face at all, capable of change. It was fixed impacable as stone in that dual expression of rejection and complacency, complacency in itself, rejection of everything but itself. No matter how much suffering it was shown, it couldn't be moved. It was the face that everyone showed to the world. It was the mask that everyone wore, the frozen gesture behind which each one hid from the truth, the deceit that became grafted on the living flesh until it was the only identity they had. There was no hope for any of them, Charlie saw, for people do not learn, cannot be taught what they have done, become inured to themselves. Failure only serves to redefine the limits of success, so that what is becomes all that might have been, and standards are corrupted by the partial realization of themselves. This mask could never change its expression, could not be moved with words. It could only be broken.

One moment Mr Whitmore was mouthing bitterly at Charlie and the next Charlie had struck him, and that one blow seemed to fuse him to the action so that he couldn't pull himself off. The restraint that had been on him snapped. Mr Whitmore fell, toppling a chair, and Charlie dropped on his knees astride him. still striking, Mrs Whitmore screamed. Harry dived at Charlie in an effort to stop him, gripping his arm. But he was thrown off violently as if by an electric current. Charlie's arm seemed to function independently. It rose and fell tirelessly and relentlessly, seemed galvanized to the act of striking, moved by more than muscle. Through Mrs Whitmore's screams and the cries of Elizabeth and Harry, it beat on, pumping blood from Mr Whitmore's face, decreasing gradually in momentum until at last it was still. Mrs

Whitmore was saying over and over again, 'That's enough, that's enough, that's enough.'

'Yes,' Charlie said dazedly. 'That's enough now. That's enough.'

And suddenly it was as if a wind had dropped in the room. The dark force that had possessed this place a moment ago, that had taken an ordinary scene and forged it into something terrible, that had swept these people into its fierce centre, surrendered them without warning, gave up the room again to quietness, and left its victims stranded derelict in their pathetic humanity. Elizabeth sat huddled in her chair, hiding her eyes. Harry lay transfixed where he had fallen, one leg buckled under him. Charlie's mother knelt on the floor, her face upraised, made into a ludicrous mask by tears. Charlie was slumped almost protectively across the dead body of Mr Whitmore. Mr Whitmore's face was wet with Charlie's tears.

Part Three

Chapter 20

UNDERSTANDING WAS A LONG TIME IN ARRIVING. FOR A while time seemed to be deferred and they were like strangers anonymous in a waiting-room. It was as if normalcy had missed its connection and all the luggage of their lives, everything they knew themselves by, had gone on ahead, where they would have to follow. But no one had the means to reach that destination or knew how they were to get there.

Charlie, as if orphaned by his own action, was like a foundling, helplessly awaiting whatever was in store for him. What was going to happen loomed before him like a closed door, against which someone else's hand had knocked. And he could only wait, powerless to turn away from or open that door.

Everything appeared grotesque and strange to his eyes, much as things must appear to the newly-opened eyes of a child, so that the chair which had fallen with Mr Whitmore had no familiar associations for him, but was a weird symbol in wood. The whole room obtruded terribly on his consciousness, its furnishings palpitating like living things and seeming somehow to grow in stature. The table was not a table, but a vast shining plain from the centre of which rose a tower of glass. The mirror was a massive burnished medallion suspended from the wall. All the familiar fixtures of the room seemed to rebel against him, to deny their ordinariness and invade his mind in fantastic shapes. The others moved before him in dim meaningless charade. His mother knelt, cradling Mr Whitmore in her lap. Would her tears satisfy his lust for grief? Her hands fluttered desperately like limed birds about his face. Her mouth, deformed with grief, spat words at Charlie. But they came to him indistinctly, confused with the sound of Harry's voice and Elizabeth's weeping, components of one continuous rush of noise like the roar of water to someone surfacing.

Then suddenly Charlie was aware of Harry's voice separately, coming to him unnaturally loud.

'Ah'll have to phone,' Harry was saying. 'Ah'd better phone. An' get John. Ah'll get John.'

'Get John. Get John,' Elizabeth said.

Harry went out into the hall and came back a moment later. His coat was open and the collar was turned inward.

'Pennies,' Harry said. 'Ah've only got three pennies.'

Elizabeth turned like a weathervane, trying to locate her purse in the chaos of her mind.

'Press the emergency button.'

Charlie listened to his own voice as if it came from a loudspeaker.

Harry went out. The front door closed. Time held them caught in it and they became no more than nervous tics, like trapped flies. Elizabeth went through and ran water on a cloth and brought it to her mother. Her mother took it and laid it on Mr Whitmore's forehead and it fell to the floor and she forgot about it. She was rocking back and forth on her haunches, moaning. Elizabeth was repeating Charlie's name endlessly. Charlie thought of the appointment he was to have kept on Monday. His mind reiterated like a prayer the fact that he was a university student. He watched the scene with stunned concern as if it were taking place in a theatre and he wanted to see what was going to happen next.

What happened was that John and Harry came in, and to Charlie their entrance was as arbitrary as in a play, in obedience to some unknown script. John was dishevelled and tieless. Shock had blanched his face and hurry had rouged it erratically, so that he entered like a pierrot. His expression of concern disintegrated as he looked round the room. The meaning of the scene seeped into him slowly like poison gas. He went woodenly and blindly towards Mr Whitmore. He crouched down. His hand went out and touched Mr Whitmore and retracted slowly and covered his own face.

194

'Jesus Christ, Charlie,' he said. 'Oh Jesus, Jesus, Jesus, Jesus Christ.'

Inside the sound of his voice, another sound began and ran slowly to a halt. It seemed to Charlie like an echo of something he had heard before, when his father was dying. That other car had arrived too late as well.

Harry went out for a moment and then there were three policemen in the room, two in plain clothes. They knew their parts all right. One of them took out a notebook. They went over and started to examine Mr Whitmore's body. One of them detached himself and came across.

'I want a statement of what happened here,' he said.

'It was me,' Charlie said. 'Ah did it.'

The policeman's eyes lit him like headlamps.

'You admit to doing this?'

'That's whit Ah said.'

'You're sayin' nothin', Charlie.' John was beside him. 'He'll speak when he's got a lawyer.'

'Easy, son,' the policeman said. 'You've seen too many pictures. Nobody's trying to force anybody to say anything. He made a statement of his own volition.'

There was a knocking at the door and a doctor came in with an ambulance-man. The room was overflowing with people. Charlie couldn't see the connection between all this and what he had felt when he hit Mr Whitmore. The terrible dark thing that had taken place in him then denied meaning. And now these men were methodically reducing it to conformity. That moment of vast freedom was being manacled with measurements and jotted notes and assessing looks. A trivial chain of reason was being forged link by link around him.

The policeman who had spoken to him called the other plain-clothes man over. He put his hand on his shoulder.

'Sam, you and Cameron wait here,' he said. 'I'm taking this one down to the station.'

'Right now?'

'Right now. It doesn't take Sherlock Holmes for this lot.

See what the doctor says. And see to the body. And get statements from everybody else here. It's too big a mogre just now to get anything here, anyway. I'll send the car back up for ye.'

'Ah'll come down wi' ye, Charlie,' John said.

'You'd better wait here, sir,' the policeman said. 'And give your statement to my colleague.'

'Ah've got no statement tae give,' John said. 'Ah only got in ahead of you. Ah'm his brither.'

'Very well, then. You can come along.'

Like a somnambulist, Charlie was taken out to the car, where another policeman was sitting in the driver's seat, and they all drove down through the town that was still asleep. In the police-station, the policeman showed Charlie into an empty room and told John to sit on a bench outside. Charlie was seated in front of a desk. The policeman went to the doorway of the room and shouted a surname. Footsteps amplified quickly in the corridor. Something inaudible to Charlie was said and the footsteps walked back into silence. The policeman came back into the room, leaving the door open, and sat on the edge of his desk. He lit a cigarette and toyed with his lighter, striking and dousing it spasmodically. The room asserted itself all at once on Charlie, was suddenly and overpoweringly there without any sense of having been entered, like places in a dream. The footsteps approached again and materialized into another policeman who had a notebook and a pencil. He closed the door and sat in a chair in a corner.

'Now,' the first policeman said, switching the other into motion with his eyes. 'I'm going to warn you, son, that anything you say now is going to be taken down and it could be used as evidence in a court of law. If you prefer not to say anything at all, that's up to you. I'm not twisting your arm up your back.'

Charlie's eyes darted about nervously until they alighted on a paperweight on the desk and fastened there doggedly.

'Well. You'd better give us the run-down on yourself. Name. Address. Age. Occupation. And the like.'

Charlie gave them like a robot.

'College boy,' the policeman said neutrally, watching him. 'Well. Suppose you tell us in your own words just what happened.'

Charlie pared weeks to minutes, put the incomprehensible in a paragraph, and told them.

'And this Mr Whitmore is what – your stepfather?'

'He's married to my mother.'

'Your stepfather, aye. She married him after yer father died?'

'Ma father divorced her.'

'I see. When would that be?'

'Look. Ah don't see what any of this has to do with it. Ah did it. Right?'

'Look, son. I'm not trying to cause you more pain than you've got. But there's not much to go on here. Ye don't seem to have any reason why. Now for your own sake as much as anything else, Ah would like to establish what it was that made you do it . . . Well?'

Charlie extended his arms helplessly, palms up, begging the question.

'Did you have an argument? A quarrel? Had he done something before this?'

Charlie's head moved evasively, as if the questions were punches.

'Did he at any time make to hit you?'

Charlie watched the cloth of the policeman's trousers where the crease had been blunted by his knees, seeing it as if through a microscope.

'Look, son. You've done something damned serious. You've killed a man. Now we'd better try to find out why it happened.'

'That's for you to decide, isn't it?' Charlie said.

'Aye. And *your* neck hangs on the answer.' The unintentional pun embarrassed his anger. His voice dropped gear. 'Look, lad. Tell us why you did it. Eh?'

Charlie stared sullenly into his question.

'For God's sake, now. You don't kill people for no reason.

There's got to be a reason. Now what was it? What did he do or say? Or what happened? Why? Why? Why did ye do it?'

'Damn it, how do I know? He was there an' Ah hit him! Maybe Ah didn't like his clothes or something.'

A sudden silence followed Charlie's words as if the room was holding its breath with shock.

'Don't go funny on *me*, son,' the policeman said, using so little breath he wouldn't have misted a mirror. 'That's the kind of sense of humour that gets people hanged.' His voice suddenly exploded. 'Damn your guts, boy! Damn them! Ah'm trying to help you. Though God knows why Ah should.'

There was a tap at the door and the other plain-clothes policeman who had been at the house looked in and nodded. The man who was questioning Charlie went out, closing the door behind him. Charlie looked across at the one with the notebook and caught him watching him quizzically. It was a look Charlie was to get used to. It seemed to assume that he couldn't look back, as if he was being seen through one-way glass. The door opened again and the two policemen came in. The one who had been questioning Charlie walked over and stood in front of him. The man with the notebook stood up and Charlie got up too.

'Well, lad,' the policeman facing Charlie said, 'that would seem to be it. You can do your talking to a lawyer.' He paused, donning his official capacity. 'All I have said, of course, has only been to determine the exact circumstances of the man's death, and how you were concerned in it. But now it is my duty to charge you with the murder of Peter Graham Whitmore. I have already cautioned you as to any statement you might make. That caution still applies.'

'Murder?' Charlie's voice seemed to dirl in the distance. The word broke through the anaesthetic of shock. The pain of that taboo word. It rang in his mind like the leper's bell.

The man who had given him the word motioned the others out of the room. Crossing to the door, he signalled in John from the corridor.

'I'll give you two or three minutes,' he said. 'And you can –' his hand spiralled doubtfully — 'talk.'

He went out and closed the door. They had two or three minutes too much. John bit on his words as if they were a rag.

'Try to take it as easy as ye can, Charlie,' he said. 'Ah mean that sounds pretty stupid. But whit Ah mean is . . . try not to brood on it too much. Ach, Ah mean . . .'

John's hands moved helplessly, trying to conjure solace out of nothing.

'Ah'll get a lawyer, Charlie. Maybe it's not as bad as it looks. Ah'll get a lawyer.'

Silence seemed to grow in every fissure of the room, like a fungus.

'We'll get ye a fair hearin' anyway, Charlie. We'll get the lawyer on to it.'

The door opened and the policeman came back in.

'I'm sorry,' he said, 'but that's it. You'll have to go now, I'm afraid.'

With nothing to say, John was still reluctant to leave, as if searching for more profound banalities. His hand grasped Charlie's arm, tight as a tourniquet, and they stood locked for a moment in each other's presence, like a masonic handshake.

'You'll see, Charlie,' John said. 'It can't be as bad as it looks.'

Before he let go Charlie's arm, he winked, and that closing eyelid was a forlorn ludicrous gesture in the bleakness of his face, belying itself like the death-twitch of an insect.

'Your brother will be in the cells here until Monday,' the policeman said as John slowly crossed to the door. 'If you want to, you'll be able to visit him there tomorrow. He'll be formally charged with murder on Monday morning at the Sheriff Court before he's taken to Barlinnie.'

'Murder!' John stopped in his tracks. 'Wait a minute. How can it be murder? It was nothin' planned. It was a fight, for God's sake. He didny *try* to kill him. You can't charge him with murder. You can't.'

'That's for a court to decide, sir. I'm afraid that's the charge we're pressing for the moment. Which is not to say that's the charge that'll stand. Charges have been reduced before. Say, to culpable homicide. Mind you, I'm not saying that's going to happen here, either. But this is the way we have to work. A charge can be reduced, you see, but it can't be raised. If we started off with a charge of culpable homicide, say, and then found out we had enough evidence for a murder conviction, we'd be in the soup. *We'd* catch it then – from upstairs,' indicating a vague celestial hierarchy. 'We're only protecting ourselves. Because the charge couldn't be raised then. We've got to do it that way, you see.'

John just stood there, impassive and desolate, his pathetic little insurrection crushed by the policeman's self-convinced logic. His hand made as if to wave to Charlie and wilted to his side. He went out.

As his back receded, the situation caved in on Charlie completely. His thoughts numbed his senses so that the things that were happening to him barely impinged on him. They took him into another room. He was finger-printed. They took away everything with which he could do himself harm, shoelaces, tie, belt. His pockets were emptied, his watch taken, and everything was put in a large envelope and filed away. At the end of it he found himself in a cell upstairs, left to the mercy of thoughts and fears and recriminations that filled his head like a forum.

Broken images flashed on his mind. He teemed with voices that railed at him, demanding attention. The night's events revolved like a carousel, whirling dizzily at times and slowing to a halt at others, filled with figures in grotesque poses and painted in the primary colours of fear, all taking place in the single location of his mind. Mr Whitmore sitting nonchalantly on a chair, his smile a subtle mockery. Elizabeth clasping her hands to her ears, shutting out her own screams. Gowdie watching. His mother holding up her hands, warding off the truth. Jim dancing, suavity in caricature. People swaying dully in a bus. Harry lying like a statue on the floor. People

200

loomed out at him horribly and receded, to a soundless cacophony of words and voices.

While his body prowled endlessly in the cell, pacing from wall to wall, sitting down, rising, stopping, moving, his mind stayed staked to its guilt. The cell did not exist separately for him, was not a distinct physical entity, having its location in a building in a street in a town. It merely partook of him, was no more than an extension of himself, a shell. It was no more than the limit to which he had driven himself. Its nature was his nature. Its edges were his edges, beyond which he could not go. It was not place, but fact, the action he had done, the action by which all other people and places in his life were denied, by which everything that had been himself was refuted. He had created this point to which nothing in his life could be related. He had impaled himself on this naked action. He had immured himself in this place outside of place, where he existed as the contradiction of himself, where everything he had been turned against what he now was. The loneliness of the cell dwindled into the vast isolation that was himself, was lost in that dark chaos that no place could impinge upon, where he was irrevocably alone against himself, where every memory had teeth and his own thoughts devoured him.

And as the cell existed for him out of place, so too it existed for him out of time. That private chronometer of precise habit, the intricate machinery of recurrent people, places and actions that regulates the passing of our days, had stopped. For him the personal concerns that preside on our lives like private zodiacs, moods that sway the tides of our blood like moons, commitments that come like punctual suns, had broken from their orbit. Present was confounded with past, old actions resurrected, faces usurped the empty air, dead words started out of their cerement of silence, and in the struggle future was eclipsed.

The time that moved outside the cell did not include him in its motion. His mind turned outside of time, functioning on its own futility, like a rat in a revolving cage. The sun that delivered morning to his window had no relevance to him. Sunday workmen who clumped past on the street outside, hoasting the first phlegm on to the pavements, moved in a different dimension from him, somnambulists in a dream from which he had awakened. The opening of the cell door evoked no response from him, a scratching on the shell.

A policeman entered, carrying a tray so that it indented a brass-buttoned belly.

'Here's a bite o' breakfast for ye,' he said.

His voice insinuated itself gently into the silence of the room, as undulating as the Highlands it came from. The haggard eyes looked back at him dully, erasing his presence. The head shook absently and a hand flicked across the eyes as if removing a speck. The policeman stood for a time, watching as if he had bought a ticket.

'Anyway, I'll leave it,' he said.

Nothing showed on the pinched face. The eyes still stared inwards, focused on whatever was happening behind them.

'Well, ye *will* fecht,' the policeman said in that gentle accent. 'It's a hard lesson sure enough. But ye maun learn it. All you kinna folk that can't keep their hands off others maun be learned.'

Something flickered like summer lightning on the face and then was gone, so that it was difficult to tell if it had really been. Charlie's eyes turned on the policeman, but whatever had drawn their attention to him expended itself in the effort of doing so. Charlie looked uncomprehendingly at him. The tobacco burning in his pipe-bowl, glowing red and fading ashen in obedience to the bellows of his breath, and the tobacco-and-soap smell that he exuded stirred Charlie's senses dimly like a childhood memory. His alien presence was a strange incursion from a life that had no connection with Charlie.

'Aye, we maun learn your kinna folk,' the policeman said. Then he went out complacently, having spoken on behalf of all good men and true.

He disappeared from Charlie's vision like a mote. Charlie's

mind was given over to its own turmoil, was caught in a civil war that no external event could influence. His concern was not directly with the fact of his imprisonment. He rethought his predicament endlessly, but without aiming at any positive effect. Already it was an automatic gesture, like the padding of a lion in its cage. It was within the limits of that fact that his agony took place. No attempt was made to see through or round his situation. The situation could only have meaning in relation to himself and at the moment there was nothing in himself that it could relate to. His identity was atomized, his thoughts were countless spinning particles that reshaped themselves into ever-changing patterns. Not until some sort of pattern was fixed could a response be established to the things around him, which at the moment were dulled by that anaesthesia to everything but itself that any intense pain throws out. The baited bear doesn't feel the gadfly. So Charlie writhed inwards on himself in a pain that was like a terrible compound of the pangs of birth and death. Many things in him screamed against their own dying, fought against the denial of themselves. Memories of happy moments invaded his mind, claiming their right to be repeated, telling him that his future should have known many more. Ambitions that had been silenced by the possessive presence of his father's death regained a hearing in his mind, now that that obsession had been exorcized in action. They assailed his mind, made all the more intense by their impossibility. They weren't the finite, logical ambitions of maturity which, being founded on reason, can therefore be rationally disposed of when their impossibility has been acknowledged. They were the infinite ambitions of youth, those dim vistas of the future which the young see shining before them with ineffable hope and which cannot be called mirage until they have been travelled, those inarticulate arterial promises that have to be lived into discredit. Now that the dark alien identity that had lived in him since his father's death had released itself, he had become again to some extent just a young man. There was a resurgence in him of the sharp sense of unlimited potential that surrounds the young like a miasma. So many things seemed to have waited for him to fulfil himself in them. There were so many places to go, names that were like mysterious private symbols to him, Rome, Madrid, La Place de la Concorde, that had always been like secret passwords to some vague Nirvana that shimmered in the future. There were simple things he was to have done, like walking down a street with a girl, being in a room where people were laughing, talking with friends. He was to have read books that illumined many things. He was to have watched so much grow and deepen around him, to learn living, to see Andy and Jim become themselves, to abide the gradual fulfilment of himself. The future was to have been the slow amassing of himself from many places, the formation in him of some great unknown identity from mysterious fragments. Ironically, this intense awareness of what was to have been realized in him came at the very moment of its ultimate contradiction, gained a vitality that made its imminent death the more unbearable. In everyone it dies, this sense of their vast and mysterious significance. But then it is a gradual process. Time administers to us gradually increasing doses of the commonplace, purging us of our fancies, until at last we are immune to all but our more practical ambitions and desires. Our lives become practical and self-contained only by starts. Reality contains us intermittently, for slowly increasing spells, so that by the time we are finally interred in it, we have become conditioned to its narrowness and hardly notice the transition. Vague grandiose intentions co-exist for a time with more mundane necessities, and then are ousted by them. The wild improbable hopes that are entertained in youth are replaced by more immediate ambitions, the absence of one only being achieved by the presence of the other, so that change presupposes adjustment to it.

But for Charlie, the process was accelerated. What may be had to become what might have been, not slowly through the assimilation of a substitute, but at once, and in a vacuum. All that he might have been was denied in one cataclysmic action, shattered, not removed by the gentle erosion of the years. Like all deaths that come in the prime, it was painful, and the pain of it was intensified by another that grew from it like a Siamese twin, the labour of bringing into being the truth that was to take its place in him, whatever it was that he had made himself.

What had he made of himself? He did not know. He did not know what had happened. He knew that a man had died and that he had killed him and that he was in a jail charged with murder, but these fragmented facts told him no more of what had happened than the wreckage tells of the shipwreck. The floating debris tells us merely that a ship is sunk, but what ship it was, or what cargo it carried, or where it was bound, or how it sank, or how many lives were lost in it, or who will wait for them, it doesn't tell. The facts of misfortune mean nothing in themselves. The vastest cataclysm means only as much as its relation to each individual involved. Disaster is a divinity we can only comprehend under private names. A city in ruins moves us less than one widow weeping. So Charlie, faced with the brute facts of what had happened, strove to wrestle them into meaning.

It was not so much that he sought to understand why he had done it as that he sought to understand what it was that had acted through him. For he sensed dimly that his own part in it was over already, finished with his action, and that personal motives could not adequately explain what had happened. It is the nature of violence to be like fire and consume the elements which feed it, so that the reasons for it are extinguished in itself. Such reasons as we form in retrospect are like the letters on the headstone. They only tell us what is not, what no longer exists. Charlie's action did not concern him most deeply in this way. His action isolated him, it is true, but it was not the fact of his isolation that mattered most. That action had been the judgment passed on him by a force far greater than himself. And it was only the understanding of that force that could make his action comprehensible. It had used him, inhabited him, goaded him, driven him, and finally manifested itself through him in a terrible action, leaving him to face a murder charge. But neither the death of Mr Whitmore nor the murder charge, nor Charlie's own predicament was the meaning of that dark force. These were no more than mere manifestations of it, themselves meaningless until it was understood. That mysterious lodestone had drawn him mercilessly to it, away from normalcy and friendship and love, through grief and despair and murder, and still, with his life in pieces about him, it was what he sought to come at. The rest mattered less than it. The cell, the impassive policeman, the intricate machinery of justice that was grinding into motion around him, the grief of his family, these things meant little to him until he had found whatever it was that dark power had to impart to him. Until it should infuse them with its meaning, these occurrences were aimless fragments, debris drawn in and thrown off by the vortex of which he was the centre.

But aimless and irrelevant as they were, they still encroached on the dark whirling void that was himself, sought to impinge on him. A little later in the morning, the cell door opened again and another policeman looked in. He lifted the tray with the breakfast untouched and shook his head.

'Pull yerself thegither now, son,' he said. 'Yer brother's here to see ye.'

The situation created for Charlie projected like a jetty into his flowing thoughts, but seemed still far away from him. As if from a distance, he saw appearing on it John and Elizabeth. The presence of Elizabeth did not provoke surprise at the inaccuracy of the policeman's statement. Where nothing cohered, the incompatibility of statement and fact was as natural as an axiom. He simply saw the two of them standing there, spruce and somehow forlorn, like people waiting to meet someone who hadn't turned up. He felt a vague, displaced sympathy for them. But it did not occur to him to give it any expression. It seemed somehow pointless, as if they were out of shouting distance.

The policeman closed the door on John and Elizabeth. They stood awkwardly in the middle of the room. The dialogue that followed was as cryptic and formal as the ritual exchanges of sentries. John asked Charlie if he was all right. Charlie's mouth said that he was all right, like a cave redounding an echo. Charlie then asked John and Elizabeth in turn and both gave the correct response. John said he was seeing about a lawyer and Charlie said they were not to worry and Elizabeth said that she had made something for Charlie to eat, extending the message-bag she was holding. It went on and on like that, like some ludicrous family game of pass-the-platitude, played out desperately against the background of the bleak walls and the policeman waiting outside and their imminent separation until Elizabeth broke the sequence. It happened unexpectedly. Elizabeth mentioned again the meal she had made for Charlie, and then realized that she had said that already, and in the moment of confusion she lost control of herself. She stopped, working furiously against herself, furrowing her brows to dam her tears. But the emotion filled up in her as palpably as liquid filling a glass until it overflowed. Her face fought to stay impassive and her body clenched on a racking sob. Somehow she managed to fix her features into something like composure, but the tears oozed on to her cheeks, like blood through bandages. She began to weep agonizingly and John had to put his arm round her and lead her out. At the door he paused and gently detached the message-bag from her hand. He said goodbye to Charlie and put the bag on the floor. The door clanged shut behind them.

Charlie sat staring into their absence. He seemed as external to their grief as the dead man is to the funeral rites. Their sorrow could be shared with each other, but not with him. He was beyond the point where these things could relate to him significantly. The message-bag epitomized their helpless love, just as the pitcher and food left with the corpse are all that his mourners can give him as token of their love. It was like the words that had been spoken in this cell, the only currency they had, but one which had no meaning here, obols in the mouths of dead men.

Every gesture made towards Charlie was nullified by his stillness, his inability to respond. He was isolated in himself, struggling for the private resurrection of understanding that would transform what had happened into meaning. The confusion of things occurring around him deepened, entangled, became utterly inextricable.

As time passed, he could not remember whether events had happened within minutes or within hours. He existed outside of any present, in a strange limbo that rested upon a subtly shifting past. Events never reached him as happening, but only as having happened. There had been the dark bumping journey with two policemen sitting with him. He had washed himself somewhere and dried himself on a rough towel. He remembered its texture on his skin. He had disembarked into a rough courtyard surrounded by high walls, another prison. Men had been watching him. A policeman had tried to get him to eat the meal Elizabeth had brought him. He had stood in a courtroom. He had been given a bath and had been dressed in anonymous corduroy clothes.

Through it all he had paced endlessly, trekking, it seemed, through a terrible emptiness where people and places were shed from him like useless lumber. Night found him still walking in that second cell, exhausted but driven on by some desperate impulse that seemed to promise him destination.

Suddenly, the tiredness of two days pressed a plunger on his pent fatigue. Sleep came like a detonation as he lay down. Thoughts thrown off drifted in isolation across his mind, a line of poetry, the image of his father's face, the date of Mary's birthday, parts of himself surrendered to oblivion. And then they too were waterlogged with sleep.

He lay on the bunk, huddled in a foetal crouch.

Chapter 21

YOU WAKE INSIDE FOUR BRICK WALLS, A CELL. AND that is all you need. You go on from there. The cell splits like an amoeba, to a bunk, a floor, a window, the shifting clouds beyond the bars. Days take shape. Morning means tea and bread, a basin of water, a tablet of dun soap, a square of gauze towel. You progress from your first sight of the gauze towel through the drying of your hands on it many times until you have become the user of the towel. Two more meals means evening. There is a twice-daily half-hour exercise, when the prisoners walk round and round the enclosed yard, a walk of refugees from reality, a trek to nowhere. There are men you come to know in this exercise period, men who walk with you regularly while the guards lounge and watch. They begin as strange presences, their faces weird in the unnatural light of their circumstance, until familiarity learns to see the wart or the broken tooth and invests them with humanity. Charges are formally exchanged like visiting-cards and friendships grow like grass in pebbled streets. There is an issue of books to read, dished out peremptorily, the iron rations of sanity. Like a chameleon you take colours from all this.

This was Charlie. This was the meaning his crime bestowed on him, the legacy of action. The dark ritual of violence in which he had sacrificed Mr Whitmore and himself had evoked nothing more than this divine indifference. The chimera of truth that he had felt haunting his father's death, whose plaintive cry he had heard demanding admittance to their lives, was by some terrible irony farther from him than ever. He had pursued its elusive presence as far as Mr Whitmore's body and he had surrendered his own identity to bring it into being. And still it had not materialized. Instead, there was only the vast waste his search for it had created. That cry came fainter now, dying in distance, and seemed a dwindling mockery.

Its departure left Charlie in terrifying loneliness. It had stripped him of himself, of friends and future, luring him towards it with promise of some deeper meaning. And now it left him with nothing but the banal functions of his body, food and sleep and the company of strangers. At first he still tried to believe that the meaning of what had happened would be understood, that the machinery that had taken possession of him would be the means of interpreting the message that was written in the death of Mr Whitmore, in the grief of his family, and in the deprivation of himself. But he learned gradually that here he had no right to be understood. Here life was reduced to the barest sustenance of itself, meant no more than its own prolongation. It gave no rights beyond itself, only concessions. It granted food for body and mind in order to keep them functioning. But it offered them no purpose for which they should function. It measured out fresh air, but only in such quantities as would suffice to counteract the lack of it.

Here one thing negated another, and each activity only existed to counteract its opposite. It was a miracle of equilibrium, the very perfection of futility. Those huge walls were a temple dedicated to meaninglessness. Each day from the endless rooms of cells men were brought forth to walk like shadows in the sunlight, but only long enough to be able to appreciate what they were not, so that their illusory freedom from futility should only serve to intensify their real bondage to it. Then they filed patiently back into their cells like macabre monks to continue their devotions to their pointlessness. And the bolts clanged home along the corridors.

Joining every day that circular pilgrimage of men on parole from meaning, Charlie came to understand their calm despair. A dull acceptance was all that was possible here. Only real people can have real emotions. And these people were not real. They were automata, mechanisms stripped to a few basic functions of existence. Each one was anonymous. Each wore the same faded corduroy clothes, which had not been made for anyone in particular. Each drank from mugs worn by other people's mouths. They were provisional people. Each one here had done the thing which didn't belong to him, small or large, had aggressed beyond himself by taking or doing. Each one here had been taken away from himself, and must wait to see what he was given back.

In the meantime, they merely existed, hung on to the periphery of living, as purposeless and elemental as a limpet. Their chief connection with reality was in the visits paid to them by their friends and families, when they pushed quiet words and hurried messages at each other through the grille. For Charlie, these visits only served to remind him of the suffering he had caused. John came every time with masochistic regularity, determinedly hopeful. Elizabeth came once with a carefully rehearsed expression of brightness, but her presence brought an even more painful tension to these meetings, with her speaking in charged whispers, and she did not come again. Andy and Jim came once, and Charlie's Uncle Hughie and some others. But with all of them, Charlie had the same feeling, though it might vary in intensity. He felt guilt. They all seemed to him people he had betrayed. They looked stunned and hurt, as if something had happened which had no right to be happening in their lives. Charlie's guilt was not only that he had killed a man. It was not just that he had introduced something ugly and horrible into their lives, something that would shadow many of their lives until they died. That was terrible enough. But then he had sensed for a long time that something terrible was going to happen if the deliberate self-deceit and the casual cruelty that he had seen implicit in their lives was to be acknowledged. The real guilt lay in what he had failed to do, more than in what he had done. For he had failed to make the wrong that he had felt be acknowledged. The terrible action had taken place, and it had left in its wake nothing but numb despair, unbalmed by understanding. To them his action was a thunderbolt that shattered without illumination, a summary judgment based upon no reasons, an edict passed upon their lives by some divine whimsy. They saw only a terrifying freak of fortune, one of the aimless hazards of living, like flood or hurricane, that come without warning or purpose out of the mysterious darkness that surrounds our lives, wreak their havoc, and are gone. They were not aware of error that had produced it, but only of the error that it had produced. They saw only a wanton wastage. They knew only the unnecessary grief, the unprovoked suffering, the fortuitous tears, and the waste of lives.

So it was that when Charlie saw them facing him through the grille he felt an awesome sense of guilt chill him. What meaning was in his action that could justify this? What right had he to have caused this havoc? They came and sat before him, bemused and stricken with an alien grief, to look at the cause of it. He felt like an oracle that had failed. What had his vision of the wrong in their lives produced but pain? What had his violent conjuration called up but misery? Where was the revelation that should have accompanied it, the understanding that was to have given meaning to the agony? He was to have been harbinger to some kind of truth, without which they could not go on living. He had cleared a way for it in their lives through a man's death, and it had not followed. There should have been something to offer them in return for the glib assurance that had been taken away – a deeper understanding of themselves, some kind of knowledge, some kind of truth.

But there was nothing. There were only the painful visits with John sitting there, a living recrimination. There were the aimless parades round and round the prison yard when they seemed to be enacting their own pointlessness, engaging in a ritual celebration of their own nonentity. There was the sense of utter hopelessness that the prison taught to all its inmates, stamped it like a motto on their minds. It was evident in the way the prisoners talked among themselves in the yard. They discussed cases. But those who had any experience did not make the assumption that their actions had any meaning for those who were considering them, or that their meaning had any connection with what was going to happen to them. They simply accepted that when you did certain things you set some force into motion and you had to abide by certain rules. But what followed was no more than a sinister game of chance. There were rules. But the rules were self-contained and need have no relevance to the pressures that had provoked your action. You simply waited while the men who knew the rules applied them to your case.

Some prisoners made forecasts among themselves about the outcome of their respective cases. Their lawyers had stressed certain points to some of them, indicating their particular importance, favourable or otherwise, with the result that they might sense their luck running one way or the other. But none of them understood what was going on and it was all so chancey that most of them tried to suspend thought on it and hold hope in abeyance until society had tossed its legal pennies and examined the entrails of their dead actions. They simply developed tricks of thought and held on to them like superstitions. One relied on the fact that he had been provoked, another on his family's need of him, another on the faith he had in his lawyer. Armed only with these, they waited, like gamblers crossing their fingers and closing their eyes while the wheel spins or the horses jump.

Charlie developed no such protective device. He submitted himself completely and honestly to the penance of afterthought that follows upon spontaneous action. The intensity of the process would not allow him to hide from the truth. He saw with terrible clarity that whatever his action meant had no bearing on what was happening now. What was happening to his action now seemed almost like a conspiracy to rob it of meaning. He was shut up here, and elsewhere, in places that he knew nothing of, men sifted facts and gathered fragments of evidence into arbitrary patterns. The only contact he had with it all was through the solicitor John had engaged for him. He visited Charlie a few times, telling him about what he called 'the progress of the case'. He was there when Charlie made his second court appearance to be charged officially with murder. Each time he came after that, he had a different 'angle' that he wanted to talk over with Charlie. He had a list of people that he was visiting systematically, taking statements from all of them. His energy never flagged. He was a young man and though he always tried to show consideration for Charlie, he couldn't quite control the sheer enthusiasm that he had in the whole thing as a case. When he came to the point of legal procedure, he had a tendency to talk with self-satisfied pedantry, quoting from statutes, savouring the sound of the official terminology. Murder must have been a rare commodity for him, and he was enjoying it.

Being with him and observing him, Charlie felt utterly despondent, not so much at the lawyer himself as at the fact that he symbolized the whole process that was taking place around him. He was quick as a compass-needle to redirect his position according to the facts. He strained statements to the sediment. He wrote sentences in his notebook, pausing over them, bolting them together carefully. Then he re-examined them, feinting at them, trying to ambush them, until he was sure that they were impregnable. He kept referring to what 'they' would do and what 'they' would say.

It was all somehow unreal, like a morality play with Charlie as the stage. His lawyer did everything possible to minimize his responsibility for what he had done. He emphasized the fact that Charlie had been drinking. He dwelt on the provocation of Mr Whitmore. He talked of filial piety until Charlie suggested that his conception of it must be fairly elastic if it could contain what he had done. He hinted at 'a temporary state of diminished responsibility'.

And the other side would be doing the opposite. The prosecution lawyer would be trying to make Charlie's action seem one of unprovoked and unmitigated violence. It did not matter what they happened to believe personally, or if they believed anything personally. Nobody made any pretence of being involved in the reality of the thing. It was all just make-believe.

Charlie could not bring himself to participate in their charade. He felt somehow as if he had played into their hands. When he had felt the injustice his father had suffered, they had offered him no means to express his feeling. They had ignored it, pretended that the injustice he felt did not exist. And when he had proven its existence by an action that they could not ignore, they isolated the action in himself, pretended that the injustice was his, existed only in the manifestation he had given it. It was as if they had let him trap himself in their own evil, and then attributed the evil to him. His action had been an attempt to pass some sort of judgment on them, and now they were using it to pass judgment on him. They made his action a means of vindicating themselves. They did not relate his action in any way to themselves. They made it all so impersonal by reducing it to this mock conflict in which they took both sides. By their skilful ambivalence, they exonerated themselves whatever happened. And they did it all with such earnestness and humanity.

The solicitor strove determinedly to make Charlie's action as insignificant as he could. As the time for the trial drew near, he promised Charlie that his 'counsel' would be coming to see him. He said it as if it was very important, a significant gesture made towards Charlie, justice sending her official representative to his aid.

But Charlie saw it as only another stage in refining what he had done to fit their own requirements, another part of the process his action was submitted to in this factory for the distortion of facts to fit society. He saw truth tethered and hobbled, helpless, lying ready for emasculation. 'Counsel' was just another name for one of those who were helping to hold it ready for the knife.

Chapter 22

IT WAS AN UNUSED CELL, REDOLENT WITH PAST MISERY and the loneliness of many men. A table and two chairs had been placed in the middle of the floor, but they did no more than offset the starkness of the stone room. The barred window relieved the gloom grudgingly, conceding a pittance of nicotined light.

Mr Bertram laid his brief-case on the table and took a few measured paces back and forth in the cell, like a general assessing the strength of his position. He checked his battery of arguments, making sure they were ready to be trained on target. He found that he was relishing the encounter. Charles Grant promised to be interesting. A working-class university student. Apparently more articulate than most of those who faced a murder charge. That was what made it interesting. Violence wasn't necessarily the monopoly of morons, but too often, he had found, it seemed to go along with a certain inability to express oneself in more civilized directions. Those who suffered from it scrawled their frustrations on society's attention the way that children chalk obscenities on a wall.

Mr Bertram lingered over the thought. It pleased him. He was a man who liked the neat abstraction, the sweeping analysis. In a world recalcitrantly irrational and incalculable, he delighted in any situation that was separable from elements of chance and uncertainty, and to which a formula could be applied. That was his reason for being here today. He could justify his presence to himself on more pragmatic grounds. Mr Edwards had been having trouble with Grant. Their client was hardly being helpful. Mr Bertram had decided to see him, but he had discouraged Mr Edwards from attending their interview. Mr Edwards would no doubt be concerned with incidental points in the case and Mr Bertram had decided that these were sufficiently clarified already. He saw this meeting as an opportunity to show Grant the image he must try to project during the trial, not as a matter of legal quibbling. Every trial followed a known formula, and Mr Bertram was pleased to reflect that he was familiar with that formula.

A warder entered, bringing with him one of the formula's components.

'Mr Grant,' he said, shaking hands with Charlie. His face troubled with sympathy for a second before it went bland again. 'As you no doubt know, my name is Alexander Bertram. I'll be representing you at your trial.'

The warder had gone out, leaving the door slightly ajar, so that the room eavesdropped on the muted sounds of the rest of the building. Footsteps came and went on the edge of the silence. Voices assailed the cell quietly and intermittently, as delicate as mice.

'Please sit down.'

Charlie sat in the chair facing the door and watched the man sit down opposite, his immaculate clothes looking sombre in this false twilight. His brief-case rested on the table, massive and thick, a leather strong-box. Charlie wondered what was in it. His own defence. The meaning of what he had done. For this was it. The final conference before his action was officially submitted for judgment. The place was appropriate to the occasion. The bleakness seemed somehow terminal, a dead-end in stone and wood. Here only fundamentals could exist, the hardest of facts, the ultimate realities. You could not bring pretence or sophistry or self-deception here. Everything but the truth broke in transit. Here all you could do was turn and face yourself. So what was the conclusion they had reached?

'My reason for coming to see you, Mr Grant, is not in order to discuss the case as such with you. I am too well aware of Mr Edwards' competence to consider that necessary. He's been in touch with you several times and he will have indicated to you the lines we'll be following. No. My real reason is a simpler one. I just wanted to see you, and let you see me. Mr Edwards tells me – let me be frank – that your attitude at times has been almost obstructive. I think I can appreciate how you feel. The legal process must seem pretty impersonal to you. So I think it's important that we should at least know each other before the trial. A courtroom is hardly the best place in which to make someone's acquaintance. Cigarette?'

He gave Charlie a cigarette and leaned across the table to light it for him. So far, so smooth, Charlie felt. It seemed a very studied performance. Straight out of the Lawyers' Handbook. Fig. 1 – Making the Prisoner Feel at Home. Remarks should be punctuated with friendly gestures, e.g. passing of cigarette. Allow him to smoke for a moment before resuming.

'I would like to give you some idea of what's ahead of you during the trial. I don't want you to be completely bewildered. Your behaviour during the trial is important. So that I want you to know what's going on. Is there any part of the procedure you want clarification on? Any questions you want to ask?'

Charlie blew out smoke, shaking his head.

'Naw,' he said. 'Only whit a' this is supposed tae have tae dae wi' onything.'

'Mr Grant. First of all. I would prefer you to speak in English. You've been to university. Presumably, you're reasonably articulate. I see no need for this . . . linguistic affectation. It's in no way to your advantage to talk as if you were on a terracing. I don't have any personal antipathy to Lallans. When it *is* Lallans. But juries are recruited primarily from the middle classes. And they tend to judge people by the way they speak. They may not try to. But it's liable to get to them.'

Charlie paused on the thought that it was difficult to see the connection between murder and the way you spoke. A remark half-formed in his mind, something to the effect that they might as well reach a decision by burning his hand and waiting to see if it festered. But it died of indifference. What was the point here? Sarcasm was too glib to have survived with him as long as this. Yet he couldn't quite avoid a hint of Eton in his voice, the ghost of former fluency.

'Oh, I see,' he said. 'I was wondering what relevance all of this had to what I've done.'

'Thank you. That's better. Actually, it is very relevant. Any jury consists of fifteen good people and true. Or as close to these prerequisites as forethought and careful pre-selection can come. But above all it consists of fifteen very fallible people. Fifteen people who are pretty ordinary. And being ordinary, they are not greatly given to self-scrutiny or to the examination of their mental processes. Now, in the strange context of a jury-room and under the special stimulus of the responsibility they bear, they will try to arrest their thought processes, to overtake instinct and study their reactions. To achieve a concentration and an honesty alien to their every-day lives. They *will* try. But how far will they succeed? It's a hard discipline. How many thoughts are pure of prejudice? How many ideas enter the mind completely unalloyed with error? And having entered, how many ideas can stay un-tainted by what is there already? By what has gathered there through years of hurried living, of makeshift thinking, of all the small necessary deceptions that people practise on them-selves. A residue remains. Something that stains whatever comes in contact with it. Bias becomes built into the mind. Do you see what I mean?'

Charlie made no answer, as if the question was rhetorical, part of some ritual in which he was not a participant, merely an onlooker. But silence was all the response the lawyer needed. His theme sustained him without the incentive of reply. The blankness of Charlie's expression was no more than a mirror in which his own conviction was reflected.

'You see. What will come together in that jury-room and in that court will not be fifteen minds. But fifteen people. And people contaminate their minds. It's unavoidable. That's what it means to be human. They reshape them to suit them-selves. They people them with their own gods. They remake the world to fit them. Institute their own laws. Enthrone

219

whims. They harness their minds to small snobberies, little prejudices. And this is what *we* are up against. This is what *we* have to deal with.'

The use of 'we' made Charlie cringe. He recoiled from it as if it were the hand of a drowned man plucking at him. He looked round the cell and its recalcitrant stone was counterpart to his despair.

'So we have to take this into account and adjust to suit. We have to try to make our actions anticipate their *re*actions. We must understand that much of their thinking will simply be rationalization from accepted points of prejudice. So it's up to us not to offend any such prejudice. Otherwise, we may effect blockages in their thinking. Don't misunderstand me. It's not that I think this aspect of it is of prime importance. Not at all. I'm not trying to say that the scales of justice balance on prejudice. Our legal system is a good one, and what matters most, of course, is the case, the two sides of it which the law presents. This will still be the jury's main concern. All I'm saying is that it will not be their only concern. The trial will be a multiple experience for them. They will be seeing and hearing people all the time. And these people will affect them not only by what they say. But also by the way that they say it. By their manner. By their very appearance. Trivial factors. Yes. But then a trial is a complex of important and trivial factors, interacting upon one another. I just want you to be aware of this. Remember that while the lawyers debate, the jury will be watching you. Small things will lodge in their minds. Your expression. The way you move your hands. Your manner of speaking. You may be creating impressions in their minds that may have some sort of influence on their thinking, however minimal. I want you to be conscious of the impression you are creating. You are playing a part. That is all. And more important than any good impression that you might create is the need not to create any bad impression. Such as your speech might have done if you had been speaking in a court there. This is what I'm getting at. Have you been following me?'

Where to? Charlie thought. Down the rabbit's burrow? To the land of make-believe, where we can play at being people? So much for truth. He could bid it goodbye here. This was as far as his action took him, this bleak dead-end. The rest was a backing-away from it, the covering of his tracks with dead leaves and twigs of reason. Why did it have to be like this? Was the truth he had wanted them to face too terrible to face? So that they had to cover it up, to obscure it with irrelevances, to make it into something different before they could bear it? Somehow what he had done had destroyed its own meaning. His action had been an attempt to halt glibness, to tear off superficiality, to make the truth be faced. Instead, it had merely created its own glibness, a greater need for superficial reasons to conceal its true nature. His truth had spawned its own falsehood. He had forced them to deny the true meaning of his action. For some things are too terrible to be acknowledged if life is to have any meaning, is to continue on a practical footing. As a wound craves bandages, the truth he had revealed to them craved concealment. And they were doing an expert job of concealment, performing immaculate plastic surgery on themselves. And what could he do about it?

'Mr Grant. Have you been following me?'

It seemed senseless to talk about it. What was talk going to achieve now? But the question was there, like a performer's hat. It was only polite to put a penny in.

'Following you? Ah widny exactly put it that way. I wouldn't exactly put it that way. You don't seem to be going anywhere. Except round in circles.'

'What exactly do you mean by that?'

The lawyer's voice had gone quiet, but its quietness was ominous with the tension of anger on a leash. Charlie felt that it was hardly worth offending him just to go on with this. Enough had been done already. Too many people had been hurt. And it all added up to nothing. What use was there in adding even one more insult to it or prolonging it in another moment's anger? But the lawyer was there. And he owed him at least an answer.

'All I mean is, I don't see any point in the part you're asking me to play. I can't identify, as it were. All this elaborate pretence. It's so trivial. I mean, what *is* the point of it?'

'I thought I had made myself clear, Mr Grant. I'm not pretending that it isn't trivial. In fact, I specifically said that it was. All right. I'm not even saying that it's going to make much difference. It might not make *any* difference. Indeed, to be quite honest with you, in a case as clear-cut as this one, I don't see that it *will* make any difference. But while there exists the slightest possibility that it might, then it is my business to consider it. And I'm trying to make it yours. While there is any factor, however slight, which might weigh in your case, however fractionally, then it is my duty to try to see that you get the benefit of it. A human being is at stake. No feather of fact can be ignored. Nothing, no matter how trivial, can be discounted if it might possibly off-set your case. And I won't let it be discounted. Not even by you. A mote is enough to blind us to the truth.'

Charlie felt smothered with protection. But what could stop this man? He was passionate in his desire to have justice for Charlie. And he couldn't see that his passion was a denial of Charlie, a gross injustice to him, presupposing that the truth of what he had done meant no more than what a few people thought of it, was subject to a few psychological gimmicks.

'I think I know what you feel, Mr Grant. You say you don't see the relevance of this to what you did. I understand. There are many other factors more important. Of course, there are. But it is in order that these other factors may be seen clearly and in true perspective that we must try to obviate marginal confusions and biases. The case as such is in our hands. Don't worry. We'll make it as strong as it can be made. Let us take care of that. But I see every case as a composite presentation to the jury. Not just words. Or ideas. But a thing of many facets. And yourself, your physical self, is one of them. Your presence. And I find your attitude to your own case alarming in the extreme. I want you to fit in with the practical requirements of this situation. That's all. Just to accept this thing as it is. And help us to make the most of what we have. I don't know what sort of vague half-formed ideal of justice you harbour, Mr Grant. From Mr Edwards, I gather that you have small patience or sympathy with the rather imperfect and makeshift version of it that we dispense. Be that as it may. It happens to be all we have available. I'm afraid you have no choice. All I ask is that you make the most of it. I want you simply to accept the negative need not to jeopardize anything we may have to our advantage by what you say or how you act in that courtroom. Just help us to see justice done. Will you, Mr Grant?'

Charlie was on the point of accepting the lawyer's terms because there seemed nothing else that he could do. But suddenly revulsion at the whole process of persistent falsification to which he had been subjected halted him in the act of affirmation. Anger rose in him against what they were making out of his action. Perhaps he couldn't stop them. But he was damned if he would agree with them, simply surrender.

'No!' he said, and his voice was almost a shout, denying not only the lawyer but everything they were doing to him. He rose suddenly in his agitation and started to pace up and down in the cell. 'No. Maybe you can make nonsense out of what Ah've done. But Ah'm damned if Ah'll help ye. Justice? Ah don't see any justice. What's justice about this? Look. Did Ah ask you to try to save ma skin? The only justice Ah want is to have what Ah've done understood. Ah want it known whit that man's death means. The man Ah killed. The same way as Ah want it known whit ma feyther's death means. You can do whit the hell ye like with me. Ah didn't ask anybody tae try to make out that Ah'm innocent or a victim of circumstances. God, Ah'm not innocent. Ah killed a man. Never mind me. All Ah want is for you to understand what's behind his death.'

'Exactly. And what makes you think that's not what we want? Of course it is. We want to know why this man was killed. What made you do it. We're trying to decide. We're trying to explain.'

'Explain! You're not trying to explain it. You're trying to explain it *away*. You're trying to find a lotta glib reasons for it. That makes it look not as black for me. You're trying tae dae everything ye can tae make it look not so bad.'

'But there *are* reasons for it. There must be. There must have been things that helped to make you do it. Your father's death. The way you resented your stepfather. Taking his place. The drink. You had been drinking.'

'Reasons. God, Ah'm sick of listenin' to the reasons you give me. You an' that other lawyer. Drink. Or misguided love for ma feyther. Or an Oedipus complex. Or God knows what. That makes it nice an' convenient, doesn't it? Because if that's all there is to it, fair enough. These things happen. It's too bad. But that won't do. Whit are ye tryin' tae make out? That Ah'm just an agent for some psychological quirk? Acting on behalf of Tennent's beer? Dae ye think that was all there was to what Ah did? Naw. It can't be explained away like that. What Ah did is burnin' me alive. An' you offer me Elastoplast. Look. Ah did something terrible. Terrible. Ah killed a man. You want to know what Ah did? Ah'll tell you. Ah went into a room an' Ah systematically beat a man to death. There is *no* reason why Ah should've done that. There's *no* excuse. There is *no* justification. Right. Do what ye want with me. Break ma neck or bury me or shut me up. Ah mean, if Ah'm just a dog that's had too much sun an' run amok, then put me down. But don't pretend that what Ah did wasn't a terrible thing. And see just one thing. One thing. See that what Ah did had tae be a terrible thing. It had to be. Because it had to show what had happened to ma feyther. An' my God, that was a terrible thing. So why pay attention to what Ah did? The only meaning it's got is to show what happened to ma feyther. There's no mystery in what Ah did. It's not worth all this consideration. Ah killed a man. You can deal with that in any way you like. But you can't deal with it and not deal with that other crime. Ah mean, Ah'm responsible for this one. So let me pay for it. But who's responsible for the other one? An' who's goin' to pay for it?

That's what matters. A lot of people are responsible for that other crime. Everybody is, who was ever glib about what a person is. Everybody who doesn't care is to blame. It's got to stop. It's got to be faced. You can't pretend that people don't matter. People need more than food and drink and a bed. They need more than material success. Everybody has to have a chance just to be a person. Everybody. Everybody matters completely. Or nobody matters. Not God. Not anybody. What's wrong here, when a man can be discounted, can be written off? An' nobody cares. What are ye goin' to do about that? That's what matters. That's what you should be concerned with. That's what everybody should be concerned with. Not with me. You should be concerned with *your* part in that other crime. Not with ma part in this one. Don't make excuses for me. Don't try to extenuate what Ah did. Nothing. Nothing can extenuate me. Not you. Not anybody. Nobody can help me now. Ah've made ma own hell. An' it's private.'

His words had forced the lawyer into a withdrawn silence, like someone taking shelter from a cataract. He was able to assimilate only fragments of what he had said, and even these seemed rough and unhewn hunks of meaning, wild, haphazard, and not a little lunatic in places. He had observed the desperate eyes, a wick of fever burning in each pupil, the broken stride that was no more than a nervous concomitant of speech and kept time to the words, the restless hands that would become suddenly crucified in appeal. The total figure was somehow reminiscent of a biblical prophet, clad in the rough skins of his own pain, wandering in a self-created wilderness, whose emptiness echoed nothing but his voice. He was reminded vaguely of a poem he had learnt at school:

> Only the echoes, which he made relent,
> Rung from their flinty caves, Repent! Repent!

'Mr Grant,' the lawyer said quietly, 'for the kind of judgment you have in mind, it's not a lawyer you want. Justice isn't a divinity. We have no absolutes. We have to wait until

225

error manifests itself and judge it comparatively. That's all we can do. It's only as far as this that our criteria are meaningful. Beyond this, no. We can pass judgment on Mr Whitmore's death. Not on your father's.'

Charlie sat down. His anger had cooled, but it had tempered his conviction to certainty.

'Then your criteria aren't meaningful at all,' he said evenly. 'You can take action on Mr Whitmore's death. But not on my father's. What good is that? It's like curing a leper of the common cold. I'll tell you something. You have no right to judge me. You have no right to punish me. If your rules can't be applied to my father's death and still have meaning, then they can't be applied to this man's death. If the laws that make this man's death a crime don't make my father's death a crime, then they aren't laws at all. If the truth they derive from isn't the same truth that governs my father's death, then it isn't truth at all.'

'Mr Grant. You seem to be blindfolding yourself quite deliberately to certain obvious differences. Something utterly intangible on the one hand. And something all too tangible on the other. An act of explicit violence. At a specific point in time. A killing.'

'You're wearing the blindfold, not me. There are different ways of violence. And different ways of killing. But does that make the thing itself different? Six years or six minutes. It only gives you more time to savour the pain. And it was tangible enough. I know it was. I was there. No. Your way of judging it means nothing.'

'On the contrary. Our way of judging it is all the meaning there is.'

They stopped talking. Words ran out, leaving them isolated in their mute convictions. They sat surrounded by the stone silence of the cell, like incarnations of twin truths that depended upon but denied each other.

Chapter 23

RON EVANS TOOK A LAST DRAG ON HIS CIGARETTE, dropped it, and gutted it with his foot, so that the tobacco shreds merged with the marl of the corridor. He looked out of the window. In the street beyond the courtyard, there weren't very many people about. Mainly women. Hurrying home to light the sacred oven. It was a boring time of day, he felt, when they all trekked home to do their devotions to their bellies. To appease the great god Guts. Two girls passed by, resplendent in print frocks. Summer was icumen in, right enough. Bringing them out like butterflies. A nice image. They emerged from the cocoon of winter overcoats to flutter in bright dresses. Very good. He was wasting his time as a hack. He watched a young woman push a pram along the street. She was coatless too, bouncing buxomly in her first post-natal bloom. 'I wouldn't mind giving your pram a refill for you,' he thought, but there was no one handy to whom to voice his wit. Only a couple of motley groups. Waiting like him.

He glanced at his watch. It wouldn't be very long until opening time. He wished to hell they would get it over with. It was a foregone conclusion anyway. They didn't have to call in Solomon for this one. Even Lieutenant Tragg would have got a conviction this time. He thought of him sitting there in the dock. Charles Grant. Charlie to his friends, and 'Charlie' was right. He was a proper one. Poor bastard. Poor, stupid bastard. Your own mother couldn't have helped convicting you in a case like this. Come to think of it, Charles Grant's mother certainly would have. She was an interesting one. She looked a fair bit of goods and yet tatty. You couldn't make up your mind just from looking at her whether she was a case of prematurely blighted early middle-age or someone who had spent her life outrunning the wrinkles, only to be caught on the home stretch. She contrived to look both well preserved and decayed, as if she had just stepped out of Shangri-la. Maybe she had. Certainly she must have had a very tidy set-up before little Charles turned boy prodigy and wanted to play at Nemesis.

Children. Who needs them? he thought. They always grew up into two-legged recriminations. They complicated every decision you made, became little consciences growing on to your life like parasites, sucking every ounce of resolution out of you, until all you wanted to do was play it safe and give them security, so that they could have all the chances their existence had robbed you of. They filled your life like overgrown piggy-banks into which you stuffed your own present so that it could become their future. And then at the end of it they turned round and told you all the places where you had gone wrong. They were impatient of the thrift you had cultivated for their sake, or they were ashamed of you in front of their friends, or they were downright intolerant of your old-fashioned interference.

They were prigs, all of them. They all wanted to believe that their parents were made of stainless steel. They didn't like to think that their parents might still know what sex was. That they might not only know it was, but might also fancy a little of it now and again from unorthodox sources was not to be considered. It was all right if you were them, but if you were their parents you were supposed to become some sort of domestic vegetable that was fulfilled in feeding their faces and looking at television. He wondered sardonically what his own eldest son would think if he knew a few of the away-from-home truths about father-figure Evans. He smiled in connivance with himself. He must take Drew aside some time and fill him in with a few of the facts of life. On second thoughts, better not. Let him hang on to his illusions as long as he could. He would find out soon enough when his own turn came.

They all had to learn. Only some were pig-headed about it. Like Charles Grant, Esquire. That was the worst kind.

The do-gooders. Holier-than-thou. Sent down specially by the divinity to sort out lesser mortals. Empowered to administer death. The upstart bastard. Who did he think he was? Evans could have told him who he was. He was a stupid little boy, suffering from a bad case of prudishness. Someone who took a tantrum because the world wasn't all peaches-and-cream and little Lord Fauntleroy. It was just too bad that someone had to die of his tantrum. Too bad for the late Mr Whitmore. Poor old Whitmore. He seemed like a smart enough bloke. He had been doing very nicely, thank you. A very good job. And just as efficient with women. So he knocked off with the one he fancied. It wasn't his fault that she was married. And why not? If he could get away with it. And he nearly did, too. Except for Charles His Holiness Grant, God's representative in Kilmarnock. Too bad, Mr Whitmore. You can't take it with you. And all because of a tantrum.

That was all it was, an overgrown child's tantrum. It was no good trying to justify it as anything more. All the clever talk was so much crap. Did the lawyer really believe all the guff he had been speaking in there, about 'social conscience' and 'hypersensitivity' and 'burden of guilt'? What the hell was he on about? You didn't have to look far for the reasons here. Charles Grant was the Case of the Classic Prig. (That was a good title. He must remember to put it on a postcard and send it to Erle Stanley Gardner.) That was all he was, anyway. Someone who couldn't face up to the fact that his mother had enjoyed a bit of extra-marital nookie. He just couldn't face it – not even when she married her benefactor and made it all legal. And he couldn't face the fact that his father was just a down-at-heel bum, who didn't know his financial arse from his economic elbow, and probably wasn't much good in bed either. What was so hard to face up to in that? Plenty of people had a bum for a father and they didn't go around killing because of it. The world was full of bums, moaners and social pimps, who never had the breaks, queuing every week at labour exchanges to live off other people's earnings. If you happened to get one of them for a father, that was too bad. You shrugged and took it.

But not our Charles. He had to go around blaming everybody else. He couldn't face it, He couldn't face anything. Some character. His psyche must be in a worse state than the Congo. Freud might have had one or two things to say about him. He would have made Oedipus look like an All-American kid. No, Charles couldn't face up to what everybody else faces up to every day. So instead, he stamps his foot and smashes a man's life like a toy. Naughty Charles. You'll have to be punished. All the grown-ups have sent you to stand in a corner while they decide what's to be done about you. Any minute now. You're due to be spanked. The spanking of a lifetime, so to speak. Any minute now.

He looked at his watch again. He wished they would hurry up. All this waiting. And for what? It wasn't as if he was even getting a good story out of it. It was all too clear-cut. No controversy. No drama. A dry courtroom exercise. He had thought he might do a human-interest piece. But he couldn't be bothered. The bastards would sub-edit it to death, anyway. It was always the same. He would be given a quarter of a column, buried somewhere in the middle of the paper. Probably beside an advert for toilet-paper. 'You can't compete with Delsey . . .' he thought, and paused, trying to finish his advertising slogan: 'You can't compete with Delsey, it's always in there at the end.' He groaned to himself, wondering if too much hanging around could damage the brain. To hell with it, he thought. He would scribble out something and phone it in. Then grab a few drinks and forget the whole thing. What did it matter, anyway?

He lit another cigarette and watched Sid Mellor of the *Sun* come along the corridor towards him, wearing his Sefton Delmer hat. Evans wondered if he had got it for his Christmas, perhaps along with a brand new toy-reporter set. Mellor was incorrigibly romantic about newspaper-work and he reported everything from murder to a meeting of the Women's Rural Institute with the same melodramatic urgency, as if the world was breathless for his words. He had come into journalism late, and he looked upon Evans as a sort of high-priest of the cult in which he himself was a novitiate of dazzling promise. Evans couldn't stand him, but he was almost glad to see him on this occasion. A spot of Mellor-baiting might help to pass the time.

Mellor stopped at his side, panting into his face like an obedient newshound, his breast-pocket bristling with as many pens and pencils as would have seen him through a detailed report of World War II, and still left a few stubs for Korea.

'I was watching you coming along the corridor there, Sid,' Evans said. 'You were walking with a pronounced scoop.'

'What's that, Ron?' Mellor's face was bright with empti-ness, a perspiring moon.

'Skip it. I haven't time to draw the illustrations just now,' Evans said affably. 'Did you get your stuff phoned through all right?'

'Eventually.' Mellor's wry expression told of the lonely tribulations of the newshawk. 'That's some phone they have through there, though. Must have been installed by Bell in person.'

Mellor gave his Worldly Wiseman laugh.

'Did you get them to hold the front page for you?' Evans asked.

'Not quite. Why? Will yours be on the front page?' Mellor was genuinely interested.

'I don't know, boy. It's a toss-up between that and Child-ren's Corner. If I play my cards right, I might even make the stop-press. Of course, that's always assuming I make the paper at all. On the other hand, I might die on the sub-editor's desk. A martyr to the Philistines. With those bastards, who can tell?'

Mellor laughed appreciatively. This was hard-bitten news-paper-talk, the idiom of the insiders like himself. It didn't occur to him that he might be the butt of it.

'No word from in there yet?' he asked with professional interest, nodding towards the courtroom.

'Well, we all know what the word is, don't we?' Evans said, abandoning irony to speak *ex cathedra*. He couldn't resist the chance to pontificate to one of his disciples. 'We're only waiting for them to get round to stating officially what we all know already. That's all that's lacking. The *ex officio* bumbles.'

'You don't think there's any chance, then?'

'For God's sake, man. Where's the get-out for him? Unless you can prove that his hands belonged to somebody else.'

'But why are they taking so long?'

'Juries, my friend. Juries. They're all the same. You'll get used to that. Think it out for yourself. There are fifteen people in there who want to have something to go home and tell their families. They're going to make the most of it. It's a good thing to have in reserve, when you want a bit of conversational attention. My life as a juryman. Man, they're enjoying it fine. Spinning it out as long as they can. I'll bet they've been taking chances each at being Perry Mason.'

Mellor laughed. Evans really had it taped. As if to show his appreciation, Mellor took out his cigarettes and offered one to Evans. Evans shook his head.

'And you can save yourself the trouble of lighting one as well,' he said. 'It's not worth your while.'

'What do you mean?'

'You won't get the chance to smoke it.'

'How do you know?'

'Because it's high time the jury got home for their tea. The fun's over. Time to return the verdict they could have returned without retiring at all. Guilty of non-capital murder. Sentence: Life.'

'How can you be so sure they'll wrap up now?'

'Because I'm psychic,' Evans said, his hand raised in a gesture of mock command. 'Sh! I can see them clearly now. The foreman is chaulkered to the eyeballs. He is asking round the table for any dissentient voices. There are none. The verdict is unanimous. Now he crosses to the door and informs the macer of his decision. The court is to be re-convened. We should be summoned about . . . Now!'

232

They waited expectantly for a moment. Nothing happened. Mellor laughed.

'So much for spiritualism,' he said, striking a match.

Somewhere a bell rang.

'I shall expect an apology in writing,' Evans said.

'Hell. That's it,' Mellor said, putting the match out. 'Come on. Come on. We'd better get in.'

Evans let him go on ahead. He noticed that some of the people who had been standing in the corridor had gone away, bored with waiting. He was tempted just to hang on out here and get the decision from Mellor. It was a formality, anyway. But after a moment he thought better of it. He would go in, just in case. You never knew. Charles Grant might yet do something that would give him a story. He might throw another tantrum. Attack the judge. Or try to hang himself in his braces from the dock. That would be nice.

He slipped into the courtroom and sat behind Mellor, near the door. Convenient for a getaway. He didn't feel like having Mellor's company over a drink. The court was assembled, only waiting for the judge. He was probably asleep, Evans thought. He looked at the jury, sitting staunch and upright, full of self-importance. He glanced from them to the dock. There he was, Charles Grant. Self-appointed representative of the arch-angels. Evans wondered how grand he felt now, sitting there in isolation. He didn't look very impressive. Only pathetic. Was this the grand finale he had envisaged for himself when he took on the role of the purifier of society? Some finale.

Evans looked round the public gallery. A couple of old women, passing sweets and pointing out the elaborate cornices to each other. A few old men who were probably here in preference to feeding the ducks. A young ned in a leather jacket, busy doing his Narcissus, stroking his sideburns. A few more very odds and ends. The others who had been here earlier had gone home. Tea was more important than this lot. Some audience. They were the only ones society could spare to take any notice of Charles Grant. The others had more important things to do. This was strictly B-picture stuff. Of very little interest. So much for the great prophet of purity. Charles Grant, this is your life.

'Court!' a voice suddenly called.

Everybody rose, and Evans dragged to his feet like a reluctant afterthought. The judge came in and took his place and Evans sat down in time with him, followed by everyone else.

Evans listened impatiently as the formal questions were put to the foreman of the jury, all the legal rigmarole that culminated in the foreman's final statement, declaimed with a sonority befitting society's spokesman: 'Guilty as libelled.' Hear, hear, thought Evans. Now it was the judge's turn. 'It is the decision of this court . . . blah, blah and blah . . imprisonment for life.' Which would really mean about a dozen years or so. Scottish courts seemed to make a very canny assessment of life expectancy.

Evans slipped out of the court with a wink at the usher, leaving Mellor to take down every cough and comma. He hurried quietly down the corridor and was glad to get out into the street. He was making straight for the pub. He would get it written out there and then see what was doing in the way of unattached women. He felt like a bit of field work tonight. In memory of the late Mr Whitmore. But a few drinks first. He had to reach the stage where the words fell into place without too much thought. This lot didn't bear much thinking about. Just as long as he could get something written about it. Anything to fill a space. What difference would it make the day after tomorrow, anyway? By that time his deathless prose would be holding a fish-supper or hanging in a toilet. That was society's final comment on Charles Grant. That's the way it goes, dear Charles. Your noble gesture will serve a social purpose after all. Perhaps not quite the one you had imagined. But things have an awful habit of not quite turning out as we had wanted. It's the way of the world. It happens to all of us. Just as it's about to happen to you. And it couldn't happen to a better fellow.

And so say all of us, thought Evans, pushing open the door of the bar.

Chapter 24

THE TWO DOORS, ONE AT EACH END OF THE LONG room, were closed, hyphenating this time between the separate progressions of their lives, putting this place in parenthesis. Beyond one door lay the city with its streets where traffic moved and people shopped and went about on private errands. Beyond the other door were the long corridors, the bare cells, the dull sheds where men laboured to futility. With a grille between them, the two of them sat on opposite sides of the table that stretched from end to end of the room like a no-man's-land. Beside the inner door, a warder stood sentry to their meeting. His face showed no interest in what they were saying, but his presence muted their voices.

'How are ye gettin' on then, Charlie?' John said.

The cliché, which grew naturally out of casual street-corner meetings and bus-stop conversations, shrivelled to meaninglessness when transplanted to this barren sliver of a room. But John had nothing else with which to mitigate the silence that lay between them like a huge slab. If he couldn't shift it, he could at least cultivate the crevices.

'Ah'm okay, John,' Charlie said. 'It's no' so bad at all now. Ah'm gettin' work tae dae. It breaks up the day. An' ye're with other blokes an' that. It's a lot better. Ah'm all right now. Really.'

The reassurance was more saddening than any complaint could have been. John felt grief to realize how much of Charlie had been lost already, how soon he had learned the limits of his cage. He was all right now. He was here for as long as they kept him, occupying his hands in accordance with their commands, his body controlled by a mind that wasn't his, while they fed him and allowed him to relieve himself and exercised him like a dog. But he was all right now. Because now they were allowing him to work, whereas before they had left him to the solitary occupation of his thoughts. Now they were letting him be among other men, whereas before they had given him only himself for company. It was simple psychology. Beat a dog with a cudgel, and a kick will seem a kindness. Already, Charlie had learned to find solace in variations of agony. Through the years ahead, he would discover content as merely a permutation of misery. Custom would wear to comfort.

John looked on helplessly at the figure on the other side of the mesh that hemmed him like a cage. The warder leaned casually against the wall, looking innocently at his fingernails, not present as a person so much as a reminder of official regulations, like a prohibitive notice. Please don't feed the animals. Charlie sat waiting for John to say something else, like a patient bear waiting to be fed. His eyes were blank, and, with the loose-fitting clothes they had given him and the faint stubble of beard and the rumpled hair, he looked as innocent and stupid as a clown. Not like a criminal at all, but like someone they had dressed up in their cast-offs to be the butt of a sinister joke. John tried to recognize the person he had known. This was his brother. He had known his laughter and his talk and his happiness and his fantastic ambitions. He could have done so much, filled so many rooms with laughter, loved women, made happiness. He could have been important to so many people. Who said it wasn't to be? Who had the right to take it from him? Why did he have to lose it? Because he had killed a man. But never before had he at any time come close to such an action, never before had he hinted at such a capability in himself, never before had he seemed in any way different from the millions of others who walked about free outside. What had happened to make him become different? This was not his own action as he had shown himself. Not his more than any other's. Then whose was it? Why had it happened? John did not know. But he knew one thing. He knew that the answer wasn't here in this room. This was no solution. This was a travesty of truth. Nothing was answered by dressing a man in these trappings and making him a mummer of guilt in this pagan ritual of expiation. On whose behalf was the expiation? The warder shifted his stance noisily, underlining his presence. John cast about desperately for some comfort he could share with Charlie.

'Elizabeth sends you her love,' he said. 'An' Margaret. Everybody misses you.'

'Tell them Ah'm askin' for them. Are Elizabeth an' Harry still all right? Ye know what Ah mean.'

'Aye. That's all right. They'll be getting engaged some time. Ah don't know when. It hasn't been mentioned just recently. But they'll be doin' it all right. Some time.'

'That's good. They'll be all right for a house, anyway. Elizabeth will get the house, won't she?'

'Aye. She should do. If she wants it. They'll have the house. That's something these days.'

'Aye. You had tae wait quite a while for yours, you an' Margaret.'

'Quite a while, aye.'

'An' Margaret's all right, is she?'

'Fine. Margaret's just fine. Really fine.'

'An' the wee fella?'

'John? Champion. Fit as a fiddle. An' a damn sight noisier.'

'He's a great wee boy.'

'He's got a new dodge now. He was at it just before Ah came oot. His mother always leaves his pram just outside the front windy. So that she can keep an eye on 'im, ye know. An' he's got this caper now. He can actually pull himself up by the sides of the pram so that he's keekin' round the hood. Laps it up, too. Thinks it's very clever. Squeals like a banshee at everybody that goes by. Ah don't know how many folk have come in the path tae blether to 'im. He just lies back there an' goos at them. Holds court like a nabob. Ridiculous. We'll definitely need to do something about 'im.'

'That's great, right enough.'

Seeing his own enthusiasm reflected automatically in Charlie, but distorted by his clown's garb and the horror of

237

his situation, John realized how grotesque his words were in this place. He had almost forgotten Charlie for a moment in his own petty pride in his son's ability to raise himself a few inches from the horizontal. He was disgusted at the callous fertility of life which in the presence of such terrible waste and destruction will still wantonly spawn pleasure in so insignificant a fact. To offset the waste of so much human life, a child gurgling inanely in his pram. A nice equation. All they had to balance the destruction was an idiot pleasure in the gradual means of that destruction. He felt terribly guilty that the only contributions he could make to Charlie's lonely hunger were such scraps from his own content. Yet Charlie seemed satisfied with that. He sat as docile as any animal, accepting these leftovers from other people's lives that John had brought him. John couldn't bear to witness it, refused to acknowledge that Charlie had come already to accept this as all that he was due. John wanted somehow to glimpse again the person Charlie had been, to waken in him some response of anger or hate or some sense of injustice that would contradict this subservience. He wanted to stir in Charlie some reaction that would show that he had at least been a man of such intensity as made him dangerous to others. He felt compelled to move him somehow, just as people find themselves striking the bars of the lion's cage, trying to resurrect even for a moment the fire that is supposed to sleep within the glazed eyes, the ferocity in the indolent paws, the power they are told is hidden beneath the mangy hide.

'Charlie. Ma mother was back through tae see Elizabeth. Ah saw 'er when she was through.'

John waited for the hate or the fury or whatever it was his words would elicit. Nothing. Only a minute gesture of contraction, a weary withdrawal, as if the lion was half-heartedly trying to get out of range of the probing stick.

'Ah think she's maybe comin' back through tae Kilmarnock to live. She might do that.'

Charlie nodded blankly. It was as if he had no right to think or feel about things any more. He had forfeited his involvement in everything except the action he had done. John had not known what his own reaction was to the possibility of his mother's returning to Kilmarnock. After what had happened, he wasn't sure that she had the right to do it. Some sort of blame for what had happened derived from her and he felt they were somehow betraying Charlie if they had anything to do with her. And he was afraid that if she did come back to Kilmarnock, she and Elizabeth might see a lot of each other, might even live together again. It should have been unthinkable, he knew. But somehow it wasn't. He could see it happening, all right. Elizabeth was desperate enough to hang on to anything that offered shelter. She needed a mother so much that even her own mother might do. Regardless of what the two of them had felt in the past, their mutual need might easily be enough to bring them together. You don't ask who else is in the lifeboat before you let them pull you in. John had not been sure what he ought to feel, anger at Elizabeth or hatred for his mother. What had happened had been so numbing that all he felt was an uncertain sympathy for both of them. He had been prepared to wait and endorse Charlie's reaction to it all. Now he couldn't bring himself to draw Charlie out any further, because it was obvious that Charlie had no reaction to it. It was simply a fact which Charlie accepted as he accepted every other fact that was imposed on him.

'She might even be considerin' living with Elizabeth. Ah don't know. She could be. Or maybe they'll get another hoose. We'll just have tae wait an' see.'

'Aye, John. We can see what happens.'

The words were not communication, but the rejection of it. They clicked mechanically into place like bolts going home. John stared at the enigma of the face across from him, sectored into fragments by the wire. It was hopeless. Coming from the trivial actions and the aimless conversations that took place beyond that door, he couldn't bring anything into this room that wasn't a mockery of what Charlie was going through. The brutal truth was that they had nothing to say to each other. They were brothers, but they might as well have been strangers who didn't even have the same language in common. The different places that they came from beyond those two doors were irreconcilable, warring opposites, and they couldn't bring them to an understanding. John sat in painful dumbness, wanting to speak, but with every remark shamed into silence by the sight of Charlie. John found the quietness racking. But he had nothing with which to break it. He could only sit and wonder how much more terrible the quietness must be for Charlie.

But, in fact, Charlie hardly noticed that John wasn't speaking. The absence of John's voice still left plenty of others, for Charlie's mind snowed with voices, and whether he was sitting here or in his cell they recurred endlessly. His thoughts were constantly grooving in the words of other people, his father, Elizabeth, Jim, Mary, Mr Whitmore, Mr Atkinson, John. Gradually over the past few weeks, he had achieved something like his own understanding of things, although it was perhaps not understanding so much as faith.

And it was a faith which enabled him to endure the long misery that lay ahead of him. It wasn't that he had come to accept these years in prison as any sort of logical sequence to what he had done. But he understood that there was no logical sequence to what he had done. Whatever this imprisonment might mean to those who had imposed it on him, it had its own meaning for Charlie, just as any event can only become coherent when translated into the terms of the people involved. For Charlie it was simply a penance to which he saw no end. There could be no end to it because the guilt he felt was absolute. Only in the act of experiencing guilt could he be absolved. To forget was to become guilty again, because the guilt was most truly not that of action but that of omission, not of doing, but of failing to be.

He was guilty of killing a man, it was true. But that was merely the pebble by which to gauge the depth of the chasm. Behind it, swallowing it, lay an infinitely vaster guilt, one of cosmic omission. He was like a hunter who sets out to snare a bird and finds that the bird is bait belonging to a mammoth. He had become the quarry of his own chase. In seeking to punish the guilt of others, he had found that guilt neutralized, swallowed up in his own.

By some terrible paradox, Charlie's action seemed to absolve his mother and Mr Whitmore of their guilt and put it on his own shoulders. Charlie had exacted payment out of all proportion to whatever it was that Mr Whitmore owed, and now his guilt multiplied itself on Charlie's back. Charlie had played at being God, had in a moment of wilful divinity released the thunderbolt, and now he was left with what seemed an eternity of retrospect in which to contemplate his action, in which to learn the harder attributes of godhead, love of the unworthy, endless participation in the agony of others, infinite understanding.

The last of this trinity was lacking, and always would be. Charlie could never understand what had happened. But in his desperate attempt to arrive at understanding, he had achieved something else which negated the need for understanding. He had discovered the sympathy with others that makes for love. The price of that love was his own guilt. For it was not until he had taken the blemish of their guilt upon himself and reincarnated in them his father's suffering that he could see them as he had seen his father. Only then was he capable of love for them. Only then could he feel for them the sympathy he had felt for his father. It took his own injustice to them to show him that they were not the wilful villains in what had happened to his father, but his fellow-victims. They were sufferers with his father from an injustice which ranged much wider than their own petty misdemeanours, making them seem innocent.

It was this injustice that Charlie had involved himself in, and it made his guilt not familial or parochial but universal. Blinded by his father's suffering, he had been guilty of the very injustice for which he had blamed others. If they had failed to realize how much his father mattered, Charlie had failed to realize how much they mattered. It was only now, when he had irrevocably denied their significance, that that significance came home to roost tenaciously in his mind. For the first time, he felt not just what it must have been like to be his father, but also the silent desperation that must have held his mother like a cage. He realized how narrow her life must have been for her, what restless dreams must have walked holes in her comfortable domesticity. He sensed what inarticulate urgency must have led to that vivid reflowering of the flesh, the heedless consummation of a new identity. The same thing had driven her as had driven his father to take refuge in pathetic dreams and had driven Charlie himself to murder. Like them, she had been unable to take life in the terms that she was given, because she had more to offer than her life could adequately express.

He saw his father and his mother and Mr Whitmore not as mutually opposed individuals but as sharers in a failure so painful as to make the distribution of blame an impertinence and an unquestioning sympathy the only valid gesture. Each stood equidistant in his compassion, seen in the perspective of their common humanity. They were simply people, and like all people they were the victims of their own nature. Like all people, they had dreams that were too intense ever to be realized, and losing their own dreams, lost compassion for the dreams of others. Being more than life could ever make them, they took from life what they could, and if they sometimes did it cruelly, the cruelty was no more than retaliation. Finding little truth, they learned to deceive, to spread words and actions around them like camouflage until they wandered lost in their own deceptions and other people's. They might have been different. In failing to have what they wanted, they might have learned to want what they had. But it was an alternative that would have debased them in the taking of it. By that criterion the bird would take the cage in preference to the sky. If they had been different, they would have been less.

Their fulfilment lay in the destruction of what was best in them, and Charlie had played his part in that destruction, not just in killing, but in denying people the right to fail on their own terms. He had been guilty towards everyone, and now the remorse he felt was universal. But such remorse is difficult to observe and Charlie made his private pantheon before which to do penance. He held in his mind the images of the people whose lives had been affected by his action, and these images were complete, as if the people they represented were dead. Like an obituarist, Charlie remembered only the good in them, and his thoughts recorded their worth like rows of headstones. Their individual natures were reiterated in his mind like masses sung for the souls of the dead in a chantry.

This ritualistic thinking occupied Charlie's mind almost completely. The rest was insignificant, an incidental mortification of the flesh. Nothing they did to him could have much effect. Just as they had been unable to help him realize the vision he had needed before, they could not now take his private vision from him. It wasn't the vision he had hoped for but it was his, forged from his commitment to his own ideals, its intensity measured by the intensity of what he had felt, harrowing, lonely, and incommunicable. To John or anyone else.

'It won't be as long as it sounds, Charlie,' John said in sudden desperation. 'The lawyer says probably no more than ten years.'

Looking at him, John saw the denial of his own words. The sentence was for life. They couldn't have set Charlie free now if they had wanted to.

'No,' Charlie said.

The warder was stirring restlessly. John stood up and Charlie stood up with him.

'Well,' John said. 'Elizabeth'll be comin' up tae see ye. An' maybe some o' yer mates. An' Ah'll be back up, Charlie.'

'That's fine.'

'Ah don't know when they'll be able to make it up.'

'That's all right. There's plenty of time,' and Charlie smiled wryly.

'Jesus Christ, Charlie. Jesus Christ,' John said.

'Ah'm all right, John. Don't worry about me.'

243

John stood staring at him, finding it impossible to leave, and eventually it was Charlie who said, 'Ah'll see ye, John,' and turned away.

John made as if to wave and the gesture withered on his wrist. He watched Charlie being led out before he turned and left himself. When he came back out into the streets, Charlie's face seemed to overhang the whole day like a question mark, a question mark that attached to everything these people were doing, to everything that John himself would do.

As he sat on the bus that was to take him home, he closed his eyes and Charlie's face loomed huge, like a terrible totem. It would have been better to forget that face. But he couldn't forget. It belonged in some way to all of them. He wondered how they could reconcile that face to their own lives, what they could do to appease its suffering.

'That's a funny man, Mummy,' a small voice said. 'Look. He's sleepin'.'

John opened his eyes and saw a small girl staring into his face from the seat in front before her mother smiled apologetically at John and turned her round to face forward. John thought of his own son, suddenly feeling how vulnerable he was. He wanted to be home quickly. He thought of the things he had to do, at his work and at home. He thought of them over and over again, like someone fingering a rosary.

NEIL GUNN 1891 – 1973
THE SCOTTISH COLLECTION

THE LOST CHART
A cold war thriller set in the Scottish city of Glasgow shortly after the Second World War, '*the Lost Chart*' moves on two distinct planes – the physical and the metaphysical.

THE LOST GLEN
The famous novel on the decline of Highland ways and values in the 1920s.

THE OTHER LANDSCAPE
'*The Other Landscape*' returns to the familiar setting of the Highlands but with a new element of dark humour.

THE SILVER BOUGH
Archaeologist Simon Grant comes to the Highlands to investigate an ancient cairn. A stranger in a strange part of the country, he finds that there are barriers to understanding between him and the people of the community.

SECOND SIGHT
The setting is a Highland shooting lodge, whose occupants are depicted in stark contrast to the local people. A violent death is foreseen. But whose? How? When? The drama is played out against a background of strange mists and elemental landscapes.

THE SHADOW
Having found sanctuary in the beautiful Highlands, Nan is disturbed by the news of a local brutal murder.

HIGHLAND PACK
Nature as witnessed by Gunn and expressed in short stories reflecting each month and season of the year.

OFF IN A BOAT
'*Off in a Boat*' logs the adventures of a man, who at a critical point of his life, throws caution to the wind, and with his wife as Crew, navigates his way round the West Coast of Scotland.
Whilst Gunn masters the art of sailing and anchorage, the Crew explores the possibilities of the camera.